ALSO BY CONSTANCE SANTEGO

FICTION
The Nine Spiritual Gifts Series:
Journey of a Soul – (Vol 1 Michael)
Language of a Soul – (Vol 2 Gabriel)

NONFICTION
The Intuitive Life, The Gift of Prophecy, Third
Edition
Fairy Tales, Dreams and Reality… Where Are You
On Your Path? Second Edition
Your Persona… The Mask You Wear
Angelic Lifestyle, A Vibrant Lifestyle
Angelic Lifestyle 42-Day Energy Cleanse
Archangel Michael's Soul Retrieval Guide
SECRETS OF A HEALER, SERIES:
Magic Of Aromatherapy (Vol I)
Magic Of Reflexology (Vol II)
Magic Of The Gifts (Vol III)
Magic Of Muscle Testing (Vol IV)
Magic Of Iridology (Vol V)
Magic Of Massage (Vol VI)
Magic Of Hypnotherapy (Vol VII)
Magic Of Reiki (Vol VIII)
Magic Of Advanced Aromatherapy (Vol IX)
Magic Of Esthetics (Vol X)

FOR CHILDREN
I am big tonight. I don't need the light!

Published By: Maximillian Enterprises
Edited By: Ana Joldes
Interior Layout: Constance Santego
Book Layout: ©2017 BookDesignTemplates.com
Cover Design: Jennifer Louie
Soft Cover ISBN: 978-1-990062-05-6
eBook ISBN: 978-1-990062-06-3
Created and published in Canada. Printed and bound in the United States of America
Ordering Information: csantego@gmail.com

Constance Santego

Prophecy of a Soul

Constance Santego has been practicing and teaching *The Nine Spiritual Gifts, Granted From Spirit,* for over twenty-three years. She lives in British Columbia, Canada with her husband.

www.constancesantego.ca

Cast of Characters

**Some of the Residents of New York City, USA
and other places.**

Alexandra (Lexi) Elizabeth Constantine: Fashion Designer in Upper East Side Manhattan. Daughter of Olivia and Marcus Constantine (Italian). Fiancée to Reverend Edward Julien Hawthorne. Her boss is Sebastian. Friends with co-worker Southern belle, Sherie.

Susannah Grace Constantine: Lexi's belated sister and now guardian angel. Lived in Dumbo (Down Under the Manhattan Bridge Overpass). Was an antique collector for Aryeh Jacob Kofman, and dated Billy Randazzo.

Olivia Sarah Constantine (Maiden name, Austin): Mother to Lexi and Susannah. Widowed Housewife. Parents were from England. Lives in Dyker Heights, Brooklyn NY.

Reverend Edward Julien Hawthorne: Mortician and Minister of a funeral home in Brooklyn. Fiancé to Alexandra (Lexi). Casandra is his secretary.

Tamara Reeve: Psychic Medium and Teacher of many of the Spiritual Gifts. Fiancée to Greg Masones. Now owns her grandmother's Brownstone in Brooklyn Heights.

Detective Ferguson 'Red' Redington: 1st grade Homicide Investigator, Manhattan Bureau – Midtown South Precinct, Shield number 1323, NYPD. Family comes from England.

Greg Masones (AKA Julian D'Angelo): Tamara's Fiancé. Accountant.

Isabella Jackson: Famous actress. Moved around to wherever her next movie was being filmed. Friends with Lexi, Edward, and Redington. Girlfriend of Belated Hans (now Erland, an Elf).

Hans Magnusson (Erland): Lawyer. Lived in Switzerland, but was from Sweden. Inherited his family's fortune. His grandfather was Olof. Became a walk-in soul to Erland in the Elemental Realm, Alfheim,

Main Angel Of Each Novel

Book 1 – Archangel Michael 'Warrior'
Companion Book - Archangel Michael's Soul Retrieval Guide.
Book 2 – Archangel Gabriel 'Messenger'
Companion Book – Your Persona…The mask You Wear.
Book 3 – Bath Kol 'Daughter of the voice,' the Holy Ghost, and Gabriel.
Companion Book – The Gift of Prophecy.

Dedicated

to Cheryl,

my first metaphysical

teacher!

Prophecy of a Soul
The Gift of Prophecy

A Novel
  3rd in the series, The Nine Spiritual Gifts
  '*The Gift of Prophecy*'
                    Constance Santego

Vol 3

The Nine Spiritual Gifts

In the New Testament my favourite story is
"The Gifts."
Corinthians 1, Chapter 12, Verse 4-11
(Maybe a little differently worded
depending on which Bible you have).

The variety and the unity of gifts
There are many different gifts, but it is always
the same Spirit; there are many different ways of
serving, but it is always the same Lord. There
are many different forms of activity, but in
everybody it is the same God who is at work in
them all. The particular manifestation of the
Spirit granted to each one is to be used for the
general good.
To one is given from the Spirit the gift of
utterance expressing **wisdom**; to another the gift
of utterance expressing **knowledge**; in
accordance with the same spirit to another, **faith**,
from the same Spirit; and to another, the gifts of
healing, through the same Spirit; to another, the
working of **miracles**; to another **prophecy**; to
another, the power of **distinguishing spirits**; to
one, the gift of **different tongues** and to another,
the **interpretation of tongues**. But at work in all
these is one and the same Spirit, distributing
them at will to each individual.
The New Jerusalem Bible

Awaken to the spirit world, for there lie your gifts granted by Spirit.

~ Constance Santego

The intuitive mind is a sacred gift, and the rational mind is a faithful servant. We have created a society that honours the servant and has forgotten the gift.

~ Albert Einstein

Fact:

All biblical references, science, legends, and myths are real *(slightly changed to fit the character.* This novel was written as a story inspired by Spirit, to give you, the reader a new perspective, a new way to learn, and a new opportunity to empower your life.

All characters are fictional.

Prologue

In religion, a prophet is an individual who is regarded as being in contact with a divine being and is said to speak on that entity's behalf, serving as an intermediary with humanity by delivering messages or teachings from the supernatural source to other people. The message that the prophet conveys is called a prophecy.

Not only is Archangel Gabriel considered an angel of prophecy, so is Bath Kol, băth kŏl.

The phrase *bat kol* literally means "daughter of voice."

In the Old Testament she is symbolized by a dove and is considered the voice of God which proclaims God's will, judgment, deeds, and commandments… She is also considered the original angel of prophecy.

Claims of prophethood have existed in many cultures and religions throughout history, including Judaism, Christianity, Islam, ancient Greek religion, Zoroastrianism, Manichaeism, and many others.

Christian scholars interpreted Bath Kol as the Jews' replacement for the great prophets. In the New Testament mention of "a voice from heaven" occurs in the following passages: Matt 3:17; Mark 1:11, Luke 3:22, Matt 17:5, Mark 9:7, Luke 9:35, John 12:28, Acts 9:4, Acts 22:7, Acts 26:14, Acts 10:13, and Acts 10:15.

Why I Believe You Should Know
This Information...

I believe we are all here on this planet to learn our life lessons and to work towards our life's purpose. After learning how to tell the difference between spirits (Book 1) and how to communicate with spirit (Book 2), the next natural gift, is prophecy (Book 3). How to see, feel, know, and hear our future.

To have an insight into our future is
a gift from God.

Chapter 1

Tamara was relaxing on the couch, watching the TV with Greg when a news break came on about a young lady who had been killed a few weeks prior. There was a request for anyone to come forward if they had seen her.

Tamara took out her phone and looked at the calendar, figuring out when she and Greg were in Jersey Shore. With her head still down, staring in disbelief at her phone, she said, "Greg, that looks like the girl who gave me the Gypsy Reading."

"What? Who?" he said as he sat up to look closer at the photo on the TV. "I can't remember what she looked like. Are you sure that's her?"

"Positive."

"That means she was killed the same day that we saw her on the beach," he said, not sure what to do next. "Do we call the police and tell them we saw her?"

"I guess we have to. We might have been the last people to see her alive."

"Man, Tamara. If anyone saw how she ran away from you, they may have thought that you had something to do with her murder."

"Greg, the TV didn't say anything about a murder, just that she had died."

"I was assuming it was a murder. You know with her being a gypsy and all."

"I am not sure what you mean, 'gypsy' and all?"

"Tamara, come on, why are you getting riled up over this. Everyone knows that gypsies are notorious for being thieves."

"Greg, we are in the twenty-first century. Really? You still believe all the folklore about gypsies?"

"You don't?" he said defiantly, defending his belief.

"Of course not. Do you even know what a gypsy is?

"Ya. A fortune teller that travels in a caravan from place to place, selling their snake oil and other trinkets. Hey, the girl we saw was doing exactly what I thought a gypsy would do."

"Wow!"

"Okay, smarty-pants, tell me your version of what a gypsy is then."

Tamara took the remote and turned off the TV. She was going to take this opportunity to set the record straight. "Greg, racism comes in all kinds of forms."

"Who said anything about racism?"

Tamara took a breath trying not to let her personal feelings get in the way of an opportunity to let a Heavenly message be heard. "Most westerners believe that gypsies originated in Bohemia, a western region of the Czech Republic."

"Ya, I heard they came from Europe."

Europeans on the other hand believed that the gypsies came from Egypt, and hence, named the new foreigners 'gyp'cies. What most people don't know is that 'Gypsies' are really Romani."

"You're telling me that they came from Egypt?"

"No. They didn't come from Egypt or even Europe for that matter, they immigrated to Europe. The true Romani gypsies came from the northwest region of India in the early fifteenth century."

"You're telling me that a gypsy is an East Indian?" Shaking his head in disbelief. "I have never heard of that before."

"It's true. Scientists have DNA proof. Look it up, research it for yourself."

"I might have to. I have never even heard of a Romani."

"In the Roma language, 'Roma' means 'a person or people.' In the Sanskrit writings, it suggests that the name derives from a form of ḍōmba, meaning, 'man of low caste, living by singing and music.'"

"Well, movies always portray the gypsy women to be dancing and singing, and the men for being 'Tinkers,' tinsmiths. Even one of my favorite female singers when I was a kid has a song about them."

"Greg, as you know, TV has a way of making us believe something even when it is fictional."

"So why do you think they have the stigma that follows them then?"

Tamara took a breath, "I believe that as a matter of survival, the Roma were continuously on the move because of the color of their dark skin and fear of slavery. The Romani people had a right to be afraid. In 1554, the English Parliament passed a law that made being a gypsy a felony punishable by death."

"What? I've never heard any of this."

"Greg, there are always two sides to a story. What I find really unfortunate, due to always being on the run, the children didn't attend school, and illiteracy became a problem. Men couldn't secure a job, and the women did what they had to do to feed their children."

"I used to think the freedom of a gypsy was cool, but the way you're talking about them, I feel sorry for them."

"They didn't have it easy, that's for sure. They were forced to leave their homeland due to invasion, only to be on the run in Europe, due to the Holocaust. It is a sad world when a Romani living in the twenty-first century is still labeled a gypsy, tramp, or thief." Tamara got up from the couch, saying, "Greg, I hope that you learned something useful from this conversation?"

"What is that supposed to mean? Tamara, ever since you got back from Peru, you have been talking to me like I was a child."

Looking at him, "I have no idea what you are talking about. I have to make a phone call."

Irritated and a bit annoyed that she didn't even notice how she was treating him, he got up and said, "Whatever, I need some fresh air."

Chapter 2

"Detective, it's me, Tamara. I was hoping you could help me."

"Tamara, it is nice to hear your voice. It's been a while. How may I help you?"

"I know it's the fourth of July weekend, and you are probably busy with family, but can we meet? I think I need to say this in person."

"Sure, I am on duty, and with the pandemic, it is actually pretty quiet around here. No parade or big parties going on today. I can come over to your place?"

"That would be great. What time can I expect you?"

"How about in an hour?"

"Can you make it an hour and a half? Greg just stepped out, and I want him to be back for our conversation."

"Sure, that will work."

"Thanks."

Tamara texted Greg to be back at her place in an hour. Then tidied up and made some chocolate chip cookies while she waited for them.

Answering the door, she let Redington in. "Hi, thanks for coming. Greg should be back at any moment." Walking into the living room, Tamara asked, "Would you like a coffee, tea, water, or a drink, or I have your favorite beer?"

"Thanks, I'm on duty, so I'll have a coffee if it's not too much trouble."

"No trouble at all. With these new gadgets, it's as easy as popping it in and pushing a button. I remember that you like yours black." Thinking back to their time together in Sweden.

Tamara brought out the cookies and his coffee.

Making small talk, Redington said, "How's Isabella? Have you heard from her lately?"

"Ya, she and the baby are good. She said that the fetus is as big as a banana and closer to the size of an acorn squash. I find it funny how a pregnant woman will compare her baby to fruit."

"Ya, but it is funny to imagine. How is Alexandra?"

"She and Edward have started to plan their wedding. I have been asked to be her maid-of-honor."

Surprised that he was jealous, he said with a bit of envy, "They'll make a beautiful couple."

"Detective, do I hear a slight tone of jealousy in your voice?"

Changing the subject, Redington said, "What did you call me over here for, Tamara?"

"I was hoping that Greg would be here. He was with me when it happened."

"Okay, Tamara, now you have my curiosity. What's up?"

Tamara looked Redington in the eyes and said, "You know the girl who died in Jersey Shore a few weeks ago."

"I heard something about it, ya. Why?"

"I think I was. . . well, Greg and I were possibly the last people to see her alive."

"Wow! I didn't see that one coming. Go on." Redington took out a small recorder and started to record what she was saying. "Is it okay if I record this Tamara?"

Looking at the recorder, Tamara took a deep breath and then said, "Sure. From what the TV says, the day she died, Greg and I had seen her on the beach. She was giving me a Gypsy Reading."

"I hope your kidding." He looked at her and shook his head. "Guess not. So, why are you coming to me with this news?"

"Well, there may be a slight problem."

"You know about her death?"

"Not really."

"What does that mean?"

Tamara shut her eyes for a moment. "Redington, I might be the cause of her death."

Redington stood up and said, "What the hell are you talking about. That is a serious admission, Tamara."

"It isn't what you think. I didn't kill her, but my energy might have."

Redington put his hands on his hips and turned slightly away from her as he started to talk, shaking his head, "What exactly does that mean?"

"Redington, you make me nervous to talk about my beliefs." Tamara took another deep breath. "I can't make someone believe what I believe to be true, but I also know what I know and can't undo the metaphysical beliefs I have. I know you don't believe, but I need you to put your personal opinions aside and help me help that girl."

Redington stopped and stared at Tamara.

"Redington, I need you to calm down and sit!"

"I'm thinking."

"She didn't deserve to die. In my belief, dark entities…"

"Ah, not you, too." Redington turned away from Tamara. "Now I know where Alexandra gets it from."

"Redington, sit down. I have a statement to make," Tamara said with an authoritative voice.

Redington turned and sat back down.

At that moment, Greg came into the house. Redington looked at him and nodded as he came in and sat down in a chair.

"Greg and I were taking a stroll along the waterfront boardwalk in Jersey Shore. I decided to indulge in some fun and have my palm read by a Gypsy reader. When she took my hand, she freaked out and ran away, screaming, saying that I was cursed."

Redington's eyes rolled, indicating so much. He couldn't believe what he was hearing.

Tamara continued, "I am afraid that she was right. I didn't know it for a few days, but after Greg and I got back home, Lexi came over and found a witch ladder under my bed."

Shaking his head, Redington said, "What is a witch ladder?"

"It is a rope tied with black feathers. It is an English belief for a curse."

"Let me get this straight. You had a curse on you, and that killed the girl?"

"I think so, yes."

"Tamara, I have heard a lot of things, but I have to give it to you. This one may be one of the craziest."

Trying to keep her dignity, Tamara replied, "I didn't bring you here to judge me. I asked you to come so we could solve a murder. She deserves that much."

"We!"

"Yes, you and I."

"Tamara, that isn't how it works. You can't help me."

"Yes, I can."

"No, you can't. You don't have any jurisdiction in Jersey, and for that matter, neither do I."

"No, but I do have the ability to astral travel and sense energy, and with your help, we can find out who killed her."

"What are you talking about?" Redington looked at Greg for help.

Shrugging his shoulders, Greg said, "Hey, don't look at me pal, I don't know how to do anything she does, but I do know if she says she can, then she can."

Redington turned off the recorder and looked at Tamara. "Let's say I believe you and that you could do what you are saying. What does that entail?"

"I need to go into a trance state and have someone ask me questions."

"That's it? Just ask you questions?"

"More or less, yes."

"Let me think about it, Tamara. I have to get approval from my chief."

"To be witness to a meditation?"

"No, to not have to arrest you."

"What? What for?"

"Involuntary manslaughter."

Greg stood up. "What the? She didn't kill anybody."

"That is not what she just said on record."

Looking at Tamara, Greg said, "What the hell did you just do?"

Staring at both of them, she answered, "I'm attempting to save a soul."

Redington picked up his recorder and put it in his pocket. Turning towards the door, he said, "Don't either of you go out of town. I will contact you shortly," and he let himself out.

"Tamara! What were you thinking?"

"I was thinking that a young girl just died, and I feel like somehow I am connected to her death."

Chapter 3

Many weeks ago, in Jersey Shore.

It was a beautiful, sunny day, and summer was just around the corner. The best season to make a living, tourist season. Kesia started setting up for the day by placing a small table with two chairs in her usual place, in the sand just off the boardwalk. She loved the sound of the ocean waves as they crashed onto the shore. It made for a surreal experience for her customers.

Kesia was just about to place her tarot deck, which originally was her great, great, great *(too many to count)* Romani grandmother Clementina's, on the dark purple crushed velvet tablecloth when she had a Déjà vu past life memory.

It was of her grandmother winning the cards from a man who had unexpectantly stumbled upon her camp.

Clementina who was sixteen at the time was part of small kumpania (band) who were caravanning from place to place throughout Bohemia. They had stopped by a creek and had set up camp. Their band was mostly made up of family members or those considered family.

It was late one night, and they were sitting around the communal campfire, singing, laughing, and dancing when it happened. Clementina's dog, Tillie started to bark. It was uncommon for a Romani to have a dog, due to the belief that pets were unclean, but Clementina had pleaded endlessly to keep the stray dog. Against her father's better judgement, he let the dirty animal stay.

Tillie had moved towards the bushes at the edge of the camp and was now growling viciously. It was pitch black and hard to see into the trees.

A man with a beard and dressed in many layers of well-worn clothes emerged from the tree line with his hands up. "Forgive me. I heard the music, and as if I were under the influence of a spell, the enchanting sound wooed me in your direction," the stranger slurred in a thick Italian accent and broken Romani. He had been drinking heavily prior to his intrusion.

Lash, Clementina's father, jumped up from his seat on a stump, grabbed a branch from the fire, and waved it in the direction of the man, saying, "Leave, you are not welcome here."

A couple of her uncles joined in. One held a shot gun pointed towards the man's heart.

"Wow, I think you have me mistaken for someone else—no need for guns. I don't want any trouble. Here, I bring gifts," the stranger slurred. A small box fell to the ground as he pulled a few trinkets from his pocket.

Clementina came forth and pulled Tillie away from sniffing the small box. Fascinated with the picture on the box, Clementina picked it up.

"Hey, not that! You cannot have that!" the stranger slurred as he tried to grab it out of her hands, dropping the other trinkets.

Clementina turned away from him as Tillie guarded her against his grasp. Looking at the picture closer, she noticed the colorful images, painted with gold and silver leaf highlights. Opening the box, she discovered similar designs painted on cards. "What are these?" she asked, bewitched by their beauty.

"Never you mind. Give them back."

"Dat (Dad), may I keep these?"

Lash came over to Clementina and looked at what she was holding.

"Please," she said as she looked up at him with pleading eyes.

"No. She can't have them. They are mine," the stranger said, sobering up fast.

Lash looked at Clementina and said, "Clementina, what do you have to trade for the box?"

"Dad, all I own is Tillie. I can't give her up. I'd have nothing."

"Well then, give the box back to the man."

Staring at the box of golden cards and then to her dog, she said, "I will bet my dog Tillie for them."

The stranger looked at her dog and said, "He will bite me. What would I want your dog for?"

Clementina whistled, and Tillie instantly sat, not barking. "Go to the man," she ordered Tillie.

The dog obeyed.

Surprised, the man petted the dog. Tillie let him, then laid down and curled up near his feet.

Lash brought over a small handmade table and placed it between Clementina and the stranger. Her uncles brought over two cut stumps and placed them one on either side.

Clementina sat down and pulled out three walnut shells and a small bead, giving the bead to the man to place under a shell of his choosing.

He sat down and placed the bead under one of the walnut shells.

Clementina started to move the shells around. This was one of her favorite games, and she was very good at it. A few moments later, she stopped and pointed for him to choose. "Your box of cards in exchange for my Tillie," she said confidently.

Knowing that he had watched the shell with the bead underneath the whole time, he was confident that he would win. Not caring to have her dog but extremely interested in keeping his cards, he touched the shell.

Clementina lightly picked up the shell.

Shocked, the stranger picked up the other two shells. The bead was under the last one. "No, that is not possible. I watched you. You tricked me." Standing up, he went to grab the box, but Lash intervened and grabbed his wrist.

"A deal is a deal, and my daughter has won. The box is hers."

"No. You don't understand. They are not normal cards."

Clementina stood up and said, "What are they?"

"They tell the fortune to the person in need."

"They can tell a person's fortune?"

"They can tell more than just their fortune. They can tell their past, present, and future."

"Fascinating! Teach me."

"No, that would take many days, and I am clearly not welcome at your camp."

Clementina looked over to her father and said, "Please, offer him to stay with us as long as he teaches me how to use the cards."

Snapping out of the Déjà vu, Kesia placed the deck on the table, just as a teenage girl came up and asked, "Will you teach me how to use the tarot cards? I will pay you."

Chapter 4

Every morning for over a week, the teenager came back to Kesia asking the same question, 'Will you teach me how to use the cards?' But this morning the girl didn't leave when Kesia said no. Instead, she unfolded a chair she had brought and sat down beside her.

"Hey, what are you doing? You can't sit here. I'm working."

"I am not breaking any laws sitting here."

"You're going to just sit there and watch me?"

"Yes. If you won't teach me, then I am going to learn by watching and listening."

"Fine. I can't make you leave, but if you bother my customers, I can."

"Fine with me," the girl agreed.

After about half an hour of just sitting there, Kesia said to the girl, "What's your name?"

"Trina."

"Why are you so adamant about learning Tarot, Trina?"

"I don't really know. I just know I have to."

"Have to?"

"I keep being drawn to the symbols. I even dream about them."

"Interesting. I haven't met anyone in a very long time that the cards are calling to." Kesia thought back to the last person, a girlfriend she had taught about five years ago. It didn't go so well.

Since the boardwalk was quiet and no one was around, Kesia asked, "How much do you know about the cards?"

"Not much. I have read a bit on the internet, but I can't seem to intuitively read them as you seem to do."

Deciding to teach Trina something, Kesia sorted the cards into five suited piles and placed them picture side up on the table. "What most people don't realize is that tarot cards are similar to a normal deck of playing cards."

Intrigued with the detailed paintings and golden worn edges of the old cards, Trina commented, "Your cards are enchanting. I've never seen this type before."

"These were passed down to me through many generations of grandmothers."

"What is the history behind your deck?"

"The story goes that the Italian Duke of Milano loved playing Trionfi, a French card game, based on trick-taking using the rule of a suit being trump, similar to Bridge, Hearts, or Whist. In the 1400s, the Duke had asked his secretary, the astrologer Marziano da Tortona, to create a symbolic card game based on Virtues and Temptations, and to add a fifth suit consisting of sixteen cards, which would trump the other four suits. Later, the game was renamed Tarocchi. Now here's some trivia that you might not know. The term tarot derives from tarocchi, which translates to "foolishness."

"Interesting, so Tarot came from Italy?"

"Yes," Kesia continued, "I doubt my cards are the original cards, but they are painted in their likeness."

"Outstanding." Trina picked up a card and looked at the detailed paintings Kesia was talking about. "Wait? Are you telling me that the deck of cards that my dad plays Texas Hold'em, or my mom plays Bridge with are tarot cards?"

"Any person who reads tarot and has memorized the meaning to each individual number in the suit could use any standard deck to tell your future."

"Fascinating. Tell me more."

"My cards are more than just a deck of cards full of pictures, they are symbolic of the times. The illustrations, also known as 'pips,' display the geography and culture of that era. Here look."

Trina looked closely at the five piles Kesia had just placed on the table, while saying, "My cards are called the Rider-Waite tarot deck and they are also symbolic."

"Oh, those are good too. I have played with them as well. These are similar to your deck, whereas each card tells a story." Pointing again at the cards, Kesia continued, "The modern-day tarot deck has four sets of suited cards, Ace to King, called the Lower Arcana, which represents the *'mundane'* secrets of life here on Earth. The fifth set is called the Higher Arcana, which represents the *'celestial'* secrets granted from the angels."

Pointing to a card with words written on it, Trina asked, "I haven't seen these before."

"They are similar to your higher arcana cards, but instead of the twenty-two 'trump cards' in your deck, my deck has only sixteen."

"Are there any cards in the standard deck that represent the trump cards?"

"The only card used is the Joker, also known as the Jester. In your deck it is called the Fool, mine doesn't use any."

"My parents are going to flip when they find out that they are playing with tarot cards."

Kesia laughed, "I wish I was a fly on the wall when you prove it to them."

Trina laughed at the thought, then looked at each suit as Kesia started to tell her about them.

Pointing to the first card pile, Kesia said, "If you were playing with a standard deck of cards, this suit's pip or symbol would be **Clubs**. In my deck, its pip is a Turtle Dove, and in your tarot deck it is a Wand, but no matter which deck you are reading from, this suit represents *virtuous or sinful communication and messages*."

Kesia pointed to another pile. "In a standard deck, this suit is represented by **Diamonds**. In my deck, it is the Phoenix. Look closely, each card also has gold coins on them. Do you see the faces? This one is of the Duke."

Trina squinted. "Ya, if I look really close."

"Your tarot deck uses the five-sided star or pentacle for this suit's pip. This suit represents *virtuous or sinful money and materialistic items*."

"How exciting."

Pointing to a third pile, Kesia said, "This next suit in the standard deck would be **Hearts,** Doves in mine, and Cups in yours. It represents *virtuous or sinful emotions*." Moving her finger to another pile, "This suit would be **Spades** in a standard deck, Eagles in mine, and notice the eagle is holding a sword. Your deck's pip in this suit is also Swords, but depending on the deck you'll see curved or straight swords. This suit represents the *virtuous or sinful actions or choices a person makes*."

Trina nodded, trying to remember what Kesia was teaching her. "Let me get this straight. Arrows or Wands are Clubs and represent communication, Pentacles or Money are

Diamonds and represent materialistic things in a person's life, Hearts are Cups and represent their emotions, and lastly, Swords are Spades and represent their actions,"

"Yep, you've got it."

Trina looked at Kesia's deck. "Hey, I don't see the page, knight, queen, or king?"

"True. My deck only goes up to ten in each suit, not fourteen like in your Tarot deck or thirteen in a standard deck of playing cards. You may have also noticed that your cards and mine use the Roman numeral instead of imperial. The Jack in a standard deck is considered the Page in your deck, and your deck has an extra card called the Knight or Cavalier. You may have also noticed in your deck that the Page has the number eleven, and the Knight has the number twelve written on it. In both decks, the Queen is the Queen, and the King is the King."

"Okay, but what are these cards then?" Trina asked, pointing to a card with words written on it. "I haven't seen these before."

"In my set, these pips make-up the fifth suit, portraying the *Gods and Heroes* from the time of the Roman pantheon. They are similar to your higher arcana cards."

"Oh."

"The only difference is that your deck has twenty-two trump cards, and my deck has sixteen cards, but no matter, both decks represent the *secrets from the universe or a higher power*."

Trina picked up Kesia's old cards and looked at them more closely. "Wow. I didn't know there was so much history involved in tarot cards, not to mention how much there is to learn."

"We've barely even started," Kesia chuckled just as a customer came up and asked if she could have a reading.

Chapter 5

The next morning Trina was back to learn more. Kesia's first customer was a lady whose husband had cheated on her and left her for a younger woman.

Trina watched as Kesia tapped the 'Rider-Waite' deck three times on the table, shuffled the deck, and then placed three cards face down onto the velvet tablecloth, which was a beautiful contrast to the cards.

Trina listened as Kesia told the lady her fate by reading the symbols on the cards.

Kesia turned over the first card. It was the five of cups. A man dressed in black was staring down at three golden wine glasses that had spilled. He did not notice the other two full glasses behind him. "Your husband is crying over spilled milk. He is pouting over what he can't have and is too stubborn to turn around and see what he still has."

The lady was almost in tears. "Before he left, our three sons moved out of the house, all about the same time. He never paid attention to our two daughters."

"I see," Kesia said, knowing that the customer is always right. She had been doing readings for as long as she could remember. Even though she was only sixteen, her years of reading the cards taught her that tarot was the next best thing to a counselor. Many people came for direction and guidance. In the hands of an experienced tarot card reader, the customer would have the answers they were seeking.

"What does the second card reveal," the lady asked.

Kesia turned over the second card. It was the 'Wheel of Fortune,' the tenth trump card in the higher arcana. "You are going to be okay. Your children will be okay. This card represents that anything is possible. It is like a lotto ticket and you've just won big."

"Oh, thank goodness. I need some good news right now," the lady said as she sank back into the chair.

Kesia turned over the last card, representing the lady's future. It was the nine of pentacles. The card was of a regal lady walking in her lush and fruitful garden. "You are going to be more than okay. You are going to be well off, financially, and you will have the time to enjoy the perks of life."

"How nice. Thank you. That makes my heart lighter already." She paid Kesia and left a large tip.

Trina came closer and said, "Hey, I noticed you were playing with a deck like mine, why?"

"I knew you would be back, and I thought I would demonstrate tarot using the same cards you would be using."

"Thanks."

Watching Kesia pick up the money, Trina was amazed at how much the lady had paid her. "Wow, she left you twice what the cost of the reading was. My dad would say that you have quite a scam going on here."

"It is not a scam. The cards reveal the person's destiny. I don't tell her anything that the cards don't tell me."

"You never make up a story so that you get more money?'

"No. I don't need to. The cards tell the story. The lower arcana tells me what is going on in the person's life and the higher arcana tells me what the gods have in store for them. Besides, why would I lie? Then I would have to face the negative karma that comes with lying."

"What do you mean negative karma?"

"God gave me this spiritual gift, and if I abuse this gift, then I will be punished. It is not worth a few bucks to have bad karma following me around, wrecking my life. Besides, I make good money helping people on their journey by telling the truth."

Trina revealed a bit about her past. "My dad yelled at me once when he saw me playing with my tarot deck. He had the minister come over to talk to me and banish any evil spirits that I might have conjured. He showed me in the Old Testament of the Bible, Deuteronomy 18:9-13 where it said, 'Let no one be found among you who sacrifices their son or daughter in the fire, who practices divination or sorcery, interprets omens, engages in witchcraft, or casts spells, or who is a medium or spiritualist or who consults the dead.' The minister had me pray with him for hours."

"I am amazed you are sitting here with me after all that."

"I can't help it. I'm fascinated by Tarot."

Kesia confessed, "I prayed to God once, asking why if I was given the 'gift of prophecy' which is written in the New Testament Corinthians 1,12:4-11, why is it wrong then to practice prophesizing, as said in Deuteronomy."

"And what was his answer?"

"The answer I received was to imagine a person who comes to me to tell their future and it comes true. Then months later, they come back for another reading, and it also comes true. The act of continually telling someone else their future creates a co-dependent person and takes away their control."

"That sounds harsh. So, you agree with the minister."

"Not quite. I believe that people come to me to hear what God wants them to hear. I empower people with my words. That is why I am here on the beach. The customers I have are tourists and probably will never see me again."

"What happens if they do come back?"

"Then I have been instructed to empower them by teaching them something instead."

"Interesting."

Chapter 6

Today, in New York City.

It's time.

A bit startled that Susannah had contacted her, Lexi answered, "Time for what?"

Your first lesson.

"What do you mean, my first lesson?"

You forgot already?

"Forgot what?"

What Gabriel said to you.

"I thought I had dreamed that."

No, it was real.

"Susannah, I don't believe in prophecy."

You will.

I doubt it. Fine. When are you expecting me to start?"

Now.

"Right now?"

Yes.

"But I am busy creating my new fashion designs. Sabastian is expecting them tomorrow morning. I still have lots to do."

You'll manage. Let's get started. Gabriel asked me to introduce you to Bath Kol. Her name means 'Voice of God.' She is one of the main angels of prophecy. Her role is to guide you towards your best future life path. Once you connect with her, you can ask her anything.

"How do I do that?"

Don't worry. I'll help you with that part.

"Good, because I don't know what she looks like. I haven't even heard of her name before."

She works with the Holy Ghost and Gabriel.

"She works with the Holy Ghost. Like in father, son, and Holy Ghost, Holy Ghost?"

Yes. Actually, many people get her mixed up with Gabriel.

"Archangel Gabriel, God's messenger?"

Yes, the same.

"How could anyone get Archangel Gabriel mixed up with a woman?"

Interesting.

"What's interesting?"

Never mind, that's not important right now.

"What isn't?"

Lexi, the important thing right now is meeting Bath Kol. Sit back and relax.

Lexi did as Susannah instructed and relaxed into her chair by putting her head back against the seat's back.

Now, take a couple of deep breaths. Great. In a moment, you are going to imagine the level of light—a part of Heaven that your spirit can reach without crossing over. Take a deep breath and imagine a robin blue-colored egg, soft light blue. Allow this color to envelop you as you enter this new level of the celestial world.

This level of Heaven is where the Seraphim angels, "Spirits of Love," the highest level to God hangs out when they are not needed to answer the prayers of a human soul.

Lexi just nodded as she relaxed deeply into the meditation.

In a moment, Bath Kol will come and greet you. Her energy is very light, very soft. One might say 'silent as the night.' She comes and goes without anyone seeing her. Her energy is transparent, where you might only notice her as a shimmer rather than ghostly.

She does not communicate in the typical way that you are used to. Tamara taught you the celestial channels, Audio, Knower, Visual, and Feeler, but Bath Kol, the Holy Ghost, and Gabriel, communicate through a frequency of light energy that most humans cannot perceive. Bath Kol communicates in the frequency of omniscience. To understand the difference, imagine all the colors of a rainbow. You do not see the beautiful colors until moisture is in the air, reflecting them like a prism, but the colors are always there. It is only your perception of the frequency of the colors that changed. The celestial channels are equivalent to the colors of the rainbow, individual of the whole. The omniscient frequency is the whole of the celestial channels, all at once. Lexi, Bath Kol is ready to meet with you now. Tell me what you see when you see her.

Lexi took a breath and said, "All I see is sparkly energy, glistening and shimmering like fresh snow on a sunny day.

Perfect. Now go ahead and introduce yourself.

"Sure. Hi, I am Lexi, Susannah's sister. She has set up this meeting upon the request of Archangel Gabriel, the teacher of prophets. I am sorry if they were mistaken, and I have taken up your time. I do not think I am worthy of such an honor. In the Bible, I have read about the prophets, and somehow, they have confused me with someone who belongs in that caliber. I am just a fashion designer from New York City."

In the softest voice, so angelic like, Bath Kol spoke these divine words, *Welcome, Alexandra, I have been waiting for this day. You have been chosen to be an Earth Angel of the Voice. You have been chosen to speak for those of us who the human soul has forgotten how to hear. Alexandra, do not underestimate the power of*

God. Creator has a plan for each of us. Part of your destiny is to deliver his messages.

Tears started to form and roll down Lexi's cheeks. Being in the presence of an angel was overwhelming. Even though Lexi knew she was imagining all of this, part of her knew that her past experience of the celestial world was true.

Dear Child of God, what question do you have for me?

Lexi took a breath, not knowing what question to ask. "Ah, I guess my question is, how do I contact you in the future?"

Good question. All you need to do is call my name and I will be there.

"That's it, just call your name?"

Yes. Now that we have been introduced, that is all that you need to do. I am your humble servant and here to help you in any way needed to make the human soul hear our message.

"Thank you. I am honored. I will create a plan, and when I am ready, I will ask for your help."

With that said, Bath Kol's energy disappeared.

Great job, Lexi. Susannah said.

"Susannah? Do you think I am ready for this challenge?"

You were born ready, little sis.

Chapter 7

June 6th, in Jersey Shore.

It was getting later in the evening as Kesia was sitting at her Gypsy Fortune Telling booth when she noticed a couple talking on the boardwalk. The lady walked over and asked for a reading.

"Hi, please have a seat."

Tamara sat down.

"Give me your hand," Kesia directed. Taking the lady's hand, she turned it slightly so she could see the palm better. As she looked, a blackbird seemed to fly out of the lady's hand, squawking at Kesia's face. Startled, she instantly stood up, yelling, "Leave, I can't read you. You are cursed."

Not listening to the lady's question, Kesia said a prayer in her native tongue, Romani, "Dear Saint Benedict, I thank God for showering you with his grace, to love him above all else, and to establish a monastic rule that has helped so many of his children live full and holy lives. Through the cross of Jesus Christ, I ask you to please intercede that God might protect me, my loved ones, past and present, my home, property, possessions, and workplace. Protect me today and always by your holy blessing, that we may never be separated from all the blessed. Through your intercession, may we be delivered from temptation, spiritual oppression, physical ills, and disease. Protect us from all that is evil. Amen."

As she said the prayer, she gathered her tablecloth and everything it was holding and ran away. Kissing a pendant hanging from her neck that her mother had given her to ward off evil spirits, she looked back at the lady.

As she was running along the beach, Trina happened to be coming her way. "Hey, what is all the rush?"

"Come on, it isn't safe here," Kesia answered as she kept running.

Trina changed her direction and followed Kesia. "Where are we going?"

"Somewhere safe."

Trina picked up the tarot deck that fell out of Kesia's velvet cloth bundle of goodies and put it into her pocket.

After what seemed like a long time, Kesia finally slowed down. Putting her bundle onto the ground, bending over from being out of breath, she looked back and said, "We need to get to my mom's house. She'll know what to do."

"What are we running from?" Trina asked.

"Evil!"

"Kesia, you're scaring me. What evil?"

"The evil of a curse attached to a feather from a blackbird."

"You believe in curses?"

"You don't?"

"Well, I have sworn at people, and nothing has happened. They never turned into a toad."

"A toad? What are you talking about? That isn't a curse you idiot. You would need a spell for that," Kesia said, shaking her head in disappointment. She really thought this girl would become her friend, but not if she didn't believe in the old ways."

"Hey, don't call me an idiot. I am not the one running away."

"Whatever. I don't have time for this." Looking around, Kesia said, "I have to go to the bathroom before we go to my mom's. I'll be right back. Wait here and watch my stuff, will ya?"

"Sure," Trina said, still hurt from being called an idiot.

Kesia walked over to the public washrooms and went inside. As she walked into the stall and locked the door, she slipped on a puddle of water and hit her head on the porcelain toilet, knocking herself unconscious.

Chapter 8

July 6th, in New York City.

He was staring at his nameplate on his desk, *Detective Ferguson Redington, Homicide Investigator.* Redington was thinking about how long he had been with the Midtown South Precinct, Manhattan Bureau when Officer Fletcher came in. In his Scottish accent, he said, "Red, the Captain wants to see you."

"Sure, I'll be just a moment."

With a smirk, Officer Fletcher added, "You better hurry. He's in one of his moods this morning."

"Thanks for the heads up, Arrow."

"Anytime."

Watching Arrow leave, Redington remembered the day Fletcher got his nickname.

It was on the first day when they were in the academy, and Redington's new partner, Davidson, had come into the locker room. "Hey, Red, hey Fletch."

"Don't call me that," Fletcher said.

"What, Fletch? Why not? I shorten Red's name. He doesn't seem to care."

"My dad is called that, and I'm nothing like my dad."

"Well, what should I call you then? Arrow, as in the meaning of your last name, arrow maker?"

"I actually kind of like that. Sure, that works."

"It's agreed, from now on, your nickname is Arrow," Davidson said as he shook Arrow's hand.

Coming back to the moment, Redington got up and walked to the Captain's office. Tapping on the door frame, Redington said, "You called for me, Cap?"

Looking up from his paperwork, Captain Sawyer said, "Red, I have thought about that proposal from the psychic." Looking down at his papers, "Miss Reeve. I would like to hear what she thinks she knows about this Jersey Shore murder."

"I thought you said it was out of our jurisdiction?"

"It was, but the mother has come forth. She lives here in Manhattan and wants more answers. With her money, she can buy that information."

"I thought it was a Gypsy girl we were investigating. How does her mother have that kind of influence?"

"No, we found the Gypsy. She was unconscious in the bathroom. When she woke up, she left the bathroom, but freaked out when she saw all the cops, and hid. She didn't go to the cops until she saw her picture on the TV."

"Then who's body, is it?"

"The girl who died is Congressman Wells's daughter. Her mother is Catherine Abeling, whose family migrated from Germany back in the early 1800s. Catherine comes from old money. Her great-grandpa was a ship manufacturing tycoon."

"I see. So, what exactly do you need from me?"

"You know Miss Reeve, right?"

"I guess you could say that."

"I need you to go and get her for me."

"And then?"

"And then I need her to do that voodoo stuff."

"Excuse me. Voodoo stuff?"

"You know. The psychic stuff."

Shaking his head in disbelief, Redington said, "Captain, you believe that stuff really works?"

"Over the years, I have seen my share of psychics. Sure, some of them are quacks, but there have been a few over the years with intel that no one but the murderer could have known. I don't know how they do it, but I am desperate, and I need to find who murdered young Miss Trina Wells."

"Sure, I can go get Miss Reeve. When do you want me to pick her up?"

"ASAP, and Redington if she won't come willingly, arrest her."

"I am sure it won't come to that," Redington said, knowing that Tamara was into this 'voodoo' stuff.

Chapter 9

$\mathcal{K}$nocking on Tamara's door, Redington and two other officers, one being Officer Fletcher, were there to take her in, willing or not.

Looking at the two men in uniform, Tamara said, "Redington, what's going on?"

"Miss Reeve, I am here to ask that you come with us willingly to headquarters, and if you do not come willingly, I am ordered to arrest you," Redington said in the tone of an officer of the law.

"Is this some kind of joke? Red, what is going on?"

Staying professional in front of the other two officers, Redington said, "Miss Reeve, please come with us," motioning for her to come outside.

Shaking her head in disbelief, she said, "I need my purse," as she turned around to go get it.

One of the officers barged in to make sure she was not going to do anything stupid.

"What the? Red, this is uncalled for. What is going on?'

"Please, Tamara," Red said, breaking protocol. "Just come with us willingly."

"I was."

As she grabbed her purse, the officer took hold of her arm and guided her out of her house.

A couple of neighbors watched the spectacle as she was put into the back of the squad car as if she was a criminal.

Smiling at her neighbor, Tamara yelled out, "Don't worry, Mrs. Edgecomb, everything is okay."

Redington followed behind the squad car in his unmarked vehicle.

Once at the precinct, Tamara was taken into an interrogation room to wait.

"Captain, was this really necessary?" Redington asked as they looked through the two-way mirror at Tamara.

"We have to know that she had nothing to do with the murder."

"I know Tamara. There is no way that she murdered that young girl."

"We have to make sure that she is legit. I don't want any wanna-be psychic detectives giving us bogus information. You know how rich that girl's parents are. They could have my badge if all this goes wrong."

"Well, let me do the talking."

"Too late. Officer Bury is handling this case."

"I thought I was going to be the one talking to Tamara?"

"No. You have personal relations with her."

"I wouldn't call it personal relations, but yes, I did spend a few days with her in Sweden, but on Miss Constantine's behalf."

Seeing the look on the captain's face, Redington turned to listen and watch from the other side of the glass.

"Miss Reeve, I have been informed that you have admitted on record that you may be responsible for the death of Miss Trina Wells," Officer Bury said as he started the interrogation.

"Wait. No. I remember the news on the TV saying that the person who died was Miss Kesia Bango, the Gypsy tarot card reader. Who is Trina Wells?"

Captain Sawyer looked at Redington and said, "What is going on? The recording you brought in said she had something to do with the girl's death."

"Captain, Tamara and I were talking about the girl who gave her a tarot card reading on the boardwalk in Jersey Shore. I assumed that is who died. No one told me that it was another girl."

"Great. Get her out of here," Captain Sawyer said to one of the other officers as he left the viewing room.

Redington quickly went out to meet up with Tamara.

"Red, what is going on?" she asked.

"Seems like there has been a mix-up."

"Are you telling me Kesia never died?"

"That is what I just found out myself. Sorry about that."

"But why did they think Trina was Kesia?" Tamara asked, confused about why she was now caught up in all this mess.

"Let me go find out. I doubt I can legally tell you much, but I will tell you what I can. I'll call you soon, Tamara." Redington motioned to one of the officers who was listening in to their conversation that he was done.

Chapter 10

"Tamara answered her cell phone, "Hi Lexi, how are you?"

"No, the question is, how are you?"

"I'm fine. Why do you ask?"

"You are not going to believe this, but I started my prophecy training."

"Your prophecy training. Do you mean intuitive training?"

"No, prophecy training."

"Who are you getting your training from?"

"Archangel Gabriel talked to me awhile back, saying that I would become a prophet. I know, that sounds crazy. I thought so too, but Susannah has already introduced me to Bath Kol."

Tamara sat down. She hadn't even met Bath Kol. "Wow, Lexi. That is big."

"That isn't the cool part. The cool part is that I now get visions. I had one last night. That is why I'm calling you."

"You had a vision about me?"

"Yes."

"What was it?"

"It's a little mixed-up, but I saw you on a beach talking to a girl. Then I saw a picture of her, like in a news flash, but she is not who you are looking for. Then for some reason, I saw Redington digging around searching for clues."

Tamara was shocked at the accuracy. "That is amazing, Lexi. There is no way you could have known any of that."

"Tamara, what percent of accuracy are we talking about, fifty percent, seventy-five?"

"No, Lexi, one-hundred percent."

"Whoot, whoot! Lexi yelled, doing a little joyful dance. "I've been practicing what you taught us in class. I guess it's paid off."

Snapping out of being in shock at how accurate Lexi was for a newbie, Tamara said, "Hey, Lexi, I think I could use your help. Are you free to come over tonight?"

"Sure. What time?"

"How about six-thirty?"

"Ya, I can be there by then."

"Hey, Lex, can you come alone. I want to keep what we are going to do really secretive."

"Sure. I'll tell Edward we are having a girl's night."

"Thanks, Lex. See you soon."

*T*amara answered the door and let Lexi in. "Hi Lexi, thanks for coming on such short notice."

"Hey, what are friends for. You dropped everything and flew to Peru. This is the least I can do."

Tamara smiled, thinking back to their adventure. "Come on in, Lex, and make yourself comfortable."

"Mmm, that smells good. Is that Chai tea I smell?"

"Yep. It sure is. Hope you want some 'cause I made enough for both of us."

"Yes, please."

Tamara went into the kitchen and grabbed a couple of beautiful hand-made pottery mugs from the shelf, and poured the Chai in. Bringing the mugs into the living room, she said, "Lex, I think you are the perfect person to help me with this."

"With the murder case?"

Tamara looked up, surprised, and said, "How did you know that?"

"Susannah told me."

"Holy cow, Lex. I think you have surpassed me in all this Celestial communication stuff."

"I doubt that, but thanks. If it wasn't for you, I wouldn't have been open to the possibility that the spirit world and all its wonder even existed. You are such a great friend and earth angel."

"You're too kind. Spirit has a way of creating opportunities for enlightened souls to advance. I am sure you would have learned it eventually with or without me, but I am glad it was with me."

"Probably, Susannah doesn't seem to be disappearing from my life anytime soon."

"No, now that she is one of your guardian angels, she will be with you for life."

Lexi smiled at the thought that coincidently her sister became her guardian angel. How lucky and blessed she considered herself. "Okay, how do you want to do this psychic detective stuff?"

"Wow. You are good. I'm impressed."

"Sorry, I wasn't trying to impress you. It's just that clear to me now."

"No. Please. Feel free to let your intuitive gifts out. I need anything and everything you got for this one."

"Okay, thanks. That means a lot coming from you."

"Here is what I know. You know when Greg and I were in Jersey Shore?"

"Ya."

"Well, remember I told you about the girl who gave me the Gypsy reading and said I was cursed?"

"How could I forget."

"Okay, well, I thought she was dead."

"What? Why?"

"I saw her photo on the TV."

"And…"

"Well, it turns out it wasn't her. There was a mix-up with the girl who really died."

"Fascinating. I see now why you said I was accurate. But how does Redington fit into this?"

"Funny. He actually came here this morning and arrested me."

"He did what?"

"Well, he didn't actually arrest me, but he and a couple of officers escorted me to the station house."

"Oh, my God. Tamara that is terrible. They think you have something to do with this?"

"Well, that part is my fault."

"I'm listening."

"I had Redington come over, and I told him that I think my curse killed her.

"Oh, my God. You didn't?"

"Ya, I know. But I couldn't let that girl's soul be lost or worse, taken by demons."

"I get it, Tamara. Okay, but who died then?"

"I don't know anything but her name, Trina Wells. I had an idea that I was planning to do with Redington's help, but now I can't since there has been a mix-up of who died. Now, I require your help."

"Sure. What do you need me to do?"

"I am going to go into a meditative state, and I want you to ask me these questions once I am relaxed and ready." Tamara passed Lexi a paper with the questions already written out. "Once you ask the questions, write down everything that I answer back."

"I can do that. Anything else?"

"Sure. You can ask Susannah, Archangel Gabriel, and Bath Kol to help us."

"Great idea." Lexi closed her eyes and asked for their help and protection. Opening her eyes, she asked, "Anything else?"

"Not that I can think of. Okay, I am going to take a few deep breaths now and prepare myself. When I nod, I will be ready for you to ask me the questions."

"Perfect."

Tamara laid down on her couch and closed her eyes.

Lexi watched as Tamara took a few deep breaths, then nodded.

Lexi looked at the paper and read the first question. Well, it was more of a statement than a question. "With the power invested in me, I, Lexi Constantine will enhance and guide Tamara Reeve's energy so that she may astral travel back in time to the day or night of this murder involving Trina Wells and Kesia Bango." Lexi was a bit surprised by what Tamara had her read. "Tamara, with your next deep breath, please allow your energy to go back in time to the day or night of Miss Trina Wells' murder."

Lexi gave Tamara a few moments to astral travel. As Tamara nodded her head, Lexi knew that she was signaling for Lexi to continue.

"Tamara, please allow your spirit to scan the day of June sixth of this year and pinpoint the murder of Trina Wells."

Lexi gave Tamara a moment.

Tamara popped out of the meditation and said, "Lexi, she was killed by… Oh my! I have to call Redington."

Chapter 11

July 1438 in the Southern Kingdom of Bohemia, Now Nosislav, Czech Republic.

Carlo had been walking for days through this part of the Holy Roman Empire, Bohemia. He recently had fled a medieval tavern in a nearby village due to an argument he had with one of the locals when he stumbled upon the sound of music playing from a band of gypsies, dancing and singing among their caravans.

Intoxicated not only from the alcohol but also from the bewitching folk song, he wandered through the dark forest to have a better look. Leaning on a tree, he peered through the branches. He watched in bewilderment at the colorful skirts swirling as the lady's hips moved seductively in front of the fire.

Moving to get a better look, his jacket got caught on a small branch. When he was trying to untangle himself, the dog from the gypsy camp started to bark.

The music stopped, and the dog came closer to the edge of the trees where he was standing. Scared that the dog had rabies or something and would bite him, he decided to show himself to the band.

It had been a while since he had spoken the Romani language. "Forgive me. I heard the music, and as if I were under the influence of a spell, the enchanting sound wooed me into your direction."

Carlo watched as a man jumped up, bumped a basket with his leg, grabbed a stick from the fire, and waved it in his direction while yelling something at him. Still tipsy from drinking, he wasn't sure what was really going on until a couple of the men pointed guns at him.

"Wow, I think you have me mistaken for someone else—no need for guns. I don't want any trouble. Here, I bring gifts." As he pulled a few trinkets from his pocket to give as a peace offering, his box of cards fell to the ground.

One of the dancing goddesses came forth from the fire and started to bend down to pick up the box that had fallen, but her beast started to bark and paced back and forth in front of her, stopping her.

Through glossy eyes, Carlo wasn't sure if he saw what he thought he saw. A snake, but not one that was native to this area. Through the light of the fire, he could see that this one had the skin of olive green with black and white bands that went all the way up its long body, it must have been fourteen feet long. Frightened by the dog, its oval flattened shaped hooded head spread out making it look even more threatening. Its eyes flashed a golden color from the light of the fire, but the scariest part was its two fangs that he could see as it hissed.

Carlo could see a man coming near, playing and waving a wooden Hindu instrument, called a pungi. He had seen one at a market but had never heard it play. The musical instrument consists of a reservoir into which air was blown and then channeled into two reed pipes. The sound that was coming out was very unique, with a high, thin tone that was sharp and penetrating, but also with a continuous nasal low humming.

Carlo watched as the snake mimicked the movements of the instrument being waved in the air.

It was very hypnotic to watch.

Suddenly the man snapped up the snake by its neck and put it into the fallen weaved basket, and closed the lid tightly.

Mesmerized by the snake-charmer, he almost missed her picking up his box.

"Hey, not that! You cannot have that!" He tried to grab it out of her hands, dropping the other trinkets he was holding.

The beast guarded her against his attempted grasp.

"What are these?" he heard her ask.

"Never you mind. Give them back."

He saw her turn to the man with the fire stick and started to talk to him in their native tongue. He couldn't understand most of what she said due to the speed she was talking.

He did hear though, "I will bet my dog Tillie for them."

Looking at her dog, he said, "He will bite me. What would I want your dog for?"

The sound of her whistle hurt Carlo's ears. The dog laid down and calmly curled up near his feet, so he petted it.

The next thing he knew, he was watching the girl place a bead under one of three walnut shells. He knew this game and tried to watch the shell with the bead.

Picking a shell, he shouted, "No, that is not possible. I watched you. You tricked me." Standing up, he went to grab the box, but her father intervened and grabbed his wrist and spoke again.

"No. You don't understand. They are not normal cards."

"What are they?" she asked.

"They tell the fortune to the person in need."

"They can tell a person's fortune?"

"They can tell more than just their fortune. They can tell their past, present, and future."

"Fascinating! Teach me."

"No, that would take many days, and I am clearly not welcome at your camp."

He watched as the girl looked over to the man and said, "Please, offer him to stay with us as long as he teaches me how to use the cards."

Chapter 12

Carlo was trying to figure out how to get his cards back when the girl and her dog came over to where he was sitting. He watched as she pulled the cards out of the box.

"Why would you use these cards to predict someone's future?"

"Cartomancy or divination with cards is used to understand your destiny. The card's imagery tells a story and depending on the cards chosen your question or your intent will tell the reader your past, present, and future. The cards reflect your emotions of what is going on in your life at this moment."

"Why would anyone care to know their fate? Aren't they happy with their lives?"

Carlo looked at the girl and smirked. She was a looker this one. Beautiful in such an exotic way. Carlo looked around at their surroundings.

"Not everyone has the story you do. A loving family, freedom, and no cares for success or money. You are truly blessed. What is your name?"

"Clementina."

"I am Carlo. I arrived here from Rome a few months ago. I was told that the land here had riches far beyond my imagination. I was as foolish as these cards." He pointed to the deck, trying to make them less desirable to her.

"They enchant me." Passing the cards to him, she ordered, "Read for me."

Carlo took the cards from her and lightly shuffled them. Fanning them out, he said, "Pick a card."

"Any card?"

"Yes."

Clementina passed her hand over the cards before picking one.

"The card you chose will represent you." Flipping the card over to see the picture, he took a moment then said, "The fifth card of the trump cards is the god, Apollo. Apollo has been recognized as a god of archery, music and dance, truth, prophecy, healing, and diseases. He is seen as the most beautiful god. He is an oracular god and considered to provide wise and insightful counsel or prophetic predictions.

He is the god who affords help and wards off evil. He is also the patron of seafarers, foreigners, and the protector of fugitives and refugees."

"So, what does that have to do with me?"

"It means that you have similar attributes to his. That you have the ability to follow in his footsteps and do what he did."

"Those are pretty words that you use to sway a girl into believing she is more than she is. True, you had me for a moment. I was taken into the story, and for an instant, I wanted what you said to be true. Fascinating."

"What is fascinating?"

"The magic of the story."

"I was only telling you what the card meant. That was all."

"Hmm. Is that all the cards can do?"

"Yes. They can only tell a story."

"Why do you have the cards?"

"Back home, in Rome, I was working for a painter who was working in the Vatican. My job was to travel from Rome to Milan to Ferrara and back again, picking up the materials he needed.

While I was staying in one of the local taverns in Ferrara, I came upon a man who was predicting the patron's futures using cards. I was captivated by the charm of the cards. As the man spoke the words describing the person's future, he would point at specific symbols on a card.

I watched him for hours that night. Finally, I asked to have him to do a reading for me. I paid the man two soldi and sat down.

He had me do what I did for you, pick a card. My card was not as omniscient as yours. I chose the four of eagles."

Clementina was riveted. "What does the four of eagles represent?"

"The eagle represents the power of Zeus. If the card is up-right, it is good and means that my life was stable but at a crossroad. My card was upside down. I was in store for some trouble. The man told me that he had traveled to China, and the word 'four' sounds similar to the word death. My card being upside down was a bad omen."

"Did you believe him?"

"Not at first. I traveled home, not thinking much of the reading. Soon though, I experienced many bad things. I was fired due to a fire that I was blamed for. I was robbed on the way home. Then when I finally got home, I was evicted."

"That's just coincidence."

"I thought so too. Having nothing to lose, I went to find the man and his card reading. It took me weeks to find him. I did odd jobs along the way to feed myself."

"What did you do when you found him?"

"I asked for another reading."

"Did he give you one?"

"No. I had no money to pay him."

"What did you do to change your luck?"

"Nothing. I couldn't afford another reading."

"So. How did you get these cards."

"After following him for a few days. I decided that my luck was so bad that I had nothing to lose, so I waited one night until he came out of a tavern and knocked him on the head with a stick and stole the cards."

"You didn't!"

"I had to. The cards had put a curse on me. I had to destroy them."

"Destroy them!"

"That was the only thing I could think of."

"What happened next?"

"The man started to come to as I was digging through his pockets. He started to yell. I grabbed the cards and fled the scene."

"Where did you go?"

"As luck would have it, I stumbled onto your camp. These cards are cursed."

"I doubt that."

"You'll see."

"Tell me what all the cards mean."

The two of them sat there discussing each card well into the night.

Chapter 13

Clementina was cleaning some dishes by the creek-side when Carlo came up beside her. As she looked up, he startled her. "You shaved."

"It was getting itchy, and one of your uncles had a blade I could borrow."

"You are younger than I thought."

"How old did you think I was?"

"Like my dat."

Carlo laughed. "He is old enough to be my dat."

"I can see that now." she blushed.

"Do you like it?" Carlo asked as he rubbed his smooth skin.

"It's okay."

"I'll take that as a yes."

Lash came down to the creek and ordered, "Hurry with the cleaning. We are leaving soon."

Carlo stood up. "Where are you going?"

"We are moving on to the next village."

"Oh." He looked at her and back at Lash. "I would like to volunteer and join your travels."

Looking at the two kids, he decided that Carlo would be trouble. "No."

As her father walked away, Clementina ran after him pleading, "Please dat, he will be handy. He knows how to work with his hands."

"No!"

She stopped and lowered her head. Slowly turning to face Carlo, her look told him everything. She liked him.

"Don't worry, Clementina. I am very good at walking. I will follow your caravan."

Clementina looked up and smiled just as her dad yelled, "Hurry. We are ready to leave!"

Gathering the dishes, she ran back to her father. Then after helping to collect the last of their belongings, Clementina hopped onto the back of the wagon and tried to spy Carlo as they left the camp.

They traveled for hours, and she was scared that he would not be able to keep up.

Her band finally stopped on the outskirts of another village. She helped her mother set up camp, looking up every so often to see if Carlo had caught up with them.

It had been a couple of days and still no Carlo. She was getting worried that he would never find them. Her heart broke a little more each day as she started to lose hope that he would ever come.

Many days later, Lash came over to her and said, "Clementina, it is time for you to find a husband. I have arranged a meeting tonight with many suitable men."

"What? No!"

"I am the leader of this band, and my word is final! You will be married tonight," he declared as he turned and left.

Distraught and in love with Carlo, she started to cry. Walking down to the creek, she sat down on a log and watched the water as it splattered against the rocks as it traveled downstream.

Pulling out the cards in her pocket, she searched for Apollo. Staring at the card, she prayed that her true love would find her before marrying another.

That night her mother helped her get dressed. She wore a skirt of many colors that flared out as she twirled. Her mother adorned her with ankle bracelets to show off her bare skin. Clementina's hair was brushed, and a long ribbon was tied into it so that it could trail down and flow when she danced. Her mother gave her a sheer silver veil to wear over the shoulder of her billowing blouse. Clementina was beautiful.

Clementina knew that the veil would become part of her dance tonight. Creating an illusion of mystery as she could use it to conceal her face as she danced. She also knew the customs of her people. She was at the age where she needed to contribute to the well-being of her people.

Finding a suitable husband who could help support the band was her parents' goal.

Clementina was to stay in the covered wagon until her father had served enough liquor to the men who had come. Not that he needed to, his daughter was gorgeous and needed no illusion to summon a husband.

She now could hear the music as it started to play. The day had turned into night, and the campfire was blazing. Food had been served, the wine had been poured, and she could hear laughter as the liquor started to do its magic.

Clementina heard her father whistle and knew it was time for her to come out and dance. Slowly getting out of the wagon while praying one last time that Carlo would save her from this fate. With no other choice, she covered herself with the veil and seductively started to move her hips to the music. She went into an altered state as she moved with the light of the fire. The music became her partner. Her body moved in ways that would entice any man.

As she moved, she could see many of the men were paying her father handsomely, trying to outbid each other for her hand.

The music kept playing, and she kept dancing. Deeper and deeper, she fell into the rhythm of the dance. Not caring anymore since she could not have her true love, she danced to help her family. It was her duty.

Chapter 14

The music stopped.

Clementina slowly came out of the twirl as a man came over and swept her off her feet. She closed her eyes as he carried her through the cheering crowd.

She was put into the back of a wagon, and a blanket was tossed onto her. She could hear the sound of a horse and could feel the movement of the wagon as it was being pulled.

The music became distant as the wagon moved further away from her family.

She wasn't sure how she felt. She had known all her life that this day would come. The boys of the band were needed for survival and would marry one day, bringing in new blood. The girls, on the other hand, were traded for supplies and would clean and dance for their husband's band. Her father had kept her as long as he was allowed. Some would say even longer than he should have. She knew that he loved her and was only following their customs.

The ride to her new husband's place was longer than she expected. So tired from dancing, she fell asleep.

The wagon stopped. Clementina opened her eyes to find that it was morning. Suddenly remembering where she was, she threw off the blanket and moved the curtain at the back of the wagon to look out.

She saw only the dirt road.

Listening, she couldn't hear anything except the horse.

She waited a few more moments thinking that at any moment, her new husband would come back to get her, but he never did.

She had to relieve herself and decided to take a chance and venture outside. Luckily, her belongings were beside her, and she put on a pair of her shoes.

Slowly she moved the curtain aside and slid over the wagon frame and landed on the ground. Looking around, all she could see was the dirt road that they had been traveling on.

She walked over to the edge of the trees and went behind a big tree to do her business. As she came back to the wagon, she still could not see her husband. Confused, she decided to look for some food, since she was now famished.

She found some bread, cheese, and an apple in a sack not too far from her belongings. She thought she smelled her mother's perfume as she pulled the food out of the bag.

It was getting late, and no one had come back to the wagon. Getting worried, she hopped up front and clicked her tongue to get the horse to move. The wagon was blocking the way, and eventually, another wagon would want to go by, she moved it only a few feet from where it had been.

Clementina waited and waited. No one returned. It was getting dark now, and she knew the horse would need water soon.

Yelling out, "Hello, Anyone there?"

Nothing. Just the soft neigh of the horse.

Grabbing a bucket, she went in search of some water. It only took a few moments. As she came over a log, she saw a hat floating by the shoreline. Running over, she picked it up.

Frantically looking for her husband. She searched up and down the shore.

Nothing.

Grabbing the bucket full of water, she went back to the wagon and watered the horse.

Deciding that she would not be safe on the main road, she hopped up front and clicked her tongue again.

She drove the wagon for a few miles before she found an area that looked safe enough to stop and sleep.

As she made camp, she heard a rustle in the trees. Scared for her life—for she had never been alone before— there was no one here to help her but herself. Grabbing a branch, she steadied herself for whatever was coming out of the trees.

Tears started to roll down her cheeks. She fell to her knees as Tillie came running over to her with his tail wagging, licking her tear-salted face as she hugged him dearly.

"Where did you come from, my dear friend?"

Chapter 15

Tillie barked and woke Clementina. Looking about, wondering if someone was near, she got out of the wagon.

No one.

She had searched the creek for a couple of days, but her husband or husband's body never appeared. She decided that he must have drowned, for there was no other logical answer.

"It looks like it is just you and me, Tillie."

Clementina hooked up the horse to the wagon and hopped back upfront. Not knowing where she was or what direction they had come from, she decided to go forward in the direction that her husband had been traveling.

Tillie ran beside the wagon and drifted off, coming back with a rabbit.

Pulling on the reins to stop the wagon, she got out and petted the dog's head as she said, "Good job, Tillie."

Taking the rabbit, she cleaned it and made a fire to cook it on. She had been taught this part of survival at least.

Giving Tillie his share of the meat. She dined in silence.

"Where are we, Tillie?"

The dog just nudged her with his nose and licked his lips, hoping for more.

As she was cleaning up, the horse made a forceful snorting sound, and Tillie started to bark ferociously. Startled, Clementina held the knife she was cleaning in front of her in case she needed it for protection.

Three men approached the wagon.

In a tongue she had never heard, one of the men said something.

Staring and not sure what to do, she motioned to shoo them away.

Laughing, one of the men got off his horse. He came closer. Clementina drew her knife and waved it in front of his face. Tillie growled and barked as he went between the man and Clementina.

A moment later, the sound of a shotgun was heard as a stranger came up behind her. She heard yelling as the man behind her was talking in the same language as the others had been.

The man got back onto his horse, and the three rode off quicker than a fox on a hunt.

Slowly she started to breathe again. Still scared for her life, she turned around and looked at the man who had shot off the gun.

The sun was in her eyes, and she couldn't see who it was. Putting a hand up to shield her face, she squinted at the stranger.

Tillie whimpered as he turned towards the man. Looking over at her dog for fear that the bullet had harmed him, she was relieved as Tillie ran over with a wagging tail.

Putting her hand down to pet the dog, she was surprised when he ran past and licked the stranger's hand.

Squinting again, she called out, "Tillie, come!"

"Clementina? Is that you?" A familiar voice said.

Her heart skipped a beat.

Her knees went weak as she recognized his voice. It was Carlo. Everything went dark as she fainted.

She felt a wet cloth on her forehead as she came to.

"Don't move. Take it easy, my love."

She wasn't sure if she was dreaming.

"Clementina, what are you doing all the way out here?"

Slowly she opened her eyes. Scared that none of this was real and she would wake up, and the dream would be over.

"Carlo?"

"Yes. It is me."

"But how? How did you find me?"

"I didn't find you. You found me."

"What?" But how?"

"The gods are on your side. Apollo must be looking after you."

"I don't understand. You didn't come to find me?"

"I wanted to. Your father hired some men, and they knocked me out and took me far away from you."

"But how are you here now?"

"You tell me. You are the one who happened upon me."

"I don't understand." Feeling better, she sat up. Putting a hand to Carlo's face, she touched him. "You are real."

"Yes."

She hugged him tightly. "I thought I had lost you forever."

"And I, you."

They stayed in each other arms until Tillie came and started to lick their faces.

"Ah. I think someone is hungry," Clementina said as she moved to get up.

Carlo pulled her tight again. "I am never going to let you get away again," and kissed her tenderly.

Their passion for one another unveiled itself, and the tender kiss led to more. Time stood still as the lovers explored each other under the star lit night.

Dawn had come, and Clementina could not be happier in the arms of her lover. Kissing him gently on his bare shoulder, she got dressed and made a fire for breakfast.

"Morning," he said as he came over to her.

Clementina wrapped her arms around him, "This is the best day of my life."

Chapter 16

July 9th, in New York City.

"Redington, I saw the man who killed that girl," Tamara was saying on the phone.

Groggily, Redington whispered, "Who is this?"

"Tamara."

Redington looked at the time, 3:30 AM. "Tamara, what are you calling for this early in the morning?"

Tamara looked at the clock. "Sorry. I lost track of time."

"You know who killed that girl. You mean Trina Wells?"

"Yes, Trina Wells. And no. I don't know for sure who the man is. I only saw him quickly."

Sitting up in bed, Red repeated what she said, "You saw him? How? Where?"

"Remember how I was telling you that I have the ability to astral travel and sense energy?"

"Umm, no."

"When I contacted you last weekend. I told you that I could help find the killer."

"No. Sorry, Tamara. I don't remember that."

Frustrated with the Detective, she said, "Whatever. Anyways, Lexi helped me, and I saw who did it."

"Lexi helped you do what?"

"Astral travel! Aren't you listening?"

"Tamara, I don't even know what that means. Did you and Lexi go somewhere?"

Almost fuming, Tamara said, "Detective, when you come to your senses. Call me," and hung up on him.

Staring at his phone, frustrated, Redington ran his fingers through his hair. "Great!"

Fully awake now, Redington got out of bed and stormed into the shower. As the warmth of the water poured over him, he started to calm down. *Man, how is it that some women can get under your skin?*

Getting dressed and grabbing a coffee on his way out, he headed over to Tamara's.

Traffic was busy even for this time of the day. In New York City, traffic was busy 24/7.

Pulling up to the Brownstone, Redington got out, still carrying his coffee. Knocking on

Tamara's door, he was surprised when it was Lexi who opened it.

"Hi. Ah. Is Tamara inside? She called."

Lexi moved out of the way and let him in.

"We both knew you would be coming." Looking over to the clock on the wall, Tamara said, "You win Lexi, here is your five bucks," and went into her purse to retrieve the money.

"You two bet on me?"

"Lighten up, Detective. If you didn't think there was anything to this, we both would have lost," Lexi said as she popped herself down on the couch.

Trying to keep his cool, he looked from Lexi to Tamara, "You said you saw the killer."

"Yes."

"Well, don't keep me in suspense. Who is it?"

"I didn't see his face, but I have a feeling that I know him, so I need you to try something."

"You're kidding, right? You phoned me in the wee hours of the morning, waking me up, getting me to come over here, just to tell me you don't know?"

"I have a hunch."

Shaking his head, he looked at Lexi, "How did you get caught up in all of this?"

"A friend to the rescue."

"Lexi, don't take this personally, but you're the kind of trouble I try to stay away from. I don't mind the drama of a good rescue, but the last two adventures, involved ghosts."

"Hey, I never asked you to come to Sweden. You decided that all on your own."

"Where is your sidekick?"

"Are you talking about Edward?"

"Ya. I thought for sure he would be mixed up someway in this crazy, what are you calling it, rescue?"

"Crazy. Now Detective, you are just getting rude."

"Hey, you two. Cut it out. We have a murder mystery to solve."

Lexi looked at Redington and said, "She's right. I am sure you didn't come here just to insult me."

Redington took a breath and shook his head, "You're right. I'm sorry. That was uncalled for. I guess I am still not quite awake." *What was I thinking? Man, I have to get my emotions under control? I don't know why seeing her triggers such a defense mechanism.* "Okay, I'm here. What is it that you want me to do, Tamara?"

Chapter 17

"First, I would like you to come and sit on the couch." Tamara pointed to a spot beside Lexi.

"Fine." Redington sat as far away from her as he could.

"Tamara, do you want me to move?" Lexi asked, noticing the obvious distance between them.

"You'll be okay there." Looking over to the Detective, she said, "Red, I need you to put your head back and relax."

"You're not going to do your hocus pocus on me, are you? I don't believe in that stuff."

"Red, just relax and take a couple deep breaths."

Redington leaned back on the couch and took a couple of deep breaths. Closing his eyes, he said, "I hope you know I can't be hypnotized."

Ignoring him, Tamara continued, "Breathe in and out, slowly. In a moment, I am going to count from three to one, and once I am at one, you will be flying through the sky."

"Uh-huh, sure I will."

"Take another deep breath in. Three. Relaxing."

Lexi and Tamara could see Redington take a deep breath.

"Two. Breathing in and out. Relaxing."

Redington's facial expressions relaxed. His breathing slowed, and his arms became limp as his left hand rolled to his side.

"One. You are now flying high above the earth. Soaring like an eagle. You can feel the wind lightly blow through your feathers. You feel so good. So free. Everything below looks so tiny. Your senses are becoming more acute. Your eyesight is focused, and you can see the faintest movement as if you were a hawk. Your hearing becomes clearer as if you were an owl—flying, soaring through the sky.

As you take your next deep breath, you will have easily flown to Jersey Shore. The first thing you notice is the smell of the ocean. Salty, with an aroma of seawater. To you, as you fly over the shoreline, the smell is welcoming and energizing.

You love the sounds of the waves as they caress the warm sand. With your wings outstretched you glide effortlessly over the beach.

As you fly over the shoreline, you spy two girls. One is holding a velvet cloth and folding table. The other is nearby.

You recognize one of the girls as Trina Wells."

Redington stirred a bit in his trance state.

"You are just an observer. You are watching as if it was a movie. With your next deep breath, you are going to tell me what you are seeing. It is June 6th, sometime in the afternoon or evening. Tell me what you see."

Lexi had a pen and paper to write down what Redington said.

"Hmm." Redington clears his throat. "I see. Hmm." He takes another deep breath. "I see two girls. They could be sisters. They look so much alike. Same height, same dark brown hair, same build, and of similar age." He takes another deep breath. They are talking. One of them leaves and goes into a building. The other sits down beside all of the stuff they were carrying." Redington stops talking for a moment.

"What is happening now," Tamara asked.

"Nothing." Redington moves a bit on the couch. "Wait! Someone is talking to the girl who is sitting."

"Who is it?"

"I can't tell."

"Is it male or female?"

"I think female. No. Male. Definitely male.

"What is happening now?"

"He is talking to the girl."

"Your hearing is amplified. You can hear what they are saying. What are they saying?"

"He is asking her to do a reading. She said no. He starts to insist, but she says she can't. He doesn't believe her. He said that he saw her on the beach earlier doing it. She starts to tell him that he is mistaken, that it wasn't her, but he is not listening." Redington straightens up on the couch but kept his eyes shut.

"What is happening now?"

"He grabbed her arm and is pulling her up. She is yelling, but there is no one around that can hear."

"What is happening now?"

"He backhanded her across the face. She is struggling to get away, but he is too strong. His grip tightens, and she starts to cry, pleading for him to let go. Saying that he has the wrong person. He hits her harder and breaks her jaw."

"Remember, you are just watching it as if it were a movie. What happens next."

"She is bleeding and unconscious, and he is searching through her belongings, looking for something. He can't find what he is looking for and so he starts to look through her clothes. He pulled something out of her pocket."

"Your eyesight is like a telescope. You can zoom in and see what he found."

"It is a small box."

"What does he do next?"

"He lifts her body up and carries her to the shoreline and dumps her face down into the water. Her head bobs up and down with the waves, she drowns."

"The next deep breath you take, the spirit of the bird enters into the man's body. It is an easy transition. You are now looking out of the man's eyes. You now can understand what the man is thinking. What is he thinking?"

Redington took another deep breath. "The cards belonged to his great, great, grandmother. He had recognized them earlier that day. He thought it was impossible but knew that they could be no other."

"What does he do next?"

"He. Ah. He walks away."

"Where does he go?"

"All I see next is a shower."

"Redington, I am going to count from one to three. When I reach three, you will be fully awake and back in your own body. One, you are back to being the bird, flying over the shoreline. Two, you are flying higher and higher. Three, your spirit has flown all the way back to this room, landing perfectly into your own body. When you are ready, take a deep breath, wiggle your toes, and open your eyes. Awake."

Lexi watched as Redington wiggled his feet. Blinking as he opened his eyes. Sitting up straighter, he said, "What was that?"

"That was astral traveling in a meditative state, with a bit of remote viewing added in."

"Tamara, that was more than meditating."

"You're correct. It was a form of sci scanning that psychic detectives use."

"How do I know what I say was real and not what I think happened?"

"How did you know the box was in her pocket and not in the velvet material?"

Redington thought back to the meditation. There was no way he knew that detail. The police wouldn't have known that detail. No cards were found. "Hmm. Good question."

"The only way we will know if what you saw was real is to ask the gypsy reader."

"Kesia Bango."

"Yes."

"I have no jurisdiction in Jersey Shore. I can't go talk to her."

"You can't, but I can," Tamara said, knowing what her next course of action would be.

Chapter 18

"How many last names of 'Bango' listed in Jersey Shore could there be?" Tamara said out loud as she was searching on the internet. None. "Dang-it! This is going to be harder than I thought."

"What is going to be harder than you thought?" Greg asked, thinking Tamara was talking to him. He had popped over earlier that morning.

"Oh, nothing. I am just searching online."

"What are you looking for?"

Tamara got a weird feeling in her gut. "Ah, it's nothing."

Greg came over to the computer and said, "You sure. Maybe I can help?"

Tamara clicked the x button on the screen just before he could see what she was looking at. *Weird. Why do I care if he sees or not?* Turning to Greg, she said, "Hey, why don't we go out and get a coffee or something?"

"Sure. It will be good to get you away from that computer and get some color on those cheeks."

Tamara smiled, but the feeling in her gut was still there.

Greg took hold of Tamara's hand as they started their stroll through the streets of Brooklyn Heights. Tamara's gut felt like it was doing summersaults.

"You okay? You don't look so good."

"I'll be fine. I just need some fresh air, is all." She hoped that was all it was.

Tamara loved growing up in this neighborhood. It was one of the oldest boroughs in New York City. There was always something interesting to see from its tree-shaded streets lined with 19th-century homes and churches, to the magnificent skyline of Manhattan from the Brooklyn Bridge.

Tamara and Greg walked to Montague Street for a relaxing snack. The hard part came when they had to decide which café or restaurant to dine at today—not to mention the distraction from the marvelous retail window displays tempting you with an impulse purchase.

Greg picked his favorite café because of its outside seating that puts you right next to the fashionable bustle of the Montague street life.

As the waiter came over, Greg ordered a local craft beer. "What are you having, Tamara? Tamara, the waiter is waiting."

Tamara wasn't paying attention as she thought she saw Kesia walk by. Turning, she said, "What? Oh, right. Please give me a moment," Turning back quickly to see where the girl had gone.

"Who are you looking for?"

Tamara's head snapped around to Greg. The feeling in her gut was back. "Ah, I thought I saw someone I knew."

"Who was it?"

"Ah, I thought it was a client of mine. I was mistaken," she responded, not sure why she was lying to him.

"What are you having?" Greg asked, looking up from the menu.

"Right." Tamara picked up the menu and stared at it. *Is it possible she is in New York?*

After ordering the 'HEIGHTS BURGER,' chargrilled with caramelized onions, smoked bacon, Gruyère cheese, and Heights fries, he asked, "What did you decide? Tamara? The waiter is waiting."

Looking up, she said, "Just water, please."

"You okay? You seem off."

"I'll be okay. I'll have a bite of yours." Tamara couldn't get the thought of seeing Kesia out of her head.

After Greg ate his meal and drank his beer, he suggested that they go to the park.

"Actually, I'd like to go home."

"Come on, Tamara, you can put off whatever work you have and take a walk along the promenade. You love seeing the stellar views of lower Manhattan from the waterfront. We can sit on one of the benches and relax."

"Greg, I am not feeling well. I really need to go home."

"Fine."

They walked in silence back to Tamara's Brownstone.

Chapter 19

Walking up the stairs to the front door, Tamara said, "Greg, I'm going to lie down. Why don't you come back later? I'll call you when I am feeling better."

"Maybe I should stay, in case you get worse?"

"No. Please, go. Then I don't have to feel bad."

"I can watch TV."

"No. Greg, I don't want any noise. Please, go."

Greg gave Tamara a kiss on the forehead and headed back down the stairs to his car.

Shutting the door, Tamara leaned her back on it. *What is going on? This feeling in my gut is telling me something is wrong.*

Walking over to the computer, Tamara sat down. Not sure why she sat down, she didn't feel like doing any work. Staring at the black screen of the monitor, she drifted back to the café. *I am sure that was the gypsy reader who walked by.*

The doorbell rang.

Getting up to answer it, Tamara tripped over a bag. Looking down, she was surprised because she didn't put it there. *Greg, one of these days, your stuff that is randomly lying around is going to kill me.*

Kicking the bag to move it out of the way, Tamara hurt her foot. Limping over to the door, she opened it to find a tiny package left by the doorstep. Picking it up, she read the name on the front, Miss T. Reeve.

Bringing it inside, she placed it on the table. It wasn't very big. It couldn't hold much more than a deck of cards. Not remembering that she had ordered another tarot deck, she opened the package. All it revealed was sand, just sand. Just to make sure she dumped all the contents of the little package onto the table, but nothing else came out, just sand.

She looked at the package for a return address but there wasn't one.

Almost jumping out of her skin as her phone rang, Tamara went to answer it. "Hello."

No answer.

"Hello. Who is this?"

Nothing.

Hanging up, she looked at the caller ID, Unknown.

The phone rang again.

"Hello!"

"Hey, are you okay? You sound weird," Lexi said, surprised at Tamara's tone of voice.

"Did you just call?"

"No. Is everything alright?"

"I'm not sure."

"I am in the area and was calling to see if I could stop by."

"Ya, sure, that's fine."

"Great. See you in a second," Lexi said as she knocked on Tamara's door.

Susannah startled Lexi by saying *Something is up, Lexi. Be careful!*

"Thanks, Sis. I will."

Tamara opened the door, saying, "That was quick."

Lexi teased, "Avon calling."

"Funny."

Coming in, Lexi said, "I have a question."

Tamara led the way into the living room and sat down on the couch without offering a drink or anything first. "Let's have it."

Sitting down beside Tamara on the couch, Lexi pulled out some drawings from her purse and gave them to Tamara.

Looking at the drawings, Tamara said, "Where did you get these?"

"I have been drifting off and getting sidetracked while I am working at home. What do you think they mean?"

Looking closer at the drawings, Tamara said, "How long has this been going on?"

"Just since the other day. When Redington came over, and you did that meditation with him. After leaving here, I went back to my place and had a couple of hours of sleep. Edward has been busy with the renovations at his place, and so I've been staying at my apartment. I've been working from home and brainstorming for new ideas for fashion week, and before I knew it, I was drawing these."

"I see."

"I was hoping you could tell me more about the meaning of the colors."

Tamara held up one drawing in particular. "What did you think when you drew this?" The page was full of dark colors, scribbles, the essence of fear, scary, almost demonic-looking.

"Actually, I was thinking about Redington and what he saw as the bird."

"I see."

Tamara looked through all the drawings again. "I think Lexi that you are doing aura art."

"Ya. I thought it might be something like that. What do the colors mean? You never taught us that part."

Tamara pointed at one of the drawings and said, "Black represents negative thoughts, power, or education. It can also mean discord or hate. Sometimes it signifies great sickness of emotional disturbance. Black is also the universal color of death, grief, and patience. On the up note, this color is worn for power and authority."

"And the other colors?"

Tamara got up and went into her office and came back with some papers. "Here. This is a description of the meaning of the colors."

Lexi skimmed over each color.

Blue: Emotional
This color represents – a sense of wellbeing. It is soft, gentle, peaceful by nature, passive and introverted. It reflects values of truth, honesty, trustworthy, reliable, and faithful. When reading a person's aura art, it means they are too self-absorbed, likes order and structure in their life. They are usually artistic, creative, loyal, and sincere. They are also harmonious, imaginative, a daydreamer, serene, and tactful. When they fall in love, they give one hundred percent of themselves. Music helps soothe their emotions.

Brown: Friendly
This color represents – a color of power, great energy.
When reading a person's aura art, it means they are logical, analytical, authoritative, inner confidence, self-assured, and self-starters. They are also, practical, materialistic, organized and steadfast, likes to get to the root of things, no-nonsense people. Usually,

money-makers and can be very impatient. They are earthy, stable, and grounded. Highly dedicated and committed to their family, work, and friends.

Green: Healing
This color represents – Renewal.
When reading a person's aura art, it means they need to communicate and require a lot of affection. They seek balance, very independent, thoughtful, adaptable, and growth-oriented. They have a lot of self-control, sympathy, and like sharing. Neither dominating nor submissive, extrovert nor an introvert. They are neat and tidy, and like parks, the coast, and open spaces. They enjoy things made from wood, clay, stone, and like to surround themselves with plants and flowers.

Grey: Ancient Knowledge
This color represents – A balance between white and black, fear, depression, as well as unused potential.
When reading a person's aura art, it means caution and is experienced as dull and somber energy.

Magenta: Regal
This color represents - kindness, gentleness, consideration, affectionate, warmth, compassionate, and love.

When reading a person's aura art, it means they are very mature with a deep understanding of life. They encourage others towards their full potential, co-operative, friendly, genuine, show unconditional love and affection. They often are involved in the caring field, such as counseling, nursing, or social work.

Orange: Action & Creative
This color represents - the energy of the sun. When reading a person's aura art, it means they are open-minded, emotional, and sensuous. They would rather "rule than serve". In a group, they mix well. They are enthusiastic, buoyant, ebullient natured, enjoy living, joyful, generally excitable, happy disposition, spontaneous, cheerful, talkative, outgoing, sociable, and warm-hearted.

Pink: Innocence
This color represents – pure of heart. When reading a person's aura art, it means these people are quiet, refined, modest, fond of beauty, gifted of great devotion, and much self-sacrifice.

Purple: Intuitive
This color represents – Spirituality.
When reading a person's aura art, it means they are extremely sensitive, non-judgmental, and are seekers of the truth. These people have a sense of Unity (love, intellect, faith).

Red: Go, Go, Go
This color represents – Energy.
When reading a person's aura art, it means they are energizing, vitalizing, heated, passionate, generous, vigorous, forceful, grounded, highly competitive, initiator, pioneer, creative, outgoing, and assertive.

Silver: Calm & Trustworthy
This color represents – peacefulness.
When reading a person's aura art, it means they are lovers of convention and formality. They enjoy challenging work.

Turquoise: Tranquil
This color represents - unfulfilled ambitions or spiritually protected.
When reading a person's aura art, it means they are sparkling with youthfulness, bringing imagination and fresh ideas to most situations. They have an attitude of 'take it in stride.' They make quick decisions and act with clarity. They have a great deal of insight and a talent to further their spiritual path. They need to learn how to be more grounded.

Violet: Spiritual
This color represents - consciousness and awareness.
When reading a person's aura art, it means that they are usually interested in all aspects of the mystical psychic forces. They have the potential to apply spirituality in a grounded way, and are willing to serve others in a healing way. They usually become healers and psychics.

White: Godly
This color represents - spiritually elevated. When reading a person's aura art, it means they are motivated, clean, pure, innocence, detached, and the color reflects all other color's qualities.

Yellow: Thinking, Smart & Intelligent
This color represents - Supersensitive people. When reading a person's aura art, it means they are highly nervous, optimistic, and very capable in business. They can be too generous. They also have a sense of reason, logic, and assessment. They grasp things easily, but can be controlling and dominating.

"So, what do you get from the one you are holding, Tamara?"
Tamara gave the drawing back to Lexi. "You tell me."

Lexi took a breath and said, "Okay. It feels dark and troublesome. Like there is a secret or something." *Careful Lexi!* Lexi looked at Tamara and said, "Susannah just gave me a warning."

Surprised because she didn't sense Susannah, Tamara said, "Why?"

"I don't know, but it is the second time since I arrived at your doorstep."

"Weird."

"Should I ask her for more details?"

"Ah. That might be a good idea."

Before Lexi could say anything else, Greg came through the door. "Oh. I thought you would be resting."

"Lexi came over just after you left."

Looking at the drawings, he asked, "What are these?"

Tamara got that icky gut feeling again, "Lexi was showing me some ideas for her Fall Fashion Week."

"They don't look like dresses?" Greg remarked.

Lexi picking up on Tamara's lie, and said, "They are just ideas for color combinations."

Greg looked at the one Tamara was holding and said, "Lexi, I think you need to rethink your idea. I don't think those colors would sell unless you are doing a Halloween theme."

"Thanks, Greg, I will scrap that one." Taking the drawing from Tamara, she put all the drawings back into her purse. "I think I should go. Call me later?"

"Ya. I will give you a call tomorrow," Tamara said as she walked Lexi to the door. Whispering, "I will tell you about it tomorrow."

Lexi nodded and said, "See you later, Greg."

"Yep," he called back from the other room.

Chapter 20

Mid July 1438 in the Kingdom of Bohemia,

Clementina was happier than she had been for years. She loved her family and missed them dearly, but Carlo filled her days with wonder and awe.

They had been traveling for many nights. Carlo decided it would be best if they escaped the possible capture of Clementina and decided to leave Bohemia. It was not safe for her here now that she was not with her band or her husband's band. The locals did not trust outsiders, and rumors moved fast throughout the countryside about the shady dealings of her kind. The color of her skin and the clothes she wore gave away who she was, long before she even spoke.

Carlo being Roman made being in Bohemia easier for him since it was the Roman Empire that ruled over these lands.

The journey was long, but he knew she would be safe amongst his people. He still had family in Rome, and he could get a job with one of his uncles and look after her there.

"I wonder what I will do once we arrive in Rome?" Clementina said out loud as she sat beside Carlo on the wagon's bench. He was exceptionally good at handling the horse.

"I suppose you will look after me."

Clementina laughed. "Well, that is obvious, but what else will I do? You know, during the day when you are working?"

"You will have to learn the language if you think you want to do anything else."

"I never thought of that. Yes. You must teach me. How do I say, thank you?"

"Gratias tibi. That is Latin for thank you. Unless you want to speak Greek. Then it is, σας ευχαριστώ."

"Oh, my goodness. You speak Greek?"

"Luckily, I came from a family who wanted me to be a priest. I went to school for many of my earlier years. Unfortunately, I was not spiritually inclined."

"What does that mean?"

"I had an eye for the ladies."

"Oh, I see. And do you still have an eye for the ladies?" she said as she tickled him.

Laughing, he said, "Only the pretty ones."

"Then lucky for me, we are leaving Bohemia."

Carlo looked at Clementina and said, "What, you don't think we have beautiful girls in Rome?"

"I don't know. I have never seen one."

"You have never met a female who was from Rome?"

"No. I've barely met any women from Bohemia. My kind is very private, and only the men travel outside of our camps."

"I didn't know that."

He was just about to say something else as he and Clementina were jolted out of the seat.

Helping her first, he then went to see if the horse was okay. It was. Walking around the wagon, he saw that a wheel had worked itself loose and came off.

It was broken.

Hearing what she thought was cursing, Clementina limped over to Carlo. She must have hurt her ankle somehow as she fell out of the wagon's seat. "Oh, dear me. I hope you know how to fix that?"

"I don't think we have the tools. I'll check." He went to the side of the wagon and opened the wooden lid to a small box that was attached to it. "We're in luck. There are tools here that will fix it."

"Oh, that is wonderful." She walked over to Carlo and said with her hands on her hips, "How can I help?"

Taking Clementina by the waist, he leaned in and said, "You, my love, can see if there is any water and make us some lunch, I am starving, and this is going to take a while." He kissed her passionately.

A little dizzy from the aftereffects of his kiss, Clementina went with Tillie to search for some water.

She didn't have to go far, as the dirt road they had been on followed a creek. Taking off her shoes, she sat down and put her sore ankle into the cool water. It helped the pain immensely.

She was startled out of her daydream by Tillie barking. Getting up and putting on her shoes, she put the bucket into the water, filled it, and limped back to the wagon.

As she got closer, she could hear two men talking but couldn't understand what they were saying.

They were riding off quickly as she emerged from the trees. Tillie had run after them, barking.

"Carlo, is everything okay? Did they help you? Carlo?"

Coming around the wagon, she dropped the bucket and went running to him, forgetting the pain in her ankle.

Dropping to his side and kneeling beside him, "Carlo!" She picked up his head and saw the blood, too much blood.

"What in God's name happened?" Screaming, she yelled, "Why?"

Between sobs, Tillie had come back and was licking her face.

Looking at the wheel, she saw that Carlo had fixed it, but it was lying on the ground. Getting up, she went over to see if she could lift it. No. It was far too heavy for her.

Walking back to Carlo, she checked if he was alive by placing her fingers on his neck. Her father had taught her that when she was still a young girl. Carlo was dead.

Clementina didn't know how long she had been sitting there, but it was now getting dark. Getting up, she was trying to decide what to do. Wait for someone to come by and hopefully help her with the wheel or should she take the horse and ride to the next town.

As she thought about the horse, she looked around. "What the?" Tillie was jumping around her as she walked over to look for the horse. It was nowhere to be found.

Screaming out loud, she collapsed to the ground.

It was light out when she came to. Tillie was lying beside her. He had kept her warm throughout the night.

Getting up, she walked to the back of the wagon and opened the curtain to find that they had been robbed. Her belongings were flung everywhere. The men had stolen everything of value. Luckily, her mother had shown her how to sew a pocket that was hidden in her skirts. She was taught to keep anything of value on her person.

Picking through the few belongings left, she bundled them up in a shawl and left the wagon, with Tillie happily following her.

She limped for miles before she stopped, due to the pain.

Making camp for the night, she looked up to the stars and prayed to O'del (the creator god of the Romani people). "My creator. Please hear my prayer. I am in need of your guidance. I am in the land of the unknown and alone, other than my dog. I am far from my people and my lover's people. I am lost in a world unbeknownst to me. Guide me with your light. Protect me with your grace."

She had heard a priest that had come upon her band when she was young say, "Amen," so she thought the word in case it would help. *Amen.*

Chapter 21

July 15th, in New York City.

Tamara was getting antsy. It had been days since she had heard anything from Redington. She still couldn't get the image of seeing that gypsy girl at the café out of her head.

That sick feeling in her gut was back again. *Something is not right about all of this. I just know it.*

Grabbing her phone, she called Lexi. "Hi. You busy?"

"Not at the moment. Edward and I have plans tonight, but I have time right now to chat. What's up?"

"I need your help. I have this sick feeling in my gut every time I think of the gypsy girl. Can you come over and help me help her?"

"Sure. I am not sure if I can do anything, but sure, I am on my way."

"Thanks, Lex. You don't give yourself enough credit. You're better than you think."

Almost half an hour went by before Lexi showed up. Opening the door before she got up the stairs, Tamara said, "Hi, thanks for coming. We'll take my car."

"Where are we going?"

"To find that gypsy reader."

Opening the passenger side door, Lexi suddenly had a thought, "Hey, I don't have time to drive down to Jersey Shore."

"No, no. We aren't going that far."

Before closing the door, Lexi asked, "How far are we going?"

"Just to a café down the street. Get in."

Getting in, Lexi had to say what she was feeling, "Something feels strange about this. I keep getting tingles on my arms and legs."

Tamara looked over at Lexi before backing up and said, "Good. That means we are on the right track."

"What do you mean?"

"Tingles are a confirmation from the spirit world that something is true, above-board, and legit."

"Interesting. I've been getting them a lot lately."

Tamara drove to Montague Street, where she and Greg had lunched the other day. Getting out, she started to tell Lexi her plan. "We are going to start at the front of that café. That is where I saw her a few days ago."

"You say she is here in Brooklyn?"

"Yes. Well, I am pretty sure it was her."

"What do you want me to do?"

"I need you to make sure I am safe. That I don't walk out into oncoming traffic or something of that nature."

Not sure about how safe this idea was now, Lexi said timidly, "What are you going to be doing?"

Tamara looked at Lexi and chuckled, "Nothing like that. The face you are making is hilarious. Don't worry. It is nothing illegal."

"Hopefully, not sinful either."

Tamara looked at Lexi again, and said, shaking her head and still smiling, "Your imagination is amazing. Come on, let's find that gypsy reader."

Tamara led the way and stood in front of the café. Closing her eyes, she said to Lexi, "Just give me a moment to pick up her energy."

"You can do that? Even when it's been days since you saw her?"

"You can always find an energy trail. It is like a bloodhound with a scent. It takes a really long time to disappear."

"I never thought about it like that."

"Imagine you are a detective, and this energy trail is a clue. You follow the clues until you either run out of them, or you find what you were looking for." Tamara started to walk in the same direction that she saw the girl walking.

Lexi jolted, not quite ready for Tamara to start walking, but followed beside her the best that she could, keeping her out of harm's way.

They walked for a couple of blocks, and then Tamara stops dead. Lexi almost bumped into her.

"What are we stopping for?" Lexi asked as she looked around.

"Her energy stops here." Tamara looked at the building. It was a Russian tea house. Smiling, she said, "Come on. She's been in here."

Opening the door, they went in.

Everything looked normal at first as Lexi looked around. It was quaint and designed in an older fashioned type of way. There was a till and a dessert counter to the left. Many small tables had pretty crochet tablecloths, with a dainty flower in a vase sitting on top. As Lexi looked further into the room, she noticed square tables at the back with people sitting opposite each other, deep into conversation. "What is this place?"

Tamara smiled, "It is a Russian tea house."

"Ya, but what goes on here?"

"People come here to get their tarot cards read," Tamara said as she went up to the till.

Pulling out some money, she said, "Two teas, please."

Lexi looked at her, wondering if two teas were code for something else, but all the lady gave Tamara was two herbal teas.

Sitting down, Lexi was still wondering how it worked. "How did you know this place was here?"

"I didn't."

"Then how did you know they do tarot cards?"

"Lexi, Russian tea houses are famous for fortune-telling."

"Oh. So, what do we do now?"

"We wait."

"For what?"

"For a gypsy reading."

Lexi looked up and looked at the people at the other tables. "Is one of the girls here her?"

"Yep."

"Which one?"

Tamara pointed over to a table.

Just as Lexi was going to say something, the waitress who sold them the tea came over. In a Russian accent, she said, "Which one of you wants the reading? Or is it both of you?"

Tamara slightly put up her hand and said, "I do. I will wait for the gypsy reading, please," and pointed to a specific person.

"Ah. Mila. Yes, she is very good. She is almost finished. Enjoy your tea."

"Thank you."

"Tamara, that is not the name I remember you saying."

"I know. Lots of places have their readers use authentic Russian names to make the ambiance better."

"Oh. That makes sense."

They didn't have to wait long. The waitress came over and guided Tamara to Mila.

Sitting down, Tamara took a breath and asked her angels and guides to help her help Mila.

Looking up, Mila asked, "What would you like? A thirty-minute or an hour tarot card reading?"

"The thirty-minute one, please."

"Fine." Mila tapped the cards three times and shuffled them, deciding to do a 'Setting Boundaries Spread' tarot card layout from one of Sasha Graham's spreads that she had learned. Remembering what Sarah had written in her book, she repeated it to Tamara, "The Great Barrier Reef, which can be seen from outer space, protects Australia's coastal shores. This spread is for you to remember how precious you are."

Tamara looked at the girl doing her reading. *Yep, the same girl. It is hard to forget a face that freaked out at you.*

"This first card represents what will help you become more self-aware." Mila turned over The Devil card. "It seems that dark energy follows you around." Looking at Tamara, Mila turned over another card, The Chariot." As I said, the dark energy follows you around. This card represents the boundaries you find hard to set up. The number seven, the Roman numeral on the top of this card, is spiritual energy. The sphinx you see here are yin and yang. Representing both good and bad. You find it hard to set spiritual boundaries." Pulling another card, Mila said, "The Hanged Man, this card represents timing. You think you are not in control of your situation, but as you can see, his arms and one leg are free. He can choose to move anytime he wants to."

Tamara looked at the cards.

Mila pulled another, "The Nine of Cups. This card represents what people should not ask of you. You should never feel inclined to give more than you can."

Tamara wasn't sure what the cards all meant yet, but she trusted that her angel helpers knew what they were doing.

Pulling another card, Mila said, "This next card is what you can ask for." She turned over the two of wands. "You have the world in the palm of your hand, yet you seek more. You have the ability to ask for more."

Turning over the sixth card that she had pulled from the deck, Mila said, "The five of wands. Your time and energy are worth protecting. You need to start looking after your needs before others."

Tamara just smiled as the girl continued.

Mila turned over the two of cups. "Your partner is supportive of you. You can count on him or her." Lastly, she turned over the eight of wands. "The first boundary that you must set is speaking your truth." Mila placed the cards in two rows of four. "Look here. You will see that the Devil card and the two of wands are opposite each other. You have the ability to ask more from the spirit world. You need to protect yourself from spiritual travelers. Your friends and family will hang around until you need them. And lastly, you should never say more than you need to."

Mila looked to Tamara and asked, "Any questions?"

"You said this is a boundary reading?"

"Yes."

"Why did you feel this spread was needed for me today?"

"I don't know. It just came to me to do this spread."

"I see. Mila? How do you know Trina Wells?"

Mila stared at Tamara and said, "I don't."

"I am sure you do, Mila. You do not recognize me, but I recognize you."

"I am sorry you must have me mistaken for someone else. I have never seen you before today."

Tamara pulled out a business card and slid it to Mila. Tamara got up, saying, "I know what happened. If you need or want my help, call me." She left a tip and went over to where Lexi was sitting.

"Well, how did it go?"

"I am not sure. We'll see. Let's go."

Lexi got up and looked over to the girl who gave Tamara a reading. She had a business card in her hand and was staring at it.

Tamara said, as if reading Lexi's mind, "She'll call."

Chapter 22

Late July 1438 in Rome

Clementina woke up to the sounds of many voices. She was in a magnificent building with marble floors, walls, pillars, and benches. Beautiful white drapes with golden thread intertwined delicately throughout, hung from framed large open windows. She could hear the bustle of busy streets and the sound of voices speaking the same language she had heard Carlo speak.

Getting up from where she had been lying, she looked around at unfamiliar and unique items. There were lifelike white statues everywhere. The ceilings must have been twenty feet above her head. Randomly placed, she saw water pouring out of the walls from what looked like monster heads into small pools. People dressed in white togas with sandals on their feet kept coming and going, never talking to her.

As she looked down at her body, she saw that she too was wearing a white cloth that was strapped over one of her shoulders, baring the other. Her feet were adorned with leather sandals. Her hair had been combed and put up into a ponytail high atop her head.

As she looked into one of the pools of water, she noticed her face, but it was not how she had ever seen it. Her lips were the color of blood, her cheeks were the color of peaches, and her eyes had black lines drawn around them, making them look mysterious.

"Ah, good. You are awake." She heard a woman say in Latin. "I am Decima. I am in charge of figuring out what to do with you."

Clementina had learned how to speak the language from Carlo. "Where am I, and where is Tillie?"

"You are in the Domus of the family, descendants of Papirii Masones. One of the most influential families in Rome."

"How did I get here, and where is Tillie?"

"You were found on the side of the road., half dead. Where is your pater familias?"

"My what?"

"Your father, brother, or husband? We found you alone."

"My husband died on the journey," Clementina said, trying not to lie if she didn't have to. "Where is Tillie?"

"You were alone. Is this a slave?"

"No. It is my dog. Slave? I do not have any slaves. Why did you think that?"

"We found a few florins along with some other coins and trinkets stashed away in a hidden pocket in your skirt. To have that much money, you must come from a wealthy family."

Clementina decided to play along. "Yes. I was traveling with my husband when our carriage broke down. As I was wandering down to the creek, thieves killed my husband and stole our most valuable belongings. With the wheel still off, I started to walk for fear that I may be attacked. The next thing I remember is waking up here."

"I see. I will inform the senator."

Clementina was served an array of fruits for breakfast.

Entering Clementina's quarters, Lucius was the great, great, great… grandson to the late Lucius Papirius Mugillanus Cursor, who back in his time was the most important Roman commander during the Second Samnite War, during which he received three triumphs.

Speaking Latin, Lucius said, "Salve, *Hello*. I heard you had a very misfortunate experience on your recent travels. My servant tells me that your husband died?"

Clementina looked at the man standing in front of her. Tall, tanned skin, dark hair, handsome. He wore a purple sash over his tunic. His mannerism told her that he was used to being an authoritative figure. Bowing slightly, she kept her eyes downward, not to let him see her lie about being a person of privilege, "It is an honor to be in your presence. I am sorry if I have caused any disruption to your family."

"Nothing of any concern," Lucius said, looking at her beauty for the first time.

"If I may be excused, I would like to continue on my travels. May I please have my belongings back?"

Lucius picked up on her accent and knew she was not from around here. "Your husband's family, they must be expecting you. Who did you say they were?"

Clementina knew she was caught. She had to think fast. *What did Carlo tell me of this land?* "He worked for the Visconti."

"I see. What were his tasks."

"Before I met him, he traveled back and forth from Ferrara, Milan, and Rome, doing business for him."

"What kind of business?"

Clementina thought quickly, "That part he kept to himself, and being a well-bred lady, I never asked. That was his business, not mine."

Lucius was content with her answers for now, but his instincts told him there was more to the story. As he turned to walk out of the room, he said, "No, you can't leave."

Chapter 23

A couple days later in New York City.

A knock at that door was heard. Tamara went over to see who it was. As she opened the door, that sick feeling in her gut came back. Standing there was Mila, the tarot card reader from the Russian Tea House.

"May I come in?"

Tamara backed up and opened the door to let her in.

"How did you find me?" Mila asked.

"I did a type of remote viewing combined with a sci scan of your energy, which I met in Jersey Shore last month. Your picture was all over the news, mistaking you for Trina Wells.

You are the gypsy reader from Jersey Shore, Kesia Bango.”

"I changed my hair color and name.”

“Yes, but your energy has a unique frequency that is like a fingerprint. No two are alike. I just followed yours until I came to an end.”

“Why?”

“Now that is a good question. Well, I am not sure why the spirit world wants me to be involved in all this, but they usually have a really good reason.”

“Your business card says that you are a psychic.”

“Yes, amongst other things. Please come in and have a seat.”

Kesia came and sat down, not knowing what else to do.

“Tell me what happened,” Tamara said, breaking the tension in the room.

Suddenly, Kesia knew who Tamara was. “You are the lady that had the curse.” Standing up, she said, “You did this to me.”

“Hey, calm down. You know curses don’t work like that.”

“They did that day. I ran from you, and then all hell broke loose. You have demons following you that are powerful. Really powerful.”

“I also have angels that follow me who are more powerful than the demons.”

“I have to get out of here. It is not safe for me here.”

"Kesia, you have nowhere to go. Sit, tell me what happened."

Not sure if she should stay or go, Kesia decided to sit and tell someone what happened. "After I ran from you, I ran into Trina. I had only known her for a few weeks. She was a nice girl. She could tell that I was afraid of something and only wanted to help me. I had to go to the restroom. I was only going to be a moment, but when I awoke, I was on the floor of the toilet stall, with a killer headache from the fall. When I came outside, I found the beach was swarming with police. All of my stuff had been moved, and Trina was nowhere to be seen, so I disappeared into the night."

"Then what happened?"

"I watched behind some trees in the parking lot next to the beach. Others had gathered there to watch as well. I heard someone say that the police had found a body in the water. They thought it was murder or manslaughter from how the girl's face was bashed in."

"Go on."

"I didn't know what to do, so I ran home. I didn't tell anyone. I was too afraid."

"Then what happened?"

"That night, I had snuck into my room, not wanting to wake my mom. The next morning, I heard my mom screaming. I ran downstairs to see what was going on, and I found my face on the morning news. Of course, it wasn't me, but my mom thought it was. Seeing me, she held me as if I was going to disappear and she was never going to see me again. The news reporter said that they found my things only a few feet away from the body."

"I can see why they thought it was you. You two look a lot alike."

"I guess."

"Why are you now in New York?"

"After my mom had phoned the police, an officer phoned asking a lot of questions. Weird questions, not just the typical ones that you would expect. He mostly asked about where the cards had come from."

"The cards?"

"Yes. He was talking about my grandmother's tarot cards."

"That is weird. What did he want to know?"

"Things like how I came into possession of them, how long had they been in the family, and did I know where they originated. Things like that."

"Then what happened?"

"Because it wasn't me who died, I went to the station house to get my belongings back, but they said I couldn't have them due to the investigation. They asked me more questions about Trina and how I knew her. I asked if I could have my tarot cards at least, and they said no. I insisted that they protect them, that they were an heirloom and that if anything happened to them, I would sue."

"That probably didn't go off so well, threatening the police."

"Actually, I was laughed at and escorted outside. The officer who escorted me out said that there was no tarot deck with my belongings."

"So, why again are you now in New York?"

"I needed to work, and since my job on the beach was ruined, I had to find another place I could work. The only thing I know how to do is read cards, so I came to New York. I have an Aunt who lives here."

"Have you heard anything else about the murder, Kesia?"

"No, but I keep dreaming of Trina."

"What is the dream about.?"

"She is running from a man who says he is after the cards."

"There is a man after your cards?"

"That is what the dream seems to be saying."

Just as Tamara was going to say something else, Greg came in, "Hi. I thought we could go out for dinner. Oh, sorry. I didn't know you had company."

Kesia stood up as if she had seen a ghost and said, "I have to run anyways. Thanks for the reading. I'll call you in a few days," and left without Tamara being able to answer.

"What was all that about?" Greg asked.

Lying for Kesia, she said, "Oh, just a girl wanting a reading. You know how kids get around grownups."

Chapter 24

"Tamara, I keep getting these dreams," Lexi said over the phone.

"What kind of dreams?"

"Well, they're not the usual kind. You know, where I'm in the dream, but really, I'm not. My typical dreams are mixed up and don't make much sense. They're more like I am watching a movie."

"Lexi, when you wake up from a normal dream, does it disappear faster than you can remember it?"

"Yes. Always. Well, that is what used to happen."

"Are you having false awakenings or sleepwalking?"

"I know what sleepwalking is, and no, but what is false awakenings?"

"They're where you wake up as normal and go the bathroom, get dressed, eat breakfast, and maybe even get halfway to work before you realize 'oh my god, I'm still dreaming!'"

"Ah, nope. Never had that happen."

"Are they more like a nightmare that terrifies you?"

"No, but I have had those before too. And before you ask, no, the dreams aren't about me being naked at school or forgetting my locker combination."

"Ya, I have had those before too. They are called recurring dreams if they happen more than once. So, tell me more, because I think what you are talking about is called lucid dreaming. Where the dream is life-like, and you know you are dreaming, but you can think clearly and control the dream."

"Not quite. I have had those types of dreams before, but this still seems different."

"Tell me about what makes this dream different."

"Usually, in most of my dreams, I am 'all' the characters, male, female, old, young, animal, human, or other. I see the dream from all perspectives: as the person, observing the person, and even watching the person from above. The dreams are always in color, but somehow not as vivid as in real life. Sometimes, I am none of the characters in the dream. I am just watching it like a movie."

"Interesting. That is not typical for most people."

"I'll tell you about the one I had the other night. It was back in the mid-1600s. I was dressed in an outfit that you would have seen on TV in a pirate show. You know, where the blouse part of the dress is white, off the shoulders, and tucks into a skirt. The skirt is darker, full length, and has a tight waist. My hair is long and flows freely."

"Yes, I have seen all the Caribbean pirate movies."

"Well, in this dream, the part that is really different is I know that I am the female character, but I am not all the other characters. It is like lucid dreaming, where I can control the dream, but I do not know that I am dreaming. It was so real. I could taste and smell the sea air. When I woke up, it was as if I was still there, back in time."

"Lexi, that one sounds like you remembered a past life."

"You think so?"

"Ya. You are describing things in extreme detail. When a person is having a memory of a past life, they are always only one person."

"I see. Okay, that makes sense. Why am I suddenly dreaming of past lives?"

"Some medical doctors believe that kind of dreaming is a unique state of consciousness that incorporates the experiences of the present, processing of the past, and is in preparation for the future."

"You think my mind is preparing me for the future?"

"Well, the average person only uses about ten percent of their brain's capabilities. It is telling me that you are developing more parts of your brain."

"Interesting. I guess with all that I have been learning about metaphysics, the celestial world, and energy, it is shifting my perspective on life."

"I think your mind is getting you ready for precognitive dreams."

"What is that?"

"Precognition is the ability to see the future, or snippets of future events that may occur."

"Seeing the future?"

"Yes. It is considered to be a form of extrasensory perception."

"ESP?"

"Yes. Don't be so surprised. You've been learning a lot about energy and how it works."

"Yes, but I didn't think I was going to be able to tell the future."

"Lexi, the last course you took from me was the start of how to read energy, past, present, and yes, future."

"Tamara, how will I know if I am having a precognitive dream?"

"You won't until it comes true. Some people get Déjà vu dreams - dreams that feel familiar and seems like you've been there before."

"Ya. I've experienced Déjà vu a few times over the years."

"Lexi, just wait until you and Edward start to have shared dreams."

"What? What is that?"

"In rare cases, people who share a strong connection may have the same dream at the same time. Twins do it all the time."

"Fascinating. Do you get prophetic dreams, Tamara?"

"Yes, but not just when I'm sleeping. I get them when I'm meditating and on purpose."

"On purpose?"

"Lexi, fortune-telling has been around for centuries. The people who do it are usually awake."

"Right. I forgot about psychics."

"There are many forms of divination. Dreams are just one type."

"What are the other types?"

"Most people know about tarot cards."

"Oh, ya. Of course."

"Not too long ago, you were learning how to read energy, auras, and psychometry. Remember, I taught you how to read jewelry, photos, and handwriting?"

"Yes, but I don't remember seeing anyone's future."

"No. I only taught you the first part of reading energy. Once a person knows how to sense and translate the energy into cognitive information, the reader can follow the person's unique energy trail backward or forward in time."

"Oh, my God. That is fascinating. When are you going to teach me that part?"

"Soon, I think you're ready."

Chapter 25

Kesia left Tamara's as fast as she could. *It can't be!*

Ever since Kesia had all her stuff confiscated by the police, she had been trying to figure out why someone would want her tarot deck.

As she hurried down the boulevard, she replayed in her head the conversation with the man who had phoned and asked her all the questions about her grandmother's cards.

"Miss Bango, I am the officer assigned to your case. I am curious about the tarot deck that was found with your belongings?"

"What would you like to know?"

"As I was recording the evidence, I noticed that the cards found on Miss Wells were very old. Are they yours or hers?"

"I'm sorry, cards?"

"The tarot deck, was it yours?"
"What did they look like?" Kesia asked, trying to gain more insight into the situation.
"They have golden edges that are worn off in many spots. The art designs are none that I have seen before."
"Do they have words printed on them such as the fool, the magician, or the world?"
"Let me see. No."
"Then they are not mine," Kesia lied.
"I see. So, do you know how she came to get the cards?"
"No. Sorry, I don't," Kesia said, lying again.
"That will be all for now. Thank you for your cooperation."

"Okay, Kesia, think," she said quietly to herself as she waited for a bus to come.

"Why would the officer at the station say that there were no cards, only to have this officer say that there were?"

Kesia started to pace as she was thinking this through. "The man on the phone described my grandmother's cards. I doubt it could be coincidental that Trina had a set of her own. No, he said they had worn edges. Even if Trina had bought a set, they would have been new."

A man who was also waiting for the bus looked at Kesia weirdly as she talked to herself.

Not caring, Kesia said, "Wait, the man on the phone said they had found the cards on Trina. What was she doing with my cards? How did she get them? Maybe she was bored waiting for me and went through my belongings? That doesn't make sense. She knew that I didn't let anyone touch my cards."

The bus came, and Kesia got on. Finding a seat near the back, she looked out the window as she was still thinking back to the policeman's conversation.

"The real question is, why did the officer care about the cards?"

As she was staring out the window, she saw a car driven by the man from Tamara's house. She instantly replayed what he said as he came in, *"Hi. I thought we could go out for dinner. Oh, sorry. I didn't know you had company."*

All the blood in Kesia's face drained out. She could swear that the man who had come into Tamara's house sounded exactly like the officer who had asked all the questions about the cards.

Chapter 26

The end of July 1438 in Rome

Clementina was treated as a guest in Lucius's house. There was no need to escape, for where was she to go?

Wandering through the house, she was amazed at the size. The walls of the Domus were painted with the most marvelous colors and designs. She imagined that it must have taken the artist months to possibly years to have completed all the murals.

As one would enter the front of the Domus, from the outside looking in, there were four small shops opening out onto the street, two on each side of the vestibulum (grand entrance hall) leading into the house. This entrance was watched by an ianitor (doorman).

Once you enter the Domus through the entranceway, you walk into the main area of the house called the atrium, which is the room where she had seen Lucius greet his guests. Clementina loved this room with its open-air ceiling displaying the bluest sky. She loved to sit in the center of the room by the small sunken marble pool and watch as the rainwater poured down each of the four inwardly slanted roof edges and out of the monster faces, filling the pool.

Her cubiculum (bedroom), which held only a bed and dresser, was off to the right of the atrium. There were three other bedrooms, four in total, two on each side of the atrium. One night she had come out to go to the bathroom, only to find many servants sleeping on the floor in front of Lucius's bedroom, which was across from hers.

As she walked further into the Domus, just past the atrium, was a short but wide-open room called an alae. At each end were large open windows that allowed the light to shine in. She marveled at the construction of the curved pillar in the center of each window, which she believed was there for support, but with his money, maybe it was only an ornamental element. This room's walls displayed intricate carvings detailing important people, events, and his family's history.

Beyond this room was the center of the Domus, Lucius's tablinum (office). Clementina imagined sitting in Lucius's office and being able to see to the entrance of the Domus, and also behind him to the back of the house. She knew from this room one could know what was happening at all times.

You could walk through his office to the second part of the Domus unless you were a woman or a servant, then you would have to walk through one of the two narrow passageways, one on either side of his office. All three of these routes led to a beautiful indoor peristyle (garden). This part of the house was much larger and taller than the first. It also had an open-air ceiling.

If she chose to walk to the left and in front of the garden, she would come upon the triclinium (dining room). The dining area had three couches, surrounding three sides of a low square table.

If she chose to walk to the right and around the garden, she passed the bathrooms and the culina (kitchen). The kitchen was staffed by servants 24/7. It had a small masonry counter wood-burning stove, and the servants would use the posticum (side entrance) next to the kitchen to come and go to the outside. This exit also had a doorman guarding it.

Her favorite route was to walk through the garden. Here many large inline columns were holding up the four segments of the roof. The garden was filled with plants, benches, another pool, shrines, and statues, which she found out later, were guardian deities. She also found out that Lucius had a piscina, which is usually a shallow basin placed near the altar of a church, which was used for washing the communion vessels. Although in this case, he used it for the reverent disposal of sacred substances back into the ground.

As she walked through the garden to the back of the Domus, she came upon the exedra, a large semicircular platform ringed with curved high-backed stone benches. She thought it would make a suitable place if one wanted to sit and have a conversation.

Clementina never in her wildest dreams would have thought that people lived like this and wondered how long she could put up this charade and play the part of a wealthy patrician.

Chapter 27

Clementina was sitting on one of the benches in the garden when Lucius came up to her. Sitting beside her, he said, "I will be hosting a large gathering tonight and require your services."

"What are you suggesting that I do?"

"I am not suggesting anything. I am ordering you to entertain the guests."

"Ordering! Am I one of your servants now?"

"You are living under my roof, and as the master of the Domus, I give the orders."

Scared to ask, for fear that he would find out that she had no idea of what he expected her to do and would kick her out onto the street, she said graciously, "I am sorry for my outburst. I would be honored to entertain your guests."

Lucius smiled slightly and walked back to his office.

Clementina stayed out of the way for most of the day as the servants set about for the gathering.

Just before the first set of guests arrived, Lucius came and retrieved Clementina from her bedroom. He marveled at her beauty.

Earlier that day, a few female servants had washed Clementina and dressed her in a stola, a long white dress that was cinched at the waist and fell to her feet. Metal clasps secured it at the shoulder. She was adorned with emerald earrings, a pearl necklace, and aquamarine and opal rings. She even had jewels sewn onto her shoes and clothing.

Taking her hand, he escorted her to the garden, where they would wait until the guests arrived. "You look beautiful," he said as he kissed the back of her hand before letting go.

Blushing, Clementina smiled.

It wasn't long before a servant came and told them that the guests had arrived. He made sure that at least ten guests were invited to the dinner party, they were his close friends, family, and associates. He had made sure that all who attended were born from marriages celebrated with the confarreatio, the Flamen Dialis, and the Pontifex Maximus.

Taking Clementina's hand again, Lucius led the way through his office to the atrium where he greeted each of his guests in turn.

The first guest he introduced to Clementina was his older sister, Octavia, and her husband, Barnabas. Next was his younger brother, Darius. She was introduced to the immediate family first, some uncles, aunts, and distant relatives. Not attending were his parents, who had died a few years prior in a horrific fire.

Lucius also introduced her to his closest friends and colleagues that he had invited for tonight's gathering.

Tonight's dinner party involved much more than drinking and eating. Many who attended were in deep conversation, and some in philosophical dialogues as Lucius stood up and said, "Please follow me."

They were all escorted outside and walked to the Temple of Jupiter. Clementina was escorted into a special room to the side, where she had to wait until everyone was seated. A servant came over and secured a red veil to her hair. Clementina played with it thinking it would make a great addition to her dance that she would entertain the guests with later.

Lucius was escorted into another room and was happy that the omina (omens) were favorable. There weren't any earthquakes or hurricanes today.

Once everyone was in place, Clementina and Lucius walked together around the altar three times. Unbeknownst to Clementina, this started the wedding ritual.

The confarreatio ceremony continued with the division of panis farreus (spelt focaccia seasoned with mola salsa that was prepared by vestal virgins). Octavia, acting as the pronuba, (Roman bride's matron of honor), gave the nubendi (couple) half of the bread each. Eating it symbolized the acceptance to share their life. Clementina was fascinated by the customs of these people. She happily ate the spelt bread. Octavia led Clementina and united her to Lucius by joining their hands and pronouncing the formula "te isti viro do, amicum, tutorem, patrem" (I give you this man as a friend, guardian, and father).

Clementina, guided by Lucius, followed by the rest of the guests, journeyed to the Temple of Juno where a white heifer was sacrificed in honor of the goddess.

Thereafter, the group returned to Lucius's Domus and were led into the dining room. The triclinium was elaborately decorated with wall paintings and portable artworks, specially placed for an elaborate dinner party. The guests were arranged according to a specific formula that gave privileged places to those of higher rank.

The dinner began with the acclaim 'feliciter' (wish for happiness addressed to the spouses). After dinner, the wedding cake called the mustaceus was distributed to the guests. Still not clueing in that she was now the wife of Lucius,

Clementina whispered to him, "When would you like me to entertain your guest? I have a beautiful dance that I can perform."

Surprised by what she just said, Lucius spit out some wine. Looking at her, he said, "That won't be necessary."

Deeply hurt by his reaction, Clementina sat up straighter and tried not to cry.

Seeing his new bride with tears in her eyes, he leaned over and said, "As my wife, Clementina, I suggest that you gain control of your emotions and entertain my guests with your smile and by standing beside me as I talk with each of them."

Dumbfounded, all Clementina could do was nod her head.

Chapter 28

After everyone had left, Clementina was escorted into Lucius's bedroom. A servant removed her clothing and jewelry. She was sponge bathed and guided to lie down on his bed.

Shortly after the servant had left, Lucius came in and unclasped his toga, it fell to the ground revealing his body.

Clementina stared at him. It was not the first nude body she had seen. He was thin but well built. His skin had the bronze glow that all Romans had, lighter than hers but not as white as the people back in Bohemia.

He came to bed and ascended upon her, doing things to her that Carlo never had.

After Lucius had finished, he lay down beside her and ordered, "Return to your room."

Clementina slowly got up from his bed and walked quietly back to her room.

Not sure what she was to do now, she laid down and fell asleep.

The next morning, she was awoken by a servant who helped her dress and escorted her outside. She was sure that she must have disappointed Lucius, for he was now kicking her out of his Domus. As she was about to turn and walk away, the servant grabbed her arm and ushered her up onto a litter carried by slaves.

Never being outside other than for her wedding, she had no idea of where she was or how big this village was.

Marveling at the businesses on the streets, she sat in awe of the new sights and wonders of the open markets emerging in front and to her sides as the litter passed through the busy streets.

To Clementina's astonishment, this village was a large city with over a million residents. Its streets were paved with stone. On the journey to wherever she was going, she passed Tiber Island, and Capitoline Hill—where she had been last night inside of the Temple of Jupiter. Later, she found out that the hill was earlier known as Mons Saturnius, dedicated to the god Saturn.

Her litter went past the Palatine Hill, where the ruler of Rome reigns. Along the journey, she saw the Imperial Palace, and attached to it was the Circus Maximus, where Clementina's litter came to a halt. She was escorted by one of the slaves up into a booth where Lucius was waiting for her.

Greeting her by kissing her hand, he had her sit beside him. Looking around, she was sitting high above the arena, which was shaped like a bullet. It was an enormous structure, standing four stories in height, half a Roman mile down each side. It could seat about two-hundred people. In the center of the racing arena, was a large central spine, creating an oval ring for the chariots to race around.

As she waited in anticipation for what was about to happen, she watched as twelve chariots, each led by four horses, were divided into four teams, often called factions. Each team was identified by their colors: blue, green, red, and white.

Lucius leaned over and said, "We are cheering for the blue team."

Clementina watched as the chariots broke out of the starting gate.

Lucius told her that the drivers, dressed in leather and with their team colors on, needed to be the first chariot to complete seven laps to win the race.

The crowd went wild as a couple of the chariots crashed. Lucius leaned towards her and said, "We call that a 'shipwreck' when there is a tangled mass of horses, drivers, and wood.

As Clementina watched, she figured out that the rules were pretty minimal. The drivers could even whip and lash their opponents and even try to pull them out of their chariots.

The people of Rome gathered not just to see the spectacles of skill and entertainment but hungered for the violence. After Augustus's time, the race laps were marked with little golden dolphins that were tipped as each lap was finished.

Lucius yelled out to Clementina, "Which chariot should we bet on?" Betting was widespread and one of the chief advantages and pleasures of going to the races.

Clementina laughed and shrugged her shoulders.

Later Clementina found out that the races were often used as a proxy for skirmishes—a way to settle minor disputes or contests between opposing parties.

After the races, Lucius sat with Clementina on the same litter back to their Domus. Leaning over, he asked, "How did you enjoy the races?"

Clementina, still high from the energy of the race, laughed and said, "I would have never in a million years thought that watching men and horses could be so invigorating. I loved it."

They had just passed an enormous round building. Clementina asked, "What is that?"

"That is the Colosseum. It is said that in the early 400s, you could watch a Gladiatorial fight. Since then, even a ruler has used it for his palace, and more recently, after the great earthquake in 1349 which collapsed the outer south side, a religious order moved into the northern third of the Colosseum in the mid-14th century and still resides there."

"Interesting."

The rest of the way home Clementina laid back onto the pillows and enjoyed the ride. Silently, she thanked Apollo for blessing her with this day.

Chapter 29

Each night since the ceremony, Clementina was bathed and guided into Lucius's bedroom, and each night after he was finished, she was dismissed. She did not understand why she could not wake up beside her husband and was too scared to ask. *I have all the riches one could dream of. . . and what I would give to be back in the arms of a man who loved me.*

The next morning Clementina was woken early to get ready for the day's travel. She found Lucius waiting for her outside in a covered wagon. One of the servants helped her up. Looking at Lucius, she said, "Where are we off to today?"

"I thought I would bring you along on my Estate tour."

"I would like that," Clementina smiled.

As Clementina peeked out of the wagon to see the sights, Lucius scolded her by saying, "A lady of your class never shows her face while in a carriage." Quickly Clementina let go of the curtain.

The first stop they made was to a small spelt farm. When Lucius came back into the wagon, Clementina saw him put his money bag beside him. "Was it a good crop this year?"

Lucius looked at her in puzzlement, "It is only July."

Clementina didn't say another word the whole trip. They had stopped at many farms throughout the day. It was nearing dusk when the wagon stopped, and Lucius told Clementina to get out. Following his order, she obeyed.

Standing before her was a Roman Villa. It was much larger than their city home. Running out to greet them was Octavia. "Welcome! I am so happy to see that you brought me a guest, Lucius." Wrapping an arm through Clementina's, with the biggest smile, she said, "I don't get a lot of city folks out here."

Smiling back at Octavia, Clementina said, "I am so happy to see you."

Entering the villa, Clementina was surprised by how much bigger it was than the Domus she was living in.

Seeing the surprise on her face, Lucius said, "I am far too busy in the city to run everything, so Barnabas, being the third son, helps me with my estate while his older brothers run his with his father and grandfather."

Clementina nodded.

Octavia showed Clementina the villa. It had multiple rooms, including servants' quarters, courtyards, baths, pools, storage rooms, and gardens. They ended the tour at a bedroom, as Octavia said, "You'll be staying here."

"We are staying overnight?"

Octavia looked at her with a raised eyebrow. "You will be staying for a week or so while Lucius continues his journey. He will pick you up on his way back." Seeing the look on Clementina's face, she added, "He didn't tell you?"

"No. It must have slipped his mind."

"You'll love it here and never want to go back to the city, you'll see."

Just then, Clementina heard the laughter of a child. "You have children?"

"Yes, come meet Arrius." Octavia led her outside, where a five-year-old Arrius was playing with a dog.

Spying his mother, Arrius threw the stick for the dog to catch and instantly ran in the opposite direction towards his mother. "Mama, he loves to get the stick. See?"

"I see that."

Tears weld up in Clementina's eyes as the dog came running back to his master with the stick. Kneeling to the ground, Clementina whispered, "Tillie."

Recognizing her and almost knocking her over, Tillie ran over and started licking her face.

Scared for Clementina's safety, Octavia yelled to a servant to get the dog off her.

"No. No. It is okay," Clementina cried. "Where did you find him?"

Octavia wasn't sure what to make of the situation.

"Sit," Clementina ordered Tillie. The dog obeyed and sat still, other than his tail.

Looking at Clementina, Octavia said, "He was shooed away many times but always came back. He laid by the door morning and night, outside the servant entrance of Lucius's Domus. A cousin of one of the house servants knew I had a son who would love him and on one of his trips dropped him off."

Clementina was petting the dog as she listened. "I never thought I would see him again."

Arrius came running over. Hugging Tillie, he said, "He is my dog. Isn't he grand? I named him Ardicus."

Clementina looked at the little boy and how he loved his dog. There was no way she could break his heart. She got up and started to walk back to the house. Tillie went to follow. "No. Stay," she demanded, and the dog obeyed.

Octavia followed Clementina into the house and said, "Thank you. He has fallen in love with the dog, and it would have broken his heart to have lost him."

Clementina looked at Octavia and said, "Do not tell Lucius of this."

Octavia nodded, knowing that even though Lucius hated pets, he would have insisted that Tillie be returned to Clementina.

Chapter 30

The next few days were wonderful at Octavia's. Clementina enjoyed her days learning how to weave and how to run a household. Watching Octavia made it seem effortless.

"I have a treat for you tonight, Clementina."

"You do? I don't know what could be better than what I have been doing."

"You'll like it even more."

"We'll see."

That evening after vesperna (their light supper) was finished and Octavia had given Arrius a kiss on the forehead and said good night, the two ladies were escorted by litter to a neighboring villa.

Getting off the litter, Clementina said, "Who are we visiting?"

"A white witch."

Clementina froze.

Octavia started to laugh. "You should see your face."

Clementina, feeling foolish, followed Octavia inside.

Darla's villa was almost as lovely as Octavia's. "You have a lovely home," Clementina said as she smiled shyly, now worried that Octavia wasn't kidding about the white witch part. If Clementina ever imagined what one would look like, Darla would be it. White long and wild hair, wrinkled skin, *she must be at least one hundred,* Clementina thought to herself.

Smiling back and with an accent, she thought she recognized, Clementina heard her say, "Thank you, that is very kind of you to say. Come in and join the others."

Clementina followed Octavia into the back garden, where she found many other women chatting with one another.

Darla announced above the noise, "Ladies, come and find yourselves a seat."

Once they found a seat, Clementina leaned over and asked Octavia, "How old is she?"

"Not as old as you may think. I heard that the sun does something to her skin to make it look like that way."

"Oh. I shall start to wear a hat more often."

Octavia giggled. "Shh. She'll hear."

Darla started to speak. "Ladies, welcome, and thank you for joining me on this full moon. As it is now our tradition to help our men out in any way that we can, I am grateful for your trust in me to honor our moon goddess, Diana. Please stand and raise your hands."

Octavia stood up, so Clementina followed her actions and turned her palms up to the sky.

"Goddess Diana, goddess of the hunt, the woodlands, and fertility."

Clementina wasn't sure, but she could have sworn she just saw a smoky version of a young lady wearing a short tunic and carrying a bow run through the garden.

"We call upon you tonight for the protection of our families and our country. Please honor us with a message."

Clementina's eyes went wide open as Darla's form took on a new persona, and she started to walk around each of the ladies here tonight in her garden, whispering for their ears only.

As she came by Clementina, she was shocked to hear her old tongue being spoken by the woman, Romani. As Darla passed by Clementina, she laid her hand upon her stomach and said to her in Romani, "He must never know," and then continued to Octavia.

Dumbfounded about what the old woman meant by that, she sat down, not waiting to be told to.

After Darla was finished, she held her arms up high and praised the goddess again before she collapsed to the floor. Startled, Clementina gasped.

"Do not worry. She will be fine. It just exhausts her to channel the goddess," Octavia said.

A few servants came in with appetizers and drinks. Clementina followed and smiled politely as Octavia introduced her to the other women at the gathering.

On their way home, Octavia mentioned, "I wish I knew what she is saying."

"You don't know what she said to you?"

"No. She speaks in the celestial tongue, and no one here knows what she is saying. It makes it even more mystical."

Trying to decide if she should tell Octavia that she was an old gypsy and was speaking Romani, she decided against it.

"She blessed your tummy, though. You will bring in a fine boy to continue our family's business," Octavia said as she rubbed Clementina's tummy.

Clementina touched her own tummy. *I'm pregnant? I'm pregnant!*

Chapter 31

1438 to 1458 in Rome

Clementina gave birth to a healthy baby boy, who was named Dominic after Lucius's grandfather. Their life was filled with days of joy as they watched the little one grow.

One afternoon, as Octavia watched Clementina waddle around, she was concerned for her welfare and said, "You must take care and not overdo it with this one, Clementina. We don't want it to be early like your first child. You were lucky that he survived being so premature."

Julian was born almost ten months after Dominic, and Clementina was happy that Lucius was able to be there to welcome his second son into the world.

The boys grew quickly, and everything seemed to be a competition between them. Dominic was tall, kind, and smart, whereas Julian was a little rascal, always trying to get his older brother into trouble.

Five years later, Clementina gave birth to a little girl. They named her Tatiana.

Life seemed blissful. Clementina loved the sound of her children playing in the garden. She loved how Lucius showed his love to the children and spoiled them rotten. Most of all, she loved being a wife and mother.

The years flew by, and the children were now grownups. Dominic had learned how to do the finances, helping with Lucius's day-to-day business and Julian hated Dominic for it.

Even though Julian made life difficult, it wasn't hard to see that he was Lucius's favorite child and could do no wrong.

Over the years, Clementina spent many hours visiting with Octavia at her villa in the country. At night when the children were asleep and left in the care of the servants, they would go and learn more about the craft from Darla.

Clementina had brought her tarot cards one evening, and Darla taught them all how to use the cards.

"I want you all to treat the cards as a reflection of what is going on in your life. As you or the person reading the cards start to shuffle them, think about what it is that you require an answer to. Your thoughts will create a vibration, and the cards as they are shuffled will resonate with this new frequency of thought energy." Darla shuffled the cards a couple more times, then said, "As I believe in a higher power, I allow the gods to answer my prayer. I pray to one god in particular, the Roman god, Mercury, also known as Mercurius. He is the son of Jupiter. Or you might have heard of him by his Greek name, Hermes, the son of Zeus."

All of this was new to Clementina. She grew up with no strict religious background as a Romani, but here many she knew followed the Roman Catholic belief.

Darla continued, "Mercury is the god of financial gain, commerce, eloquence, messages, communication, including divination, travelers, boundaries, luck, trickery, and thieves. He also serves to guide souls to the underworld. He is the god who wears winged shoes or a winged hat. He is the fastest messenger of all the gods. The staff he holds in his left hand is the caduceus, a rod with two snakes intertwined and wings at the top. He is also seen with a cock or rooster. Mercury is the herald of the gods and is the go-between for mortals and the divine. He will send and retrieve your messages."

Darla asked Clementina to think of something that she wanted an answer to.

Clementina started to think about Lucius and why he never let her sleep in his bed.

Darla turned over a card. "The first card is the god Cupid. This card means that you desire affection." Darla turned over another card. It was the king of Virtues. "Clementina, this card represents your husband and his virtues. Speaking from experience, I will tell you that you are loved. The Roman men are different from other men. Where you come from, you are the only wife. Here he may have more than one and may have concubines as well. Consider yourself lucky. Lucius, from what I know, only has you. He does not love another."

Clementina was shocked at the accuracy of Darla's words. How did she know all of what she said? Clementina had not told her of her thoughts.

Reshuffling the cards, Darla said, "Ladies, the cards reveal how you are feeling. The emotions of your thoughts, wishes, wants, and desires. Nothing more. The cards will change as your moods change. If you are stressed about something, it will show up in the cards. As you heal and grow, the cards will always reflect your shift in energy and emotions."

Clementina put up her hand.

"Yes."

"Darla, when should I use the cards?"

"Good question. Anytime you have a problem or issue, the cards will reveal how to find a solution, guidance, or a new direction. The cards pick up on how you are feeling right this moment, and if you ask the right question, the cards can show you what to do about it.”

“That’s good to know. Thank you,” Clementina said as she took her cards back from Darla.

The rest of the evening, Darla talked about other enlightening subjects.

Chapter 32

1459 in Rome

Clementina was in her room shuffling her cards when Tatiana came in.

"Mater (mom), what are you doing?"

Clementina looked at her teenage daughter and said, "It is time that you learned the craft. Come over here and shut the door."

Over the next few weeks, Clementina taught Tatiana all that she knew about the tarot cards and how to use them. She also told her about her gypsy heritage from Bulgaria.

Tatiana was fascinated with all of it.

As Clementina put the cards into a hole in the wall that was behind the dresser, she said to her daughter, "We must keep this a secret. It is not safe for you to flaunt your gifts of the craft. Others do not allow a woman to possess power, let alone the ability to tell the future. Times are changing, and praying to the old gods is even becoming a sin. You must promise me you will be careful and not reveal what you are learning to your father or brothers. They would forbid you from ever learning it. They will consider it witchcraft, which is a crime."

Nodding, Tatiana said, "But we are not doing spells. I do not understand what they are afraid of. The cards hold no power. They are simply made of paper."

"Tatiana, promise me."

"Yes, I promise." *But I don't understand what the big deal is about.*

The next time the family visited Octavia while Lucius and the boys were on another round of visiting tenants of their estate, Tatiana was invited to come along to Darla's.

Clementina introduced Darla to her daughter.

Tatiana bowed her head slightly as she said, "Thank you for having me. I am excited about tonight's festivities."

As Darla took the young girl's hand, shivers ran down Darla's back. Looking into the girl's eyes, she said, "You are destined for great things, but your most precious gift will be what you teach your children and their children. Never forget where you came from." Smiling, she led them into the garden where the others were waiting.

After everyone was seated, Darla said, "Ladies, I am afraid this will be our last evening together. I will not be hosting any more of these festivities."

The other ladies in the room showed their displeasure with a slight cry of despair.

"It is not safe to gather as we do. The officials are starting to do witch hunts and putting anyone to death for practicing what they believe to be pagan crafts." Darla looked over at young Tatiana. "We must teach our young what we have learned and pass down the knowledge to our children."

Clementina looked at Tatiana and grabbed her hand, and gave it a little squeeze. The disappointed look on her daughter's face told her everything.

As they left Darla's, Tatiana ran up to their hostess and thanked her with a hug. "It feels like I have known you my whole life. Like we are kin or something."

Taking a step back and a gentle hold of Tatiana's face, Darla said, "Child, we are all sisters in the ways of the old gods. You will be okay. Trust your heart and know what is true." She then kissed Tatiana's head and said, "Good night."

In the litter back to Octavia's home, Tatiana leaned in and hugged her mother and aunt. "Thank you for trusting me with this knowledge. I will treasure this night forever."

As they came into the Domus, they heard screams.

Running to see what the commotion was all about. The three ladies came to a sudden halt as they looked down at Lucius's dead body.

Clementina fell to her knees as she went into hysterics seeing her husband's blood.

"What happened?" Octavia ordered.

One of the servants started to stutter with fear. "He… col . . collapsed."

Looking for her sons, Clementina yelled, "Where are the others?"

"We… do . . do… not know," the servant answered. "They… did . . .did not… come back with him."

"Where could they be?" Clementina said as she looked up at Octavia.

Worried now for her own son and husband's welfare, she got up and started ordering people around.

Coming back to Clementina and Tatiana, she said, "I have ordered the servants to go and find help. Everyone will be looking for them."

With tears rolling down her face, Tatiana went and helped her mother into a chair.

It was hours before someone returned with some news.

"Mistress, the others are being held captive by the Roman army. It was said that your brother's youngest son tried to kill his own brother."

Looking now at Clementina, he said, "Your husband tried to stop it and got in the way."

Clementine managed to say through her tears, "What are you talking about? My son's?"

"It started with the Mistress's son, Arrius. He was joking around with his cousins about not being real brothers."

"Oh no," Octavia said.

"What is he talking about, Octavia?" Clementina demanded.

"A few days ago, one of the tenants came by and said that he was at your house earlier and that he found it odd how Dominic doesn't resemble anyone in our family."

"There must be more to it than that, Octavia, for Arrius to bring it up."

"I am so sorry, Clementina. If I knew that this would ever have happened, I would have never said anything."

"Octavia, tell me what happened."

"Later that same night, we were talking amongst ourselves, and Barnabas started to do the math. He agreed that there was a chance you were pregnant before you came to Rome, and Dominic was a bastard."

Just as Clementina was about to say more, Barnabas and Arrius came into the Domus.

"Where are my sons?" Clementina yelled as she did not see them with them.

"Julian is being detained," Barnabas said. "You must leave now, Clementina. It is not safe for you here."

"What are you talking about?"

"We have Dominic in a carriage waiting for you."

"What, why?"

"It is not safe for either of you two. Julian is pressing charges for fraud and theft. It is a crime for the firstborn to play the role of an heir when he is not of the blood of his father."

"This is crazy. You have known Dominic all of his twenty-one years. There is no way to prove that he is not Lucius's son!"

"The law does not see it that way. You would have to prove that he is Lucius's son, and you cannot."

"How would anyone know that?"

"The servant who cleaned the sheets on Lucius's bed knows that there was no sign of you being a virgin."

Clementina turned to Tatiana and said, "Get your things. We are leaving."

Barnabas stepped in the way and stopped the girl from moving. "No, she stays here with us. She is Lucius's blood and she will remain here."

"Octavia, do something!" Clementina begged.

Barnabas grabbed hold of Clementina's arm and led her out to the carriage, where Dominic was bound and gagged.

A servant gagged and tied Clementina up and sat her beside her son.

"Take them north, and let them go once you are outside the city limits," Barnabas ordered.

"And, if either of you ever returns, you will be hung."

As the carriage started to move, Clementina leaned her head onto her son's shoulder, with tears running down her cheeks.

Chapter 33

August in New York City.

Redington was at his desk, looking at the evidence he had about Miss Trina Well's murder. Even though this was not his case, he could not help but wonder about her mysterious death.

The meditation he had at Tamara's of being a bird flying over the crime scene in Jersey Shore came to mind. *It seemed so real. What was in that box?*

Redington picked up his cell phone and called Tamara.

"Did you find new evidence about the murder?" Tamara said since she knew who was calling because of the caller ID.

"Hi to you too. No. Is there any way you can contact Kesia?"

"Ah, I think so, but don't you already have her info?"

"Yes, but I am not the official on her case. I was hoping you could set up a meeting for the three of us to get together."

"I think I can do that. Let me call you back."

"Great."

Not even five minutes later, Tamara called back. "Can you meet me at the Russian tea house on Montague Street in about an hour?"

"I can make that work. See you soon."

"Hey, Red? Thanks."

"No problem. Ever since the meditation, I can't seem to get this case out of my head."

As luck would have it, there was an open parking spot in front of the café for Redington to pull into.

Tamara started to walk over to his car as he was getting out. "Kesia works here, so I thought it would be good for you to get to know her on her home turf."

"You make me sound like I am hard to deal with."

Tamara just smiled.

"Great, I guess I will have to work on that."

As they entered the café, Tamara got a weird feeling like she was being watched.

Kesia walked up to Tamara and gave her a hug. "Thanks for everything you are doing."

"Spirit seems to have gotten me involved, so I will do my best to help you out." Turning to Redington, she said, "I would like to introduce you to Detective Redington."

"Nice to meet you, Detective," Kesia said, looking into his eyes.

Feeling like he was being probed, he said, "I am sorry about your friend, Trina. Did you know her long?"

"Nothing like bedside manner, Red," Tamara said as they sat down at a private table.

"Right. Sorry, just not good at small talk. So how long did you know her?"

"Not that long. A few weeks, I guess. She would come by and watch me do tarot."

"What happened to you that you didn't see the murder?"

"Red! That is a little harsh, don't you think?"

Looking at Tamara, he said, "Do you guys want answers or just for me to be polite?"

Kesia piped up, "I need answers. Tamara, I can handle this, don't worry." Looking at the Detective, she said, "I went to the restroom and slipped on some water. I hit my head and passed out. When I woke up and went outside, it was swarming with the police. So, I took off and watched from behind some bushes."

"You don't know who the murderer was?"

Pausing, Kesia answered, "No, I don't think so."

"What is the pause for?" Redington said but changed his question to, "If you suspect anyone, who would it be?"

Kesia dropped her head.

"It is okay to say who you think it is, Kesia. I can protect you," Redington told her with great confidence.

"But who is going to protect her." Kesia looked up at Tamara.

Shocked, Tamara said, "Why are you worried about me?"

Redington asked again, "Who do you suspect?"

"Her fiancé."

Tamara just stared. She was in too much shock to say anything.

Redington looked at Tamara and then back at Kesia. "What makes you believe Greg did it?"

"His voice. When I was at her house, and he came over, his voice was the exact same as the officer who phoned me and questioned me about the cards."

Tamara's mind was swarming with so many thoughts all at once. *No, it can't be.* The weird feelings she got around him lately came back. Coming to her senses, she said, "But why would Greg kill someone?"

"That is a good question. There are three reasons why someone murders, for money, for love, or to cover up a murder." Redington answered as he wondered what to do next.

Kesia, defending her suspicions, added, "The Officer on the phone wanted to know about my great grandmother's tarot cards."

Tamara wondered, "Why would Greg care about some tarot cards? He has access to as many as he likes at my place. I have all kinds."

Redington scratched his head as he was thinking. "All right, at the moment, you two are safe. Greg doesn't know you suspect him. Here is what we're going to do."

The girls leaned in as he said, "I will put an Officer on Greg to watch what he is doing. Tamara, tonight go stay with Alexandra. Kesia, do you have a friend you can stay with?"

"Red, I think Kesia should stay with me. She will be safe at Lexi's."

"Is that okay with you, Kesia?"

"Sure."

"Fine. I will follow you to Lexi's place, Tamara."

"Sounds good, but I have to stop at my place first to get some things. Kesia, you can come with me."

"No, I'll drive her," Redington said as they walked outside. "Tamara, it could be Greg. Thinking back to the meditation, it could be him. He's similar in size and has the same color hair as the guy I saw."

"Red, there is something else weird that happened."

"This must be good if you think it was weird."

Tamara gave Red a look to say, watch it. "I received a package in the mail. It was an envelope full of sand."

"Sand?"

"Yep, just sand."

"Like sand that you would find in Jersey Shore."

"I guess it could be. I never thought of that."

"I'll follow you home and pick it up if that's okay."

"Sure."

Redington pulled in behind Tamara's car, got out, and followed her inside.

Tamara went over to where she had hidden the envelope and almost tripped over the bag on the floor that she had kicked a few days ago. Giving Red the envelope, she bent down to pick up the bag. As she did, some sand from the bag fell onto the floor.

Redington looked from the envelope to the floor. He didn't spill any. Putting the envelope down on a table, he picked up some of the sand from the floor and put it beside the envelope's sand, *same type of sand.* Taking the bag from Tamara, he opened the bag. Greg's clothes were inside, as well as more sand. "Tamara, I'm going to have to take this with me. I will wait while you get some clothes to take with you to Alexandra's."

Tamara didn't know what to say but did go and get some things to bring with her.

Once they were outside, she got that same weird feeling, as if someone was watching her.

"Call Alexandra and tell her we are coming. Don't worry, I'll be right behind you."

Chapter 34

Lexi was getting anxious, waiting for Tamara to show up.

The new doorman for the apartment building rang up, "Miss Constantine, you have a guest, a Miss Tamara Reeve. Would you like me to allow her entrance?"

"Yes. Thank you, Elwyn. I have been expecting her. Is Detective Redington or Kesia Bongo with her?"

"No, ma'am, should I let them up when they arrive?"

"Yes, please do. Thank you, Elwyn."

"My pleasure, ma'am."

A few moments later, Lexi's doorbell rang. Upon opening the door, Lexi said, "What's going on?"

"Thank you for letting us come here on such short notice."

"No problem, I am working from home anyways, and I am not at Edward's place since it's still under construction. He is so secretive about the whole thing. He won't let me see it until it is finished."

Tamara tried to force a smile.

Noticing, Lexi said, "What is it. What is going on?"

Not being able to hold all the mixed emotions in, Tamara started to cry.

"Oh, my. Here let me help you. Come and sit on the couch." Lexi grabbed a box of tissue and set it down beside Tamara, knowing that she couldn't pass her one due to Tamara's belief that it would be telling her to shut up."

Tears flowed as Tamara tried to tell Lexi what was happening.

"You are telling me that Greg may have killed someone. You don't believe that, do you?"

Tamara shrugged her shoulders.

Just as Lexi was going to say something else, her doorbell rang. Getting up to get it, she shook her head in disbelief.

Lexi let Redington and Kesia in and motioned for them to go and sit down in the living room with Tamara.

Red sat beside Tamara and said, "We don't have any proof yet."

Tamara just nodded and wiped her face with a tissue.

"This is why I didn't want to say anything," Kesia blurted out. Looking up, she noticed the painting on the wall. "Where did you get this from?"

Everyone looked.

Pointing at the painting, she asked again, "Where did you get this?"

"It was a gift from a friend. Why?" Lexi asked, curious now.

"My ancestral grandmother painted it in the 15ᵗʰ century."

"What! No way," Lexi exclaimed as she got up to read the signature.

"Tatiana Masones." Kesia said.

"Yes. That is correct," Lexi confirmed.

"My mom has a painting similar to this one hanging in our living room. It is said that my ancestral grandmother kept her Father's clan name.

Lexi looked at Tamara and said, "What is it with me and paintings?"

"Some people just have all the luck," Redington said jokingly.

Tamara snapped out of her sadness and stated, "There is obviously a reason why you have this painting, Lexi. Spirit works in very mysterious ways, but there is always a reason."

Redington looked down and shook his head, "Here we go again." Looking up, he said, "Okay, let's say there is a reason that 'spirit' magically decided that this painting needed to be here, so, what is it? And who is that in the painting?"

"Archangel Gabriel," All three ladies said at the same time.

"Hmm. Where are his wings? I thought angels had wings," Redington rationalized.

"In the bible, there is no mention of Gabriel having wings. For that matter, there is no mention that he was even an Archangel," Kesia clarified.

"True," Tamara agreed.

"So, what is so important about this painting then?"

"Gabriel is the angel of communication. He is God's messenger. He delivers messages between the human world and the divine."

"Uh-huh, okay then." Redington was having a hard time believing how he got caught up again in this religious, metaphysical stuff.

Lexi looked at Redington and interjected, "Don't you find it coincidental that there is a painting in my apartment that Kesia's ancestor painted? Come on, Red, that has to be proof of a sign from Heaven, even for you."

Redington was getting uncomfortable with all of this spiritual talk. "I admit, it is weird."

Lexi smiled at him, then looked over at Tamara, "So, what do we do now?"

Tamara looked at the painting and then back at Kesia. "Tell us about this painting."

"Well, I am not sure what you want me to say. I was told that my ancestral grandmother, Tatiana had learned the craft from her mother, Clementina. That there was a tragedy in the family, and her mother and oldest brother were sent away. There is not much else known about them after that. I was told that Tatiana had passed down the knowledge of the craft to her children and grandchildren and that we are required to do the same. Since she could not pray to the old gods or let anyone know about the craft, she started painting divine beings that the church would allow."

Redington interrupted. "What is the 'craft' that you are speaking of?"

"The 'craft' is the abilities people like Moses, Daniel, David, and Jesus possessed. It is well known that Jesus and his mother, Mary, had divine abilities," Kesia answered before the other two ladies could say anything.

"Mother Mary had abilities?" Redington said, getting caught up in the story.

Kesia smiled, "Well, how many women do you know that can stay a virgin and get pregnant?"

"Touché."

"There are nine spiritual gifts granted randomly at birth. They are the gift of Wisdom, Knowledge, Faith, Miracles, Healing, Prophecy, Distinguishing Spirits, and both Tongues - Speaking and Interpreting. Jesus learned the 'craft' of performing all of them."

"You're telling me Jesus was taught how to do all of those spiritual gifts?"

"Yes. They are still being taught to this day. There are many stories of people protecting and passing on this divine knowledge, like the Templars and Masons. Even other cultures have learned from the sacred Sanskrit scrolls, such as the East Indian Yogis and Buddhist Monks."

"Let me get this straight. You are telling me that people today can do what Jesus did?" Redington said in disbelief.

Lexi cut in on the conversation, "Red, it is true. Tamara has been teaching me how to do what Jesus did."

Redington looked from Lexi to Tamara. "That meditation you had me do, is that part of these teachings?"

"Yes," Tamara nodded.

"Wow! This will take a bit to wrap my head around," Redington replied.

Kesia continued her story about the painting, "Notice that there is a blurry spot hovering behind Gabriel." She got up and walked over to the painting. "Notice here." Touching the area that she was referring to.

"Ah, I hadn't paid attention to that. I thought it was just part of the background," Lexi said, getting up to look closer. "What does it represent?"

"It represents Bath Kol. The voice of God," Kesia said proudly as she was able to share her knowledge about the meaning of this painting.

Redington cleared his throat, "Who or what is Bath Kol?"

"She is of the highest order of angels, even higher than an archangel. She is a Seraphim, the close rank to God," Kesia smiled with delight.

Tamara smiled at the abundance of knowledge coming out of someone so young.

"I am scared to ask, what does she do?" Redington enquired.

"She, Gabriel, and the Holy Ghost communicate divine messages, just as the gods, Mercury or Hermes was believed to do back in ancient times."

"And how do they do that?" Redington asked, trying to make sense of all of this.

Kesia answered him with, "Many individuals get these three angels mixed up. For those that can sense spirits—most cannot distinguish the spirits (*tell the difference between them*)—they just assume who came. A lot of people get Gabriel and Bath Kol's energy mixed up. That is why you hear stories of people not sure what sex Gabriel is. I sometimes get Bath Kol, and the Holy Ghost's energy mixed up because they are both vaporous and quiet, whereas Gabriel usually appears as a man and speaks clearly to me."

Tamara added, "Actually, many people believe that Gabriel is the Holy Ghost. I am not sure if that is true, but who am I to say if it is or isn't."

Kesia continued, "As you might know, the Holy Ghost can enter your body and bears witness to your spiritual beliefs. The other two do not enter your body. Though, all three can guide you in your decisions and protect you from physical and spiritual danger. I do not think that the Holy Ghost is Gabriel. They are too different."

Lexi added, "Archangel Gabriel came to me in a dream and spoke to me about becoming a prophet."

"You're kidding, right?" Redington couldn't believe all that he was hearing.

Lexi nodded and gave Redington one of those looks, as if you better not judge me. "Tamara teaches that Gabriel is the teacher of prophets."

Redington looked over to Tamara, "Is that true?"

"I believe that it is. There are stories that are told today of people having experiences that science cannot explain, and similar stories are also written in the Bible."

"Okay, but what does all of this have to do with this painting?" Redington asked again.

Chapter 35

Lexi went into the kitchen and popped two premade pizzas into the oven. Coming back with drinks for everyone, she passed them out.

Kesia looked at the painting. "This one is different from the one my mom has."

"How so," Tamara queried.

"This one doesn't show anything behind Gabriel. In my mom's, he is standing in front of a doorway."

"Can you tell me the details about the doorway," Tamara insisted. "It might be the key we are looking for."

"Funny pun, Tamara. Key. . . door," Redington teased. From the look, she gave him, he added, "Lighten up. I thought it was funny."

"Let's try something," Lexi suggested. "Why don't we do a meditation and ask Archangel Gabriel?"

Redington stood up, "Okay, this is my cue to leave. You guys can tell me what you find out later."

"Wait, the pizza is ready. Let me get you a piece."

"I can pick something up later. I can't hear any more about this weird stuff. I have to get back to the real world and find a murderer.

"Too bad that the world you choose to live in, Red, is corruption, violence, and homicide. I like our version better, inner peace, love, and spirituality," Lexi teased.

"Uh-huh, from what I have witnessed so far, Lexi, you seem to get caught up in all kinds of dark mischief," Redington smirked as he thought about the adventures they have had together.

"Oh, my goodness. You're right. I do find myself in situations that are dangerous." Freaking out now, she turned to Tamara. 'What does that say about me?"

"I believe that God has a reason behind everything. Think about what has happened to you since your sister Suzanna's death. You have been on a quest to find answers ever since. One thing happens, and then you learn more. Then that leads you to learn even more. For some reason, God has you learning the nine spiritual gifts granted by spirit."

"When you put it that way, it is pretty exciting."

Kesia smiled at Lexi's enthusiasm. Ever since she could remember, all this 'weird stuff' was normal day talk in her family. "You don't know what you are missing, Detective. Pretty cool things happen in meditation. I'm ready Tamara, let's get this party started."

Lexi gave Red a light punch in the arm. "Come on, don't be a party pooper."

Redington grabbed a piece of the pizza and walked out the door, mumbling, "Call me later and tell me what you come up with."

Finishing the last bite of her pizza, Tamara said, "Get yourselves comfortable and focus on receiving a message from Archangel Gabriel, Bath Kol, or the Holy Ghost. There is a reason we have all been brought together here in Lexi's living room. With your next deep breath, you will meet one of these divine beings, and they will forward a message to you. Something important that you need to hear. I will speak again when it is time to come back to our reality."

Tamara stopped talking and let everyone receive whatever message it was that they needed to hear in the meditation.

About twenty minutes went by before Tamara said, "With your next deep breath, you will thank the divine spirit that delivered your message. . . You will remember in detail what you must share with us. . . and with your next breath you will wiggle your toes and open your eyes. . . coming fully awake. . . feeling wonderful and blessed."

Lexi and Kesia opened their eyes at about the same time.

Lexi cooed, "Mmm, that was marvelous. I love the feeling I get after being in a deep meditative state. I always feel so refreshed when I come back to a beta state. Meditation seems better to me than having a great night's sleep, and I love my sleep."

"Me too, Tamara, your voice is so soothing," Kesia added.

"Thank you. I have to agree. The feeling is amazing. So, what message did you two get?"

"Tamara, I think you should go first. What message did you receive?" Kesia said, wishing to know how these ladies can help her.

"My message was from Archangel Gabriel. He always comes to me in a male form. I love to receive his counsel. It is always wise and exactly what I need to hear. The message I received was this. For many years now, you have had the ability to prophesize. It is time to teach others more than just to read tarot cards. It is time to teach how to read energy without anything but your mind."

Lexi sat up straighter. "I am ready to be one of your disciples. In my meditation, I was invited to speak with Bath Kol again. Her energy is the softest I have experienced from a spirit so far. It is as fluffy as a cloud. All I feel when I am in her presence is love and peace of mind. She makes me feel whole. Her words are like whispers blowing through the air. You don't hear them, but you know they were spoken. Somehow the message she speaks resonates to your very core. If you asked me what she said, I would not be able to repeat the words, for she does not use a communication form with words. It is even different than what you would think a telepathic person uses. It is a frequency of energy that is none like we know here on earth. I think one would call it omniscient."

"What did she share with you, Lexi?" Kesia asked, getting impatient.

"Oh, right. I will do my best at translating what she said. Prophecy is a crazy business. People wish for a positive outcome, but sometimes, just knowing the outcome can shift the results from good (unconscious path of events) to bad (conscious path of events). *Meaning that when you didn't know the path to your immediate future, you went about your day as you normally would, and all that was to be, would be. But now that you know the path to your immediate future, your energy will shift because of knowing, and unfortunately, that could mean a worse outcome.* I think what Bath Kol meant was that you are best off to set the outcome you intend, like goal setting or something like you would learn in a positive thinking book. The laws of the universe are pretty straightforward, what you think you create. Your deepest emotions are what trigger your future. All that you feel drives you to your immediate and future actions."

"Wow, that was deep," Kesia said as an epiphany hit her. "Tamara, that day on the beach when I read your cards. It scared the bejesus out of me, and from what Lexi just said, I am the one that created that outcome."

"No, Kesia. You are not in control of my destiny. I am the one who came to you first, remember? You didn't seek me out."

"But Trina's death. If it wasn't for me, she would be alive."

"That is hard to say. Many spiritualists believe that your destiny is your destiny. When it is your time, there is nothing that can stop it."

"Kesia, what message did you receive in the meditation?" Lexi asked.

"I am not sure who came, I think I could feel a presence, but I didn't receive a message."

"That is strange," Lexi said as she turned to Tamara and asked, "Why wouldn't she get a message?"

"I am sure she did, but sometimes when we are distraught, our emotions block our intuitive hearing," Tamara replied as she asked her spirit guides for more guidance.

Before she could say anything else, Lexi sat up straight, and with a frightened look on her face, she yelled, "Oh, my God, he's here!"

"Who is here?" both Tamara and Kesia said at the same time.

Before she could answer, there was a knock on her apartment door.

Chapter 36

"Who is here, Lexi?" Tamara said with as much calmness as she could muster.

"Greg."

A knock came again from the door.

"What? That is impossible. He didn't know I was coming here."

Afraid for her life, Kesia whispered, "What the heck? What do I do now? He can't find out that I am here. He'll kill me."

Tamara looked at Kesia and was about to say, no, he won't, but wasn't sure that was true. "Go hide in the bathroom in Lexi's bedroom. We'll come and get you when it's safe."

Kesia ran to the bathroom as Lexi got up to answer the door. Peeking out the hole to see if she was right, Lexi wasn't surprised that she was.

Lexi started to open the door just as he knocked again and started to say, *"Hey, guys, it's…me, "* and she had the door fully open by the time he finished his sentence with, *"Greg. "*

"Hey Lexi, how are you doing? I brought pizza," he said as he more or less barged in without an invite.

"Greg, that was so very kind of you. We were in a meditation and barely heard you knock."

"That explains the wait. Hi Babe. I thought I would surprise you and come join in on the fun. It feels like we never get to hang out anymore."

Tamara smiled and patted the seat beside her.

"Here, let me take that." Lexi took the pizza box and set it down on the kitchen counter beside her left-over pizza. Grabbing a plate for him, she set it down beside the box and then opened the cupboard to get another glass.

"How'd you know I was here?" Tamara said, trying to act normal.

"You told me earlier," He lied.

"Oh, right. Silly me," she replied as she patted his leg. "I've been so busy lately. It must have slipped my mind."

"Greg? Who let you in?" Lexi asked. "They never rang up to inform me that you were coming."

"Hmm. I don't know. Nice chap, though. I told him my fiancée was here, and he said something funny. He asked which one was my fiancée, Miss Tamara or Miss Kesia?"

Lexi almost spits her drink out, but gained her composure and said, "Wow. Someone is getting fired."

Looking around, Greg said, "Where is she anyway? I don't see her."

Thinking fast, Tamara said, "She left."

"That's funny because I asked him if anyone had left, and he said only Detective Redington." Getting up off the couch, he started to walk around. As he did, he said, "Now why would you have Kesia here, Tamara? What are you all up to?"

Hearing everything that was going on in the other room, Kesia came out of the bedroom and said, "Miss Tamara, sorry I took so long. I'm ready to continue." Looking at Greg, she said, "Oh, hi. Are you joining us?" Then went over to the couch, sat down, and slouched back, shutting her eyes.

Playing along, Lexi added, "Greg brought pizza. Want some?"

Kesia opened her eyes and popped up from the couch. Heading towards Greg and the counter, she said, "Thanks, man," grabbed a piece, and took a big bite.

Not sure now what to make of the situation, Greg said, "What is she doing here?" Referring to Kesia.

"I told Lexi about Kesia's intuitive gifts, and she asked if she could meet her. Once we got together, we decided to practice fortune-telling."

"By meditating? That is what Lexi said you all were doing before I arrived," Greg said, trying to catch them in the lie.

Not lying, Tamara said, "I was introducing them to the Spirits that help a person with prophecy. Greg, are you okay? Why do I feel like I am on trial?"

"Why don't you guys practice by telling me my fortune? I would love a reading," Greg said as he sat back down on the couch. "Here, use these."

Greg pulled Kesia's great grandmother's tarot deck from his pocket.

"What the! Those are my cards," Kesia screamed.

Chapter 37

1975 – 2000 in Rome, Italy.

As luck would have it, Serena D'Angelo, the last female child born from Tatiana's ancestral line, gave birth to a baby boy. She had always wanted many children and named him Julian, after her ancestral great uncle.

As she counted all his tiny fingers and toes, she said, "Don't worry, my sweet, you will have a sister to play with one day." He was so beautiful and healthy.

As she was lying in the hospital bed, the doctor came in and bluntly said, "It is with my deepest regret that I must inform you that there was a complication to the birth. We had to remove your uterus. You will not be able to conceive any more children."

Tears started to flow down her cheeks as she realized the meaning of his words. What was she going to do now? She was the last female to be taught the craft. It was supposed to be her job to teach the next generation.

Over the years, she watched Julian grow into a fine boy, but something was missing. Something felt funny. She couldn't put her finger on it, but her gut instinct told her that he was destined for something different than what she hoped for him.

On his sixteenth birthday, Julian had another vision. This time he was walking down a busy street in America.

These visions had started many years ago, but he always put them off as imaginary dreams and paid no attention to them. This one seemed different, so real. He could even smell the freshly baked bread from the vendor selling pretzels.

He was older in this vision, maybe forty or a little older. He had cut his hair and wore it now in an adult fashion, like someone you would see in business. He was looking for something, something that belonged to his family.

He started having this same vision over and over again. It wouldn't go away.

One day, he was sitting at the kitchen table when his mom came in, talking on her phone. He heard her say, "Just a second, let me get my cards."

He watched as she pulled some cards out of her sweater pocket and started to shuffle them. She flipped a few over and started to touch them as she talked to the person on the phone.

Once she was done and hung up, he asked her, "What were you doing?"

Almost jumping out of her skin, for she had not seen him sitting there, she said, "It is called tarot."

"It sounded like you were giving the person on the phone advice."

"I guess in a way I was."

"Why would they be calling you? You're not a counselor."

"True, but sometimes I help people when they are desperate for answers."

"May I see the cards you were using?"

"They are for the women in our family. Men are not taught the craft."

"Craft? I don't understand. Why am I not allowed to see the cards?"

"To be honest, I don't know why the men in our family aren't taught."

"Okay, then read my tarot?"

"What? That is silly. You don't need counseling as you call it," she stated and then left the room.

Julian was now fixated on learning the mystery of his mother's cards.

As the years passed, he had a ritual of sneaking into his mother's room when she was sleeping and take the cards, always returning them before she awoke.

Playing with them, he studied each card in great detail. He became obsessed with the cards. His mission was to learn everything he could about them.

Just before his twenty-fifth birthday, his mother died. Now, you have to understand that Italians are very family-oriented and dramatic people, so many of his aunts were screaming and crying. The immediate family stayed with him for dinner, and then visitations at the house began. At least 20 people came the first day. These visitations lasted for hours.

He watched as one of his aunts sprinkled salt around the home and knew someone would do the same on his mother's chest. It was believed to stop evil from entering the body.

Distraught over her death, he never noticed the cards being removed from the house before his mother's funeral. Julian knew that many Italians have superstitious beliefs about death, especially the fear that a dead person's soul never really leaves the earth and that their soul might wish to come back. He also knew that one of the rituals his family would have performed to allow his mother's soul to leave the earth successfully, was to bury her with some of her favorite objects, like her tarot cards.

On the day of her second viewing and desperate to have the cards back before his mother was buried with them, Julian told his uncle, Enzo, at the funeral home that he wished to be alone with his mother's body.

His uncle knew that he had a small window of opportunity. Once the period of mourning is over, many Italians will not speak of the dead, as they do not wish to summon them back to earth. He had to talk to Julian now about his mother. "Yes, yes. That will not be a problem, but I need to ask you something."

"Sure. What is it?" Julian was antsy that someone else may find the cards and take them. He prayed this would not take long.

"You may not know this about your mother, but she was special."

"Of course, she was special. She was my mother."

"No. I mean gifted."

"Gifted?" Julian didn't know that others knew about his mother and her prophesizing.

"It is a long story, and we do not have time here to talk about it, but I need to know where she may have kept her tarot cards?"

"What? Where she kept her tarot cards. Why are you asking such a question as this?" *Porca miseria! I thought the cards were with her body. If he hasn't seen them, then where are the cards?* Julian ran past his uncle and entered the room holding his mother's body.

The casket was open, and there were a few people standing in line to pay their respects. Barging past the line, Julian leaned in and started searching his mother's casket.

"What in heavens are you doing?" His aunt screamed out.

Ignoring his relative's comments and questions, he frantically searched her body, nothing.

His uncle was by his side now and pulled him back, saying, "The cards are not there. Come and sit down."

Julian let his uncle guide him to a seat.

"So, you know about the cards? Obviously, you do not have them, or you wouldn't have made a scene."

"No. I don't have them, and they are not at the house.

"I see. Well then, we do have a dilemma. Those cards have been in our family for over five hundred years. It is said that, unlike most tarot decks, this deck is what holds the prophesying ability."

Julian looked at his uncle, "What do you mean the cards hold power? In all my research, it is the reader that has the ability, not the cards."

"Not these cards. They have been blessed by the divine. They resonate with the person who is requesting the reading, and the gods answer their prayers."

"The gods answer their prayers?"

"Yes. There are sixteen god cards, and whatever gods are turned over actually grant the individual their true life's desire."

"Uncle, we have to get those cards back!"

"Yes, but it may come at a cost."

Chapter 38

2001 in Rome, Italy.
2001-2015 in New York City

It had been almost a year since her death, the mourning period was almost up, and one thing was for sure, their Italian relatives and friends would never allow them to speak about his mother again, in case it brought her spirit back from her grave.

Time was of the essence.

Julian knew that on November 2nd, he could visit the graves of any relative or friend as long as he brought with him candles and chrysanthemums. Even Churches hold special services for the dead on that day, and small children are given toys and presents by the morti. But he still would not be permitted to speak her name.

Julian came rushing into his uncle Enzo's study. "I have a lead on the cards. I overheard a friend of a friend talking about some tarot card session that her friend had in the USA."

"A friend of a friend's friend?"

Julian waved his hand, "That's not the point. The point is the cards are in the States."

"Are you sure about that?"

"Yes. Positive. I can feel it in my bones that the cards are not on this continent."

"Well, that may explain why we can't find them."

"Uncle, I need to go to America. I need to find those cards."

"Julian, our time is almost up. There is not enough time for you to get to the States and find the cards."

"Ah, but there is, uncle."

"How so?"

"In the US, they do not believe the same about the dead as we do. There I can speak about my mother and her cards all I want to."

"Interesting. Here is what I propose. I will arrange for your travel, a job, and a place to stay. I have friends in New York City, but you will have to change your name. I do not want any family here to know that you are dishonoring our beliefs. I do not need the curses that your aunts will bring to our family if they find out what you are doing."

"Agreed. When do I leave?"

A week later, Julian was on a flight to New York City. Just before he landed at the JFK airport, a flight attendant came and passed him a note. "You must have friends in high places to get this delivered up here."

Smiling at her, he said, "Darling, if you only knew."

After she left, he looked down at the note. On the front was written, 'For Greg Masones.'

He decided that from that day forward, he would take on the persona of a spy, and this new name was one of his aliases.

Walking off the plane, he was greeted by a man holding a sign with his new name written on it. Holding up a hand to gesture that he was that man, he was escorted out of the building by a couple of men that looked a lot like they were mafia. *What kind of business is my uncle really in?*

It didn't take long for him to find out.

Taking one look at Greg, the man wearing a Dormeuil Vanquish II suit said, "Let me make this clear. You are here because of my friendship with your uncle. I owed him a favor, and he is collecting. You had better be as good as he says, debt or not, you will be out of here.

One of Genovese's guys showed Greg to his new office. Sitting down at his desk, Greg caressed the fine workmanship of the vintage

Italian olive wood tabletop. *At least working here, I can still enjoy some comforts of home.*

Greg's first assignment was to learn all that he could about the Genovese family business. He didn't realize how sheltered a life that he had been living. He had no idea that his family back home had connections like these. And who was his uncle if this guy owed him a favor?

Family secrets, he was learning all about them, especially now that he was a family secret.

He worked his butt off, proving to his boss that he could do the job. He wasn't a mobster or anything. He became an accountant and a very good one at that.

On his off time, he continued his search for his mother's tarot cards. It had been many years since he first arrived, and nothing, not even a crumb.

It was during one of his crazy hunts to find the cards that he met her, Tamara Reeve. He had been to dozens of readers searching for the cards. She had surprised him. As she flipped over the cards, unfortunately, not the ones he was looking for, she said, "You have been on a quest to find something very important to you, priceless in fact. You are close to finding it."

Greg got shivers. "Tell me more."

"You are on the right path to what you are looking for. This card here, see, it means that you will take a short journey for what you seek, and there you will find it."

Excited now, Greg asked, "When? When will I take this short journey?"

"First, you will take a wife."

"A wife, I don't even have a girlfriend. I haven't had the time."

"I can only tell you what the cards tell me."

"What else?"

"That is all. The cards do not tell me anything else."

"Great, another flake reading the cards. Why I listen to you people, I will never know." Getting up to leave, she added one more thing.

"Greg, your mother is here with us."

Chapter 39

2015 Same day in New York City

"What did you just say?"

"Your mother, I think it starts with an 'S'. For Sara, Sabrina, something like that.

Greg sat back down. "Serena."

"Ah, I was close. I never seem to get the full name, but I am usually close."

"Fascinating. She is here with us right now, in this room?"

"Yes."

Greg looked around. He couldn't sense her. "Does she have something to tell me?"

"I think so."

"You. . . think so?"

"Her energy is a bit fuzzy. I am trying to connect so I can communicate with her."

"Try harder."

"She says you get visions. Is that true?"

Greg was shocked. He hadn't had any visions since he had moved to New York. "Not lately."

"I see. She is telling me that you need to clear your mind and start to receive her messages."

"How am I to do that?"

"You are going to think that I am after your money, but honestly, you can go to any other person you choose. You need to start taking intuitive classes."

"I suppose you teach on the subject of metaphysics?"

"Like I said, you can go to anyone you choose."

"Answer my question."

"Yes."

Greg thought about it for a moment. "When is your next class?"

"This Friday, at seven. Here's the address."

Greg took the card she had written the information on. "What is the cost?"

"Tell you what, this one is on me."

"How very kind of you," Greg said, trying not to let his sarcasm show.

When Greg got home, he searched on the internet for everything he could find on Tamara Reeve. *There was no way she knew who my mom was or that I have visions. She might be the real deal.*

Friday night, Greg made sure he was at Tamara's class. He was a few minutes early and found a seat next to a lady in her fifties.

"Fresh meat." Winking at Greg, she said, "Hi, I'm Lillian."

Greg looked at her and said, "Hi, I am Tamara's future husband."

That shut her up.

From that day on, Greg was determined to win over Tamara's heart. Because of a vision he had the night before, he now knew that to find his cards, he needed her help.

For the next year, he went to whatever class or lecture she was offering and helped her in any way that he could.

Finally, he asked her out on a date, and she declined, saying that she was flattered, but she didn't date students.

He stopped going to her events and started to send her flowers and poems. Then he stopped altogether. He decided she needed time to miss him.

Another year went by before he 'coincidently' ran into her.

He had been stalking her, not in a creepy way, but in an online kind of way. He knew her schedule. It was posted on her website. He knew she was going to be helping at a charity event, which led to the perfect opportunity for him to run into her.

He planned it perfectly. He found out what table at the auction she was manning and made sure he was helping at the one beside her.

"Hi, Tamara, fancy meeting you here."

Tamara looked over, "Greg, hi. How have you been?"

"Good, thanks, and you?"

"Ya, good." Tamara nodded her head, not sure what else to say.

Greg played it cool and didn't say anything else. He knew they were going to be there for hours. He had time to make his move.

Throughout the day, Greg looked over a couple of times and smiled. Tamara smiled back. He played the role of a person who believed in the cause. He would have won an Emmy.

Just before the charity event was over, someone came over to the helpers and said that there was a dinner planned for everyone that helped and to meet in the blue room at six.

As they were packing up, Greg walked over to Tamara and said, "I don't know if I am going to the dinner. Are you going?"

"I wasn't planning on it."

"Well, we do deserve a free dinner for all the work we did. We could go together."

Tamara looked at him and smiled. *He was charming.* "Sure. I'd like that."

One date led to another, and soon, he had won Tamara's heart, and they became a thing. It didn't bother him to date someone he didn't love. He didn't love anyone, not after his mother died. His obsession with finding the cards was all that he had true feelings for.

He would have won an Oscar for the part he played as a devoted boyfriend.

After knowing her for five years and being with her for the last three, he finally proposed. *She did say that to find the cards, I needed a wife. Who better than a psychic?*

His visions had slowed down. He wasn't getting messages about the cards anymore. Panicking, he asked, "Tamara, can you do a reading for me?"

Smiling, she said, "Sure, is there any particular reason?"

Lying, he said, "No, not really. It has been years since you did a reading on me. I was just wondering about my future."

"You mean our future?"

"Ya, our future."

"Here, come and have a seat at the table. Let's see what our future holds."

Tamara shuffled the cards then gave them to Greg to shuffle.

"You know the drill. Think about what your question is and pick a card, any card."

Greg closed his eyes and thought about his mother's tarot cards. *Where are they?* Greg picked a card and turned it over. It was the eight of cups.

"Hmm, interesting. It means that you should abandon your quest and walk away. Leave behind everything you are feeling, all your emotions. Just walk away."

"It is saying to walk away. Like to leave you?"

"Ah, let's see. Pick another card."

Greg did as she asked. It was the two of pentacles.

"You have two choices, and both are rocky. See the waves and boats in the background?"

"Ya."

"Both choices will determine your future. Pentacles represent the materialistic world, your work, business, trade, property, money, and other material possessions. You need to find a balance, or you will lose everything."

"That doesn't sound like me." He lied again. He flipped over another card. It was the page of cups.

"There is an opportunity coming up for what you seek."

This card made Greg happy. *At last, a card that gives me hope.*

Greg flipped up another card. Knight of swords.

"You're about to take action."

"When?"

Tamara took hold of a pendulum that was lying on the table beside her. Counting the motion until it stopped, she said, "Three."

"Three what?"

"Three days, weeks, months, possibly years. That part I never know for sure. Let's use the pendulum. Is it three days?"

The pendulum answered by turning in a clockwise motion, Tamara's movement for no. "No. Does it mean three weeks?"

They both watched the pendulum.

"No. Does it mean three months?"

The pendulum started to swing a no answer but changed to a straight line."

"Crazy yes, but yes. within three months."

Greg could handle that. He gave Tamara a kiss and said, "Thank you."

"So, do I get to know what you were asking?"

"Nope, it's a surprise."

"Well, I guess I will find out in three months anyways." She picked up all the cards and tapped them on the table as she straightened them and put them back in their velvet bag.

Chapter 40

New York City

"Jersey Shore? Why do you want to go there?" Greg asked, not sure why they had to get away. His visions always showed him holding the cards in New York City.

Tamara rubbed her head, "Greg, I really need to get away. I have been having these headaches and they are interfering with my job." She went over to him, and with her best flirtatious smile, she said, "Come on, I'll make it worth your while, and if that's not good enough, there is a spa we can go to."

"Fine, but don't expect me to play in the sand with you."

Tamara smiled. *Now that would be something to see, Greg playing.* "You might surprise yourself."

The following weekend he drove the two hours to Sea Girt, New Jersey. Tamara had booked them into a grand Victorian seaside Inn near the Jersey Shore. *What I do for her. One day all of this will be worth the wait.*

He smiled as they started to take a walk. "Hey, Tamara, I'll be a moment. I forgot something in the hotel room. I'll be right back."

Heading back towards the hotel, he bent down and picked up some sand. Going to the front office, he asked for an envelope and, as a joke, mailed it to Tamara. *There, she'll think it's romantic.*

As quickly as he could, he ran to catch up with her. He found her standing on the boardwalk, staring at the beach.

Coming up to her, he said, "Sorry that took longer than I expected."

"No problem, I was enjoying the sights."

They walked a bit further along the boardwalk.

Stopping Greg so she could get a better look, Tamara said, "Hey Greg, look at that. A Gypsy reader."

"Go ahead Tamara, knock yourself out and indulge in a reading," Greg teased her.

He watched as Tamara sat down.

The young lady proceeded to look at Tamara's palm and suddenly let it go. He heard the young lady cry out, "Leave, I can't read you. You are cursed."

Then he heard her say something in another language and watched her gather her tablecloth and everything it was holding and run away. That is when he saw the cards. His cards, the cards he had been searching for all these years.

Greg quickly ran over from where he was standing and said, "What was all that about?" as he was watching the young lady run away with his cards.

"I don't know. She took one look at my hand and let go. She let it go as if it was diseased. She said I was cursed."

He watched as Tamara looked at her hand.

"How weird, you of all people would know if you were cursed. Wouldn't you?" Greg asked.

It seemed like forever before he had a chance to get away from Tamara.

Leaving Tamara at the hotel, he made an excuse to go outside and walked back to the beach where the girl had read Tamara's palm, then continued to walk in the direction that the girl had run.

The gods were on his side. He found the girl and all her stuff sitting on the ground by the beach restrooms.

"Oh good, I found you. Can you do a reading for me?"

"No."

Greg started to insist.

"I can't."

"Of course you can. I saw you on the beach earlier doing it.

She started to tell him that he was mistaken, that it wasn't her, but he grabbed her arm and pulled her up. She started to yell, but there was no one around that could hear.

He was so close to getting his mother's cards that there was no way he was leaving this beach without them.

The next thing Greg knew, he backhanded the girl across her face.

She struggled to get away, but he was too strong. She started to cry and pleaded for him to let her go. Saying, "You have the wrong person."

His obsession with the cards made him go crazy, and in his blind frenzy, he hit her harder and broke her jaw."

Her body went limp, and she started to bleed. He frantically started searching through her belongings, looking for the tarot cards. Not finding them in the purple tablecloth, he started to search through her clothes. Eureka, he pulled them out of her pocket.

Coming back to reality, he realized he had killed her. Panicking, he lifted her body up and carried her to the water, and dumped her face down.

Looking around, he saw that nobody was near and could identify him or know what he had done, so he left her there with her head bobbing up and down in the water.

Entering their hotel room, he said, "Tamara, I'm back. I'm going to go take a shower."

Before he did, he stuffed the cards into his bag, sand, and all.

Chapter 41

Present day in New York City

"*I* don't think so, little lady. These are my mother's cards."

"No, you stole them from me. They are my cards!"

Knowing that he stole them from the girl he dumped into the water, he said, "Actually, I found them in the pocket of your friend. It looks like she was going to steal them from you. Lucky, I came by and retrieved my belongings before she got away with them."

Tamara couldn't believe what she was hearing. "Greg? What are you talking about? How are these cards yours?"

Looking at Tamara, he was grateful that the charade was over. "I have been searching for these cards for over twenty years. They were my mother's."

"No, he is lying. They were my mother's, and she passed them down to me," Kesia yelled out.

"That is impossible."

"Ask my mom. She's been teaching me my real genealogy for over a year now. That is when I received these cards."

"What do you mean your real genealogy?"

"I found out last year that my mom was adopted. Her parents, Florentina and Cyrus Bango are not her real parents. They adopted her from Italy in 1970."

"Why would I care about knowing this? That doesn't answer why the cards could be yours. I know for a fact that the cards are only passed down to the females in my family, and my mother, Serena D'Angelo, was the last living female in our family tree to receive these cards."

"Greg, you never told me your mother's name," Tamara said, still in shock over what was happening.

Greg looked over to her and said, "I changed my name when I came to America. Masones is a long-ago family name."

Lexi looked at the painting. "As in Tatiana Masones?"

"Yes. How do you know that name?"

Lexi pointed to the painting.

Greg turned and looked at where she was pointing. Chills ran down his back. "Where did you get this?"

"It was a gift from Isabella."

"How do you know this painting?" Kesia demanded from Greg.

He said to her as he walked towards the painting, "My mom had one similar, but hers had a blue angel standing in the background."

Not sure what to make of the situation, if she should be terrified that Greg had appeared mysteriously, or if she was safe. He wasn't holding a gun or anything, so Lexi said, "Let me get this straight. The two of you both claim that Tatiana is an ancestral grandmother."

"Yes," they both answered at the same time.

"Greg, what happened to your mother's cards?"

"They were taken when she died. Someone stole them from my house."

Kesia interrupted, "It sounds to me that the cards were given to the next female in line for them."

Greg started to fume.

"Greg? Is it possible that Kesia's mom is your sister?" Tamara asked.

"What? No. I would have known about that."

"How old is your mom, Kesia?"

"She just turned fifty."

Turning back to Greg, Tamara said, "She is only a few years older than you. You wouldn't have been born yet. Your family might have never mentioned to you that your mom had a child. It happened lots with children being born out of wedlock."

Greg thought back in time and remembered a story about his mom going overseas to study for a while. "This is absurd. I would have known if my mother had another child."

Just as he had enough of this, Lexi got a call.

Chapter 42

Before she could answer it, Greg headed for the door and left her apartment.

Seeing the call display, Lexi bluntly said, "Hi, Red. You have to get here right away!" and hung up.

"Well, that explains a lot," Tamara said, still in shock. "How could I be so blind. I should have known."

Lexi grabbed Tamara's hands and said, "You are still human, and you were in love. Love is blind, and we don't always see what is right in front of us."

"Even the great prophets couldn't see everything in their own future," Kesia added, trying to make Tamara feel better.

Looking over to Kesia, she tried to smile but couldn't.

There was a knock on Lexi's door. Getting up, she peeked through the peephole. It was Redington.

Opening it, she said, "What? The doorman lets anyone in now."

"Hey, I am not anyone. I showed him my badge and insisted he not call up in case it would worsen your situation."

"Oh. Okay then, but I am definitely going to have a talk with the owners about the new doorman."

"So, what is the urgency? You said get over here right away."

"Greg was here."

"What? Where is he now?"

"He left when you called. We don't know where he went," Lexi answered.

Standing up, Kesia blurted out, "Detective, he admitted taking the cards from Trina. He had the cards with him. We saw them. They were my cards."

Looking at the girls, he asked, "Is that true? He had the cards?"

Tamara nodded, and Lexi said, "Yes. He pulled them out and asked for a reading. But Red, that is not the crazy part."

Redington looked at Lexi, waiting for her to continue.

"He is related to Kesia. Tatiana is both, Kesia's and Julian's ancestral grandmother."

"You two are related?" He said, looking at Kesia now.

"I don't know that for sure. But he seems to believe that the cards belong to him."

Tamara said, "It is possible. Kesia told us that her mother was adopted and that it was her mother who gave her the cards last year."

Looking back to Kesia, "Well, that doesn't make him innocent. He is now a fugitive on the run for murder." Redington said as he picked up his phone and walked out of Lexi's apartment.

Chapter 43

Greg left the apartment and started to drive directly to Jersey Shore. He needed answers. Knowing that the cops would be looking for his vehicle he made a call. "Boss, I need a favor."

Within five minutes, Greg was met by one of Genovese's guys and traded vehicles. As Greg drove away, he noticed the guy had started to change the plates on his car. *Hate to know what favor I am going to have to pay for this one.*

Greg drove the two hours to Sea Girt. As he was pulled into town, he got a text message from his boss saying where Kesia's mom lived.

Driving up to the address, he got out of his car and went and knocked on the door.

He thought he had seen a ghost. There was no mistaking who the lady was when she opened the door. She was the spitting image of his mom.

Not waiting for an invite, he barged in. "We have to talk."

"I was wondering when you would show up."

"You know who I am?"

"Kind of."

"What does that mean?"

"You're older, but you still look a lot like you did at our mother's funeral."

The room seemed like it was turning, and Greg's body started to feel like he was going to pass out. It was all too much. All these years, he had been searching for the cards, and now he had them. All to find out that he had a sister.

"Let's see the cards. If you are who I think you are, then you have the cards."

Greg pulled the cards out of his pocket.

Florence thought back to how she received the cards. *Florence, named after her adopted mother, looked at Greg. It was a secret that upon Serena's death, that her daughter would be contacted and given the names of her birth parents.*

When she found out about her birth mother's death, she flew to Rome and went to Serena's funeral. No one questioned her being there. She looked like family.

While she was at her birth mother's house, a small girl around the age of five came running up to her, "Aunty Serena, you are supposed to be dead. Read the cards to me again." The little girl pulled on her hand and dragged her to a quiet area in the house.

Florence sat down where the little girl told her to and accepted the cards. Looking at them, she noticed that they were a very old deck of tarot cards. She hadn't seen this type before. They had birds and gods instead of the high and low arcana. "Where did you get these?"

"Silly, they were in your room, where you keep them."

As someone came closer and called out to the little girl, the little girl said, "I have to go, my momma is calling me. We can play later."

Florence put the cards into her pocket and forgot about them as she was looking for Greg, but couldn't find him after the funeral. Family members said that his uncle Enzo had sent him away to boarding school, but they didn't know where the school was located.

Greg held the same cards. They were the ones she mistakenly took from Serena's home.

"Come sit down. We have a lot to talk about."

As Greg came in and sat down, he stared at the painting of Archangel Gabriel on her wall. "So, it is true, you have a painting from our ancestor as well."

"Yes, I found it while I was researching my genealogy."

Standing up, Greg said as he passed her the tarot deck, "Here, these belong to you. My quest is over."

Walking out the door, he said, "I am sorry for the trauma I caused Kesia. If I only had known."

Getting into his vehicle, he made one last call. "Sir, I need another favor."

Chapter 44

Red had called it in and gave Greg's information to his captain. Every cop in New York City was now looking for him. Trina Well's family wanted justice for the person who had killed their daughter.

Thinking back to Lexi's apartment, *what is it with these paintings? How do they keep finding their way into her life? Is it possible that there is a God, and angels that help us here on Earth?*

Redington shook the thought out of his head. *Hogwash. If there was a God, why then allow all this chaos? What's the purpose?*

Redington lightly banged his forehead a couple of times with his hand. *What am I doing even contemplating this subject? I'm a cop, for Goodness' sake. A homicide detective, for that matter. If it wasn't for chaos, I wouldn't have a job.*

After he was finished at the precinct, he was back at Lexi's apartment building.

"Please ring up and tell Miss Constantine that Detective Redington is here to see her."

"Will do, Sir."

As Red headed into the elevator, he was met by Reverend Hawthorne.

"Redington, what brings you into the neighborhood? Is Alexandra in trouble again?"

"You haven't talked to her?"

"I was joking. What? Is she in trouble? I've been so busy renovating my place, we haven't had time to see each other. It's a surprise for her, and I don't want her to see it until it's finished."

The elevator doors opened before Red could say anything else.

They walked to Lexi's apartment together.

Red went to knock.

"I have a key," Edward said, showing the key.

"Trust me. She'll want a knock."

Lexi opened the door to find both of them awkwardly standing there.

"Come in. Edward, it's nice to see you," Lexi said, giving him a quick peck on the cheek.

"So, I hear you haven't told Edward about the last few hours."

Looking at Edward, Lexi said, "I didn't want to bother you. I know you are busy right now."

"What? What's going on?" Edward asked but added silently *this time?*

Ignoring Edward, Redington said, "Tamara, we haven't found him yet, but we will."

"Found who?" Edward asked, trying to figure out what was going on.

"Greg. It's a long story. Come have a seat," Lexi said as she guided Edward towards the living room couch.

Sitting down, Edward said, "Hi. I'm Reverend Edward Hawthorne, Alexandra's fiancé, and you are?"

"Kesia. Whose Alexandra?"

"That is my full name. Lexi is a nickname."

"Oh," Kesia said, looking at Lexi. *A Reverend? She is going to marry a Reverend.*

Redington asked Tamara, "How are you holding up?"

Tamara looked up from the couch and solemnly replied, "I can't believe that I have been going out with someone who could commit murder. I was going to marry him."

"If it helps, many people have the ability to perform the act of murder. I see it all the time. Regular people have a moment of insanity, and bam, just like that, someone dies." Redington reasoned.

"That doesn't help, but thanks anyway."

"So, what do we do now?" Kesia asked just as her cell phone rang. "It's my mom."

"Actually, that is a good question," Lexi said, agreeing with Kesia.

"We'll find him. Until then, there is nothing for you all to do," Redington answered.

"Wow! You guys aren't going to believe this. Greg was just at my mom's."

"What? When?" Redington moved in closer to her.

"Get this. He gave her back the tarot cards and left."

"When? When did he leave? Did she get the number on his plates?"

"She said that she is okay and that she knew that one day he would figure out who she was."

"Your mom knew about him?" Lexi asked, astonished.

"I guess so."

"Kesia, did she say anything about where he was going?" Redington said as he wanted to shake her to answer him.

Looking at the Detective, she said a bit snarky, "No."

"I have to go. Edward, it's your job to look after the girls," and with that, he headed out the door.

Edward insisted, "Can somebody please catch me up? What is going on?"

Chapter 45

"Greg, Tamara's fiancé, killed a girl and is on the loose," Lexi said, trying to catch Edward up.

Edward made the sign of the cross. "What is this world coming to? Greg, no way."

"I know, right."

"I wouldn't have guessed that in a million years."

Changing the subject and not wanting to think about the last three years with that man, Tamara said, "Lexi, when we were in Han's grandfather's library, didn't you read something about the world of Vanaheim where there were gods and goddesses that can see the future?"

"I might have. It's been a while. I don't remember."

"Well, I do. You were reading about Yggdrasil being the Tree of Life and the worlds that connect to it."

"Oh, ya. I do remember talking about the nine worlds. What about it?"

"I was thinking that I need to practice seeing my future."

Edward asked, "I thought you could already see futures. You do it all the time when you do tarot."

"Yes, it is easy to read a stranger's future. You don't have any emotional connection to the outcome."

As she was searching the internet on her phone, Kesia said, "It says here that the Aesir and Vanir had a war. The Vanir tribe of Vanaheim and the Asgard tribe of Aesir became a single pantheon."

"What is a pantheon?" Lexi asked.

"The word pantheon is Greek and means a temple of all gods," Edward answered.

"Oh, you are so clever, Edward," Lexi said with a sexy smile.

Kesia shrugged her shoulders and made a face at Lexi. "Honestly, you too, get a room."

Lexi blushed, and Edward had a grin from ear to ear.

"Seriously, you guys. I need to figure out what my future holds," Tamara tried getting everyone back on track.

"Sorry, it is just that I haven't seen him for a while, and he is just too cute," Lexi said as she batted her eyes at Edward.

"Tamara, I think it is Freyja that you want to ask for help in seeing your future," Kesia said looking down at her phone.

"Why do you say that?" Tamara asked.

"It says here that she is honored by the gods themselves as their own sorceress. For it was she who taught the gods the art of seiðr, 'seething.' The craft of cursing, prophecy, shamanic rites, and necromancy."

Edward had never heard of Freyja. "Is she from Vanaheim?"

"Yes, until she was captured by the Asgard."

"It also says that she assists other gods, creatures, and mankind in intense situations with her feathered cloak that transforms her into a falcon. Where she can fly to all the other worlds."

"Why do you think that she is the deity that Tamara should call upon, Kesia?" Lexi asked.

Looking at Lexi, Kesia answered matter-of-factly, "Because Freyja can get the information needed from anyone in any world."

Looking at Tamara, Lexi said, "That is an interesting concept. Kesia, you might have something."

"Lexi, can I use your laptop?"

"Sure. Let me get it." After retrieving the laptop, she gave it to Tamara. "What are you looking for?"

"I need to know more about her. What she looks like. That sort of thing."

"Why?"

"It is easier for me to conjure a Spirit that I know something about."

"Oh."

Kesia added, "Tamara, it says here that Freyja is a beautiful blondish, redhead, with a body that any male Viking couldn't look away from."

Tamara found a site that described Freyja's family, she read it out loud, "She is the twin to her brother, Freyr, and was the daughter to the Vanir leader, Njord. Now, this is what I needed to know. It says that Freyja introduced the gods to seidr, a form of magic that allowed practitioners to know and change the future."

"What is so special about that?" Edward asked.

"It said, 'change' the future."

"How is that going to help you?" Lexi asked, trying to figure out why she thought changing her future would be of any benefit. "I thought you said that tarot cards only told you what path you are on. . . Oh, I get it. So that you can get off this crazy path with Greg and choose the best path for you. Is that it?"

"Close, but that is not the only reason."

"There is another reason? What is it?"

"You'll see."

Chapter 46

"Guys, I have to go," Tamara said as she quickly closed the laptop and stood up.

"Do you think that's a good idea, Tamara? What if Greg comes back?"

"I'll have to take my chances."

"Can I catch a ride home with you?" Kesia asked.

"Sure."

"Guys, are you kidding me? I think that you need to stay here, with Edward and me. At least until Redington says it's safe to go home."

"Sorry, Lexi. I can't wait. This is far too important."

"Edward, do something!"

"What am I going to do? Tie them up."

Lexi tried again as Tamara started for the door. "Well, at least take us with you."

Looking back at Lexi, she said, "Fine, get your stuff and let's go."

"Can I come along?" Kesia asked.

Tamara looked over at her as they rode the elevator down and said, "Why not."

Getting into Tamara's car, Edward asked, "Where are we going?"

"My place."

"Well, I guess if Greg comes back, he'll have to kill all of us."

Lexi looked at Edward and said, "Really, that is all you could think of saying?"

"I get nervous under pressure. You should know that by now."

The ride back to Tamara's was in silence.

Once everyone was inside, she went into her office to find something.

"Can I help you find what you are looking for?" Lexi asked as she slowly popped her head into the room, not sure if she should intrude.

"Um, I am looking for a magic key."

"You're kidding, right?"

Looking at Lexi, she said, "You're the one who asked."

"What does it look like," Lexi said as she walked into the room.

"It is brass and funky looking, like an old-style skeleton key."

"What does it open?"

"A door."

Just as Tamara had said door, Edward had entered. "What kind of door?"

"A fairy door."

Shaking his head, he said, "Why do I even ask."

"Tamara, are you going to summon Hans?" Lexi asked, knowing that he was the only elf she knew about living in the fairy world.

"You guessed it."

"How can a ghost help you?" Edward asked, even though he wasn't sure if he wanted to know the answer.

"He's an elf now, not a ghost. He became a walk-in. His soul walked into an elf's body when he ascended to Alfheim."

Standing at the door with Edward, Kesia said, "I didn't know that was possible."

"Souls can do quite a few things once they leave an Earthly body."

"I guess. I just didn't think they could take over an elf's body," Kesia said, fascinated.

"A soul is a soul and has no race in its true form. It can be reborn into anything. A walk-in is just a soul choosing not to be a baby again. The elf he became would have been on the verge of dying for the exchange to happen. He didn't possess the body without its consent."

"Well, that is good to know," Edward said thankfully.

"I found a key! Is this it?" Lexi said excitedly.

Tamara came over and took the key from her. "Perfect. It is."

"Now what?" Lexi asked.

"We unlock a door."

Everyone followed Tamara into the living room.

Bending down near the fireplace, she picked up a tiny wooden door, which was about six inches tall, with a knob and keyhole. It looked so whimsical and mystical, decorated with gems and flowers.

"What is that?" Edward asked.

Kesia answered him, "It is a fairy door."

"But I thought you said we were getting Hans from Alfheim. Don't you need an elf door?"

"A fairy door opens to the elemental world. From there, we can go to Alfheim."

"We?" Edward said with unease.

"Yep, I am not going to let you guys miss out on the fun."

"I was worried you were serious," Edward said as he took a step backward.

"Don't worry, Edward, we're not going to do it here at my place."

"Oh good. Hey, wait! Where are you going to do it?"

"Funny you asked. From your place."

"Tamara, that isn't funny."

"I'm not kidding. We need somewhere safe that Greg would never think of, and since I will be with all of you, I'll leave my phone here, so he can't track me."

"Lexi, what have you gotten me into this time? Man, all I wanted to do was take you out for dinner. I wasn't planning on a show first."

Lexi gave him a hug and said, "When it comes to traveling through the celestial world, you have become a wizard at it."

"Ha, ha. I can't even say no because she drove."

"I'll just be a moment. All I need is some rosemary and hollyhock, and then we can go," Tamara quickly said, as she went to go get them.

Chapter 47

Once at Edward's Funeral home, Tamara entered and said immediately, "Edward, we'll use the counseling room with the circular couch. I love the art there! And besides, it is becoming our thing." As she entered the room, she placed the fairy door in an upright position against the far wall.

"Our thing?" Edward asked with an inquisitive face.

"Well, you know what they say after three times."

"No, what do they say?"

"That you just signed a subconscious agreement."

"A what?"

"A subconscious agreement."

"I heard you, but what is it?"

"Let's say you have an issue with something that someone else is doing, but you don't say anything and let it happen. Maybe you were in shock, or you were too embarrassed. As in this room, if you had a problem with us using it, you should have said something."

"I did!"

"But you let it happen, and then you should have definitely said something the second time."

"I did!!!"

"But you let it happen, and now you are letting us use it a third time. So, it now becomes a subconscious agreement that it is always going to be okay for us to use this room."

"Fine, just let me go tell the staff that I will be using the room and not to disturb us."

"Great idea. Thanks, Edward!"

Edward gave Tamara a look to say, 'but you don't win, I am choosing to let us use the room,' and walked out the door.

Kesia turned from looking at the art and asked Tamara, "Hey, what happens after the fourth time? What if someone changes their mind and doesn't allow the situation to happen again?"

Tamara smiled, "The person looks like a jerk."

"But they are just putting their foot down."

"It's too late. They should have done that the first time. At the very least the second time."

"So, what you are saying is that if you let something happen more than once and don't fix the problem, then it is the person with the problem's fault and becomes a jerk if they try to fix it later?"

"Yep. After the second time, if a person doesn't fix the issue they are having with a situation, it becomes a subconscious contract with the other person or persons, insinuating that the situation is okay."

"You're telling me that a person who is abusing you is allowed to keep on doing it?"

"Morally no, but technically yes."

"But what if it is a child or someone weaker?"

"In Spirit's eyes, it's all the same. There are no older, smarter, stronger. . . just universal laws."

"That sucks."

"Kesia, everyone has a choice to change a situation."

"I don't believe that. What about a child or a person being sexually abused? What choice do they have?"

"One belief is that the soul chooses their life lessons when they agreed to this lifetime's purpose and path. It was part of their destiny."

"I guess," Kesia said, thinking about karma. "It still sucks."

Edward came back into the room and said, "Okay, we have two hours, and then the room is needed for a client."

"Then we don't have any time to waste. Let's get started."

Chapter 48

Once Edward was settled in the room, Kesia asked him, "What is all the construction about?"

"It's a secret."

"Why?"

Lexi touched Kesia's shoulder and said, "Don't feel bad. He won't tell me either, and I'm his fiancée."

Tamara broke up the conversation by saying, "Okay, y'all, we have to get started. Find a seat and get yourself comfortable." Once everyone was seated, she said, "Lexi, I am going to start the meditation. Listen carefully to how I use the fairy door. You never know when you might need to use it."

"Sure. Okay." Lexi felt a little uncomfortable but said, "I take on this new challenge."

"You are so corny sometimes, Miss Constantine," Edward said as he took her hand

and kissed it. "I love that you take a scary situation and turn it into a challenge."

Kesia tilted her head so she could see them and asked, "Edward, why do you think using a fairy door is scary?"

"Past experience. Everything I do in this room when Tamara is here seems to be scary."

Just in case what he said had any merit, Kesia rubbed a pendant of Archangel Michael she was wearing. *Protect me from anything evil, please.*

Tamara started the meditation by saying, "Now that you are comfortable, close your eyes, and take three deep breaths."

Edward was the last one to shut his eyes and breathe deeply. *God, please protect my friends and me from any harm.*

Tamara went on by saying, "Angels, guides, and our fairy friends, please helps us on our journey today. We need to speak with Erland."

Edward interrupted the meditation by asking, "Tamara, remind me who Erland is, please."

"Erland is the name of the elf Hans's soul took over."

"Oh, right. I forgot. Thank you, I am ready to continue."

"When you take your next breath, imagine that you are the size of a pea. In a moment, you will be astral-traveling out of your crown chakra and joining me in front of the fairy door, which is at the base of the far wall. Go ahead. Take a breath."

Tamara gave everyone a moment to do what she had requested.

Sensing the other three souls, she continued, "With your next deep breath, the fairy door will open. Hold hands as we enter through the portal to the level of elementals. Now, take a breath, and imagine that you went through the fairy door."

Tamara waited for Edward's energy to come through.

"Edward, no need to worry yet. We haven't even begun the exciting part."

"Funny, Tamara. I'm here, aren't I, but how did that big key open this little door?"

"It didn't. It is a metaphor and a talisman."

"Oh."

Lexi gave his hand an extra squeeze.

"Wow, this place is amazing," Kesia said in awe as she saw the fairy realm for the first time.

It was early morning, even though it wasn't at home. The sunlight was piercing through the trees, and the landscape in front of them seemed like the lushest forest one had ever seen. With the bushiest, greenest, softest, frilliest of ferns, whose delicate leaves protected the forest floor.

Kesia had never seen a fern up close and was amazed at how its foliage curled at the apex of each blade. Each frond (branch) of the plant reminded her of a roller coaster ride with many twisty turns.

The ancient oak trees towered above and were covered in moss. The air here seemed so fresh and new, as if this forest was pure and innocent from ever having had any harmful contamination of any kind.

You could hear the sweetest bird songs ever sung and the faintest sound of laughter in the distance.

As she pointed in the direction of the laughter, Tamara whispered, "Don't make any noise. We don't want to scare away the fairies. Follow me."

Kesia, Lexi, and Edward followed her through a fern path that led to a small clearing.

Surprised at what she saw, Lexi squealed, "Oh, my!" as she covered her mouth, trying not to make another sound.

Too late, they looked her way.

Chasing each other and laughing were a tree nymph and a satyr.

Whispering, Kesia said, "Wow, a Dryad or better known as a tree nymph. I never thought I would see one in this lifetime. My mom has told me stories about how the goddess Diana is a friend of these specific fairies."

"Why do you call her a Dryad? All I see is a beautiful, although slightly tinted green naked young woman."

"My mother said Dryads are an ancient Greek myth and are also known as a wood or tree nymph, nature spirit, or Hamadryades. Each Dryad's life is tied or bound to a tree. Since the only trees here are oak, the one we are looking at is an oak tree nymph. While her tree flourishes, so will she, but when her tree dies, so will she. These types of oak Dryads are usually connected with river-side trees and sacred groves. To answer your question, Edward, a Dryad can change form and become a beautiful young maiden."

"She disappeared. Where did she go?" Edward asked in shock.

Kesia answered again by saying, "Into the tree. She can step into any oak tree and disappear from our view. She can't go far, though. Remember, she is tied to her own tree."

"Oh, my God, he is coming at us," Lexi screamed.

Coming towards them was a very naked half-man, with ears, legs, and a tail resembling a horse with a snubbed nose. He looked savage, carnal, and brutish.

"Is that a faun coming at us?" Lexi asked.

"No, they are half-goat," Kesia said as she stood up to run but had no idea where to go. Thinking quickly, she said, "We need to make a sacrifice."

"What?" Edward said as he stood up, scared out of his mind, because the guy looked like he was going to kill them.

"Tamara, dream up some wine that we can offer him," Kesia said as she remembered what her mother taught her about these mythical creatures.

"Ah, good idea." Tamara closed her eyes, and instantly, a craft of red wine appeared into her hands. Standing up, she called out, "Hello, sorry for our intrusion, we mean no harm. We have some wine for you."

Lexi tuning into the moment, decided to transform herself into a seductive female.

Edward's eyes almost popped out of his head.

The satyr stopped as he saw Lexi. If there was anything, a satyr liked more than wine, it was a beautiful woman.

Unhappy that she now had competition, the tree nymph appeared.

"Great! Now you made her mad. If it wasn't bad enough that we had to deal with a mad satyr, now you made it worse, we now have to deal with a jealous nymph," Edward complained.

Kesia yelled out, "Tamara, this time conjure some milk and oil. She likes that."

Lexi called out to Edward, "Fast, think that you are a horny half-man, half-goat."

"What? Are you mad!"

"No. Do it. She'll be attracted to you."

"For goodness' sake, Tamara, get us out of here. I've had enough of this nonsense," Edward yelled just as the tree nymph was about to attack Lexi.

Tamara had to think quickly. "Everyone, hold hands, NOW!"

Chapter 49

Lexi opened her eyes. "What happened? Did I die?"

"No. I brought us back through the fairy door to our world," Tamara answered as she quickly made sure everyone was back.

"That was too close, Tamara. Lexi could have gotten hurt," Edward said as he moved closer to Lexi, making sure she was okay.

"Hey, Tamara? What would happen to us if we got hurt over there?" Kesia asked as she kissed her pendant.

"Well, to be honest, I am not exactly sure. Some people believe that what happens there is like a dream, where others believe that if you get hurt there, you get hurt here."

"I see."

"I can't do it again. I can't go back. Tamara, it's too much," Edward said as he looked at

Lexi. She could have gotten hurt. *We can't take that chance.*

"I can't make you go, Edward. Only you can decide that for yourself, but I do have to go back there," Tamara said as she moved the fairy door to another wall.

"I'm in," Lexi said.

"Me too," Kesia said as she snuggled back into her spot on the couch and closed her eyes.

"This is crazy," Edward said as he shook Lexi. "Alexandra, it is too dangerous. We don't even have any creatures to ride."

"Good idea! That's it. I'll call a ride for us to get to the fairy city," Tamara said as she also went back to her spot on the couch. Looking at Edward, she said, "You in Edward? We don't have much time left. Your staff will be knocking soon."

"What? No. I didn't mean that. Come on, you guys, it's not even real."

"Then what are you scared of?" Kesia asked. "Let's do this."

Tamara started the meditation. "Take a couple of deep breaths. Edward, if you are in, take a breath, and if you're out, you know where the door is."

As he laid back on the couch, Edward said, "Fine. I'm in if Alexandra is. Someone has to protect her,"

"This time, y'all will have a ride waiting for you on the other side of the fairy door. Take another deep breath, imagine holding hands. Here we go, size of a pea, and through the open fairy door."

Waiting on the other side was Phantachus, the Pegasus Lexi rode into the Void, the night mare that Edward had ridden to retrieve Isabella, and also waiting were two eight-legged horses like the one Odin rode.

"Kesia, you will be riding this beautiful silver one. Her name is Lettfeti, which means light-foot, and I will ride her golden brother, Natan. Okay, everyone, mount up."

"But, Tamara, I have never ridden a horse. Does it matter how I get on?"

"I know that a western rider gets on from the left side of the horse, but Kesia, all you have to do is imagine being on Lettfeti, and you will automatically be on her back."

"Good to know. Thanks."

Once everyone was mounted, Tamara said, "Take us to the fairy city, please."

Lexi clicked her heels against Phantachus three times.

Edward grabbed hold of the night mare's mane and held on tight.

In an instant, all four mythical horses were up in the air and riding at lightning speed towards the Kingdom of Astovodal.

As Phantachus started to descend, Lexi could see the vast countryside of Astovodal. It went on as far as the eye could see. As she got closer, she could see fairy gardens with shimmering bright colored magical flowers and enormous vegetables. She smiled as she saw the tiny wings of the fairies flying around busily as they were planting and tending the crops.

Closer to the fortress, she could see people doing all the things you would see in a medieval movie. There was a market filled with mystical and magical goods and wares. Many items were being sold, but she had no idea what they would be used for.

As Phantachus landed close to the entrance of the fairy castle, she was in awe of its grandeur. It wasn't quite what she expected, not that she knew what a fairy castle was supposed to look like, but this castle's walls were made of shimmering gold. Ivy vines grew towards the four turrets, twisting and turning in all directions as it climbed. As she expected to see a moat and water, it appeared, as if by magic. *Right, this is my imagination. Anything is possible,* she thought to herself as the other horses landed.

All the riders got off and stood in front of the castle.

"What do we do now?" Lexi asked Tamara.

Chapter 50

"Hello," a beautiful lady about the size of Lexi's hand whispered as she flew closer to their group. The tone of her voice sounded like soft music flowing through the air.

She had sparkling green eyes, the color of emeralds, long flowing blond hair that was tied back and adorned with a flower crown. Her dress was made of many sheer layers of opal-colored silk, and her perfume reminded Lexi of gardenias.

Tamara took the lead. "Hello, we are from Earth and request to speak with your Queen Freyja. Please tell whoever is in charge that it is vital that I speak with her."

In her sing-song voice, the fairy answered, "She is not here."

Desperately needing a meeting with Freyja, Tamara said, "I understand that she lives in

Alfheim, with her husband, Freyr, who is also her brother."

"She is not here," repeated the tiny fairy.

Lexi said quickly, "Tamara, ask to see Erland."

The fairy's wings started to beat faster, her dress changed color to blood red, which now matched her eyes, and her voice became evil as she hissed, "How do you know Erland?"

Taking a step back, Tamara said nervously, "His soul is a friend of ours, and we knew him when he was a ghost on Earth. I am the one who helped him ascend to Alfheim."

The fairy grew twice her size and ordered, "Leave. Now!"

As a swarm of fairies carrying weapons swooshed in from nowhere, creating a circle around their group, Edward backed up, saying, "Guys, I think we are not welcome here. Get on your horses."

Lexi turned and mounted Phantachus as the others mounted their horses. Clicking her heels three times, Phantachus obeyed and was off like a lightning bolt.

Tamara sent a telepathic message to the other three. *We need to find Erland. Follow me.*

Within moments Lexi was flying high in the sky, higher than a plane would fly, almost into the ethers.

As Phantachus started to slowly descend, Lexi saw a magnificent estate, a regal manor fit for a king.

To Lexi's surprise, they did not land near the estate. Instead, they landed near a modest dwelling near a creek.

"Who lives here?" Edward asked as he dismounted.

"Erland. I should have thought of it sooner, but because I was thinking of the fairy door, I assumed I needed an escort from one of the locals," Tamara answered.

A slender, very fit, six-foot tall man walked out of the building. He had unnaturally beautiful golden hair and perfect skin that seemed to glisten brighter than the sun as he moved closer. His eyes were a sparkly silver-grey. Even though he had pointed ears, he was stunning, way more attractive than any man Lexi had ever seen on Earth.

Erland stood as if he were a god, and his voice, when he spoke, sounded as if he was in your head. *Tamara, is everything alright with the baby? Why have you come?*

Kesia was confused, "What baby?"

"Erland, I apologize for our unannounced arrival. Isabella and the baby are fine. This is about me. I need your help," Tamara answered, ignoring Kesia's question.

Are you prepared to honor the way of the elves?

"I am," Tamara answered as she bowed her head.

"Hi, Hans, I mean Erland," Edward said. "It looks like you've been faring well. Hey, what is the problem with you and the fairies?"

Erland squinted his eyes in a manner that stated to leave that topic alone. He wasn't ready to talk about how she wanted him as a husband and was insulted when he declined. Changing the subject, he looked towards the other travelers and said in their minds. *I have been well, thanks. Hello, Lexi nice to see you again. And who is this young one?*

Tamara introduced Kesia.

What have you brought me as an offering, Tamara?

"I have brought a picture of Isabella and the baby."

"Tamara, how could you have a picture of the baby? It hasn't been born yet," Lexi asked.

From her pant pocket, Tamara brought out two pictures and gave them to Erland.

The group watched as he caressed the photos.

Lexi had to twist her neck to see the pictures. One was of Isabella, looking radiantly pregnant. Lexi guessed she must be almost due by now. The other was an ultrasound picture of a baby still in the womb.

A tear fell to the ground, as Erland smiled and said, *Thank you, Tamara. I accept your offering. How may I help you?*

"I need to see Freyja. I must speak to her. *Tell me more.*

Chapter 51

Erland gestured for them to have a seat.

Startled, since there was no patio seating when they first arrived, Edward had a seat next to Lexi. *I might be able to get used to this magic stuff after all. It comes in handy.*

"It is such a long story, do you mind?" Tamara took Erland's hand and placed it on her forehead. "This is much faster."

Edward leaned over to Lexi and asked, "What are they doing?"

Lexi shrugged her shoulders, and Kesia answered, "She is having him read her memories."

"Oh, that would be faster," Edward said, liking this logic.

I see. You wish to meet with Freyja to change your future. Is this correct?

"Yes," Tamara said solemnly.

You know she does not meet with just anyone. And not only will you need an offering worthy of a Queen, but you will be asked for a sacrifice of some kind. Are you prepared for that?

"I am."

Give me a moment. Erland went into his home and came out with a funny-looking gourd.

Edward chuckled, "That reminds me of a book series I read when I was a teenager. I loved them. Don't tell me we pop a hole into the gourd and peek in for our soul to visit Freyja while our bodies stay here?"

Erland looked at Edward and said, "That is absurd. Besides, your soul is already here, and you have no body."

"He has a point, Edward. It is our soul that astral traveled through the fairy door. Our bodies are still on the couch at your place," Tamara confirmed.

Feeling a bit embarrassed, Edward inquired, "I'm still confused about all this hocus pocus stuff. How are we all able to have the same dream in our meditation, Tamara?"

A little surprised that it had been almost a year since his first meditation experience, and he just thought now to ask. "Edward, have you ever heard of Hemispheric Synchronization?"

"No."

"Some people use audio sound waves to create change in a person's brainwave activity, creating both sides of the brain's hemispheres to synchronize. Once your mind knows how to do this action on its own, it can reproduce the procedure without using sound."

"So, now explain that in plain English, please."

"When your brain's frequency is at a certain hertz, you can sync to other people's thought waves."

"But I didn't learn how to do that."

"I did, and since you are in my meditation, I linked us."

"Oh. Good to know. Can I do this on my own without you?"

"Yes. Now that you have done it, and may I say many times, your subconscious knows how to do it again."

Interrupting, Erland said as he passed her the fruit, "Tamara, you need to take this gourd with you to Freyja. It makes her favorite pie."

"Really, pie? It has no special power?" Edward asked.

Tamara laughed, "Edward, not everything is magical, you know. Some things are practical, like food. Even gods like to eat."

Lexi gave Edward a kiss on the cheek and said, "You're so cute. Thanks, I learn a lot from your silly questions."

He smiled at her and said, "I am glad someone finds my ignorance useful."

"Tamara, only you girls can go to Freyja. She won't be as cordial if Edward is there."

"What? Wait, no way. If Alexandra is going, then I am going."

"Have it your way, but if you want to come back alive, then I suggest only letting the girls go," Erland warned.

"What? Why? She doesn't like men?"

"She is a Vanir god, and you are of no significance to her because you are human."

"But the girls are human. Will they be safe?"

"They should be."

"They should be?"

"Yes, as long as they can perform her request, they will come back here safely."

"Perform her request?" Edward was now very concerned. "What request?"

"My gourd is not an offering. It is a gift. They will have to make an offering or sacrifice that she finds suitable for Tamara's request of her."

"Wonderful, just wonderful. Well, what am I going to do while they are away? Sit here and twiddle my thumbs?"

Bluntly, Erland said, "I thought you could keep me company, but if you would rather twiddle your thumbs, then be my guest."

"Edward, don't be rude. Apologize to Erland," Lexi said quickly so that Erland wouldn't leave.

Looking at Lexi, he realized how childish he was acting, "Sorry, Erland, I just get so worried about Alexandra that I forget my manners sometimes. I would love your company."

Erland nodded and said, "Okay, ladies, Freyja is waiting for you."

Chapter 52

*A*s they thought her name, the three ladies were instantly teleported to her in her private chamber in the temple.

Surprise was an understatement. "Holy Hannah!" Kesia said, smiling. "Wish we could do that back at home."

Lexi commented, "I don't know. That could be dangerous. You never know where you might end up. People could be in interesting places at any given time, like bungy jumping, except you won't have the equipment."

"I'm sure there are rules, and with practice, you could travel anywhere in an instant."

Just as Lexi was about to say something else, one of Freyja's guards stepped forward, with his battle sword drawn, and yelled, "SILENCE! Bow to the Queen, you low-life mortals.

Insulted by the racism, Lexi declared, "Well, of all the nerve."

The guard pulled back his sword to swing at Lexi's head, just as Tamara screamed, "No! Your majesty, please, we are here in peace. Please, excuse our ignorance of your customs. I have a gift."

Sitting in an elaborate chair fit for any queen, Freyja raised a hand, and the guard beside her stopped his advancement and went back to standing on guard beside her. "You may present yourself."

Tamara moved forward and revealed the gift. "Erland asked if I would give you this gourd. He says it produces your favorite pie."

Recognizing the gourd at once, Freyja smiled and said, "His horticultural knowledge from Earth is astounding. Only he can produce fruit like this."

One of Freyja's servants came and retrieved the gourd.

"I was also told that you require an offering and a sacrifice. May I offer my services?"

"No."

Taken aback, Tamara was devastated since she didn't have anything else to offer.

"I demand the service of your servants."

Tamara looked from Lexi to Kesia, "Your majesty, there has been a misunderstanding. These are my friends, not my servants."

"It is of no concern to me who they are to you. I demand their service."

Scared that Lexi and Kesia were the sacrifice, she said, "Your majesty, I cannot sacrifice their lives in exchange for changing my future."

"I never said I was going to kill them. I demand an intuitive reading."

"Your majesty, I am far more experienced in the field. I can offer you a reading."

"Guard, tie a gag around this one. She doesn't shut up."

The guard moved behind Tamara and tied a cloth around her mouth so that she could not speak.

"Now, for my reading. Come, have a seat at the table."

A table with chairs appeared in front of the queen's chair as if by magic.

The guard escorted the three ladies to their seats.

Gesturing to Kesia, Freyja said, "You go first."

"I need my tarot cards," Kesia said, not knowing how to do a reading without them.

"What are tarot cards?"

"Stiff paper about this size." Kesia brought her pointer fingers and both thumbs together to create a rectangular. "Each card has drawings and symbols painted on one side."

"Never heard of those." Turning to Lexi, she said commanded, "Then you do the reading."

Looking at Tamara, pleading for help, Lexi said, "She hasn't taught me how to do a reading without tools."

"What tools do you require?"

"She taught me how to read a person's photo."

"What is a photo?"

Surprised that the queen didn't know what a photograph was, Lexi hesitantly said, "Ah, it is a glossy piece of paper with a snapshot of a person's essence."

"Never heard of that before. Sounds like torture. Capturing a person in a photo. What else can you use?"

Lexi thought back to Tamara's class. "Um, I can read your signature."

"What is a signature?"

Lexi shook her head in disbelief. *How could she not know what a signature is?* "It is your first and last name written down with a writing tool, like a pen or pencil on a piece of paper."

"I do not have a last name, and I do not have a pen, pencil, or for that matter, paper. What is it with you mortals and paper? Everything you two are talking about concerns paper."

"Oh wait, I can read your aura."

"What is an aura?"

"It is the colored light that emanates from your body."

"Oh, that will be sufficient, go ahead, read my aura."

Happy to find something that she could do, Lexi took a breath and shifted her eyesight.

Staring at the queen, Lexi asked, "Can we dim the lights, please? I think it is too bright in here."

Freyja clapped her hands, and the lights faded to a soft glow.

Lexi stared again to see Freyja's aura. Turning to Tamara, she said, "I don't see her aura. I don't think she has one."

"Are you telling me that neither of you can give me a reading?" The queen said, getting impatient.

With pleading eyes, Lexi said, "Please, let Tamara help me. I am sure she has a way to do a reading for you."

"Fine. Guard, take off her gag."

The guard moved to Tamara and removed the cloth.

Looking at Tamara, Freyja asked, "Is there a way that they can give me a reading?"

"Yes, it is called an energy reading."

"How does it work?"

"The reader uses their sixth sense and decodes your energy field that is being transmitted from your body."

"What tools do they need?"

"None."

"None?"

"That is correct. They do not require anything except their own mind."

'Well then, I would like to have you guide one of them in reading my energy field."

Tamara looked at Kesia and said, "I am going to share how to do it, but I am going to have

Lexi read Queen Freyja's energy field. Lexi has been taking my classes and will know what I am talking about."

Kesia nodded her head in understanding.

Looking at Lexi, Tamara said, "Lexi, take a couple of deep breaths and relax, but keep your eyes open."

Waiting a few seconds for Lexi to relax, Tamara continued. "Now, if we had a paper and pen, I would ask you to write the initials P, Pr, and F on the left-hand side of the page, above one another, with space in between. They stand for past, present, and future."

Lexi nodded.

"Lexi, in your mind I want you to look at the queen, your intended thought is about her past only. This means to think of her past one year ago to her birth as you look at her. Now pick an age. Any age." Tamara gave Lexi a second to shift her thoughts. "Normally, I would have you write out the first thing that came to your mind, but since we don't have a paper and pen, just tell us."

From taking Tamara's classes, Lexi knew she had to go back an instant before her conscious thought came to her mind. She knew that intuitive energy is lightning quick, and the human mind tries to decipher with logic, but logic is not usually the correct answer. So, she took a breath and backed up a millisecond before her conscious thought came. Lexi knew her subconscious picked up the true answer. "I see a different world. It's not this place, and it is not Asgard, though you have ruled from there as well. I have watched movies that portray Odin's and Thor's world, and it looks nothing like that."

Fascinated by what Lexi was saying, the queen leaned in.

"In this world, I see a man standing beside you. He looks like you, but he has a boar with him."

"You are seeing my brother, Freyr."

Lexi refocused and looked at Freyja's eyes and said, "Ah." She then dis-focused and continued to stare at the queen's energy field. "This world is beautiful. It actually looks like Earth, in which it has a sun, rain, and wind. I see figures growing crops and fishing."

"You are seeing the world Vanaheimr, where I came from before the Æsir war," The queen answered.

Looking at the queen's eyes again, Lexi said, "I see." Then looking back to her energy field, she continued with the reading, "They are calling you something I don't understand. It sounds like volva."

"Völva pronounced Vølve. It means wand carrier. In English, you would say, seeress, seer, or witch. I believe in your Norse religion, that it was a female with the ability to tinker with the seidr – magic pertaining to destiny and its 'weaving.' It is a person who has the ability to alter and manipulate one's desire and fortune."

Tamara interrupted by saying, "Lexi, stay focused, don't get caught up in the story. She confirmed what you are seeing, now move on to the present. Switch your focus to her present situation back on Earth, that would be the last year to today. Here, I am not sure what a year is equivalent to, so just pick up her energy over the last couple of days. What do you sense now?"

Lexi took a breath and shifted her thought and intent to the queen's present situation. "I see her meditating, or what looks like meditation. She is consulting someone that I cannot see. I can hear her talking about you, Tamara."

Tamara looked at the queen. "Is what she is saying true?"

Surprised by Lexi's abilities, Freyja said, "Well, your student is good. No one has ever been able to. . ."

Lexi interrupted, "Wait, I know who she is talking to."

Freyja turned from Tamara to Lexi, "Impossible!"

Lexi blurted out, "Bath Kol. She is talking to Bath Kol!"

"Impossible, there is no way you would know that, unless. . . unless she has talked to you."

"She has, just recently," Lexi said.

"If this is true, ask her what we were talking about. I give you permission to ask her about my personal affairs."

Lexi took a breath and closed her eyes. *Bath Kol, as you may already know, I am here in Alfheim with Freyja. She has given me permission to ask you what you two were discussing about Tamara. Please tell me, and thank you.*

Lexi waited for an answer. She almost missed it. It was quieter than a whisper.

You are a long way from home Lexi, be careful not to get stuck there. We were discussing the sacrifice Tamara will have to make.

Thank you, Bath Kol. It is always a pleasure speaking with you.

Lexi could feel a warm glow come over her. "Bath Kol said you were discussing Tamara's sacrifice."

The queen stared at Lexi in disbelief. "Amazing. I haven't heard of a mortal being able to communicate with her. Truly amazing."

"What about her sacrifice?" Lexi asked.

Tamara interrupted again, "Lexi stay focused. This reading is about the queen, not me. It is time to move to her future."

"Right. Wow, that is hard to do. It is so easy to get caught up in her drama."

Tamara nodded but said, "Take a breath and focus on her future."

Lexi shut her eyes and took a deep breath to clear out the queen's present energy, and shifted her focus into her future. *Her future. What would a queen want to know about her future?*

Bath Kol, may I ask for your help in predicting the queen's future?

Yes.

Please tell me what I need to say to the queen.

*She needs to hear about. . .*There was a mass of information that came to Lexi's mind within an instant.

Thank you.

Opening her eyes, Lexi said, "There is to be a war between the fairies and the elves, one elf in particular. She says that you must not take sides. That this war is because of us." Lexi put her hands over her mouth. "Oh, my God. Tamara, this war is because of you."

Chapter 53

"A war? Who said that there was going to be a war?" Freyja demanded.

"I figured that if you could talk to Bath Kol for future events, then I could also. It was Bath Kol who told me what to say about your future."

"Guards, take away these two ladies!"

Lexi and Kesia were escorted out of her chambers.

Looking at Tamara, Freyja said, "Do you know why you could not do the reading for me?"

Sitting up straighter in her chair, Tamara answered, "I believe it is because I am not myself lately. My personal life has affected my emotions, and I am not a clear conduit at the moment."

"Precisely. You have come here to ask me not about your future as most do, but to change your future."

Tamara nodded her head, yes.

"That is a big request. It requires a big sacrifice. Are you sure you want to proceed with your request?"

"Yes." Tamara had no other desire. She could not go back to her world and live with the knowledge of Greg and his betrayal.

"I see. Love is fickle. The human soul lives by emotions, not by logic. Bath Kol and I have been contemplating your request. She has had to ask the heavenly father on this matter."

"I didn't know it would come to that."

"Tamara, you have been able to manipulate energy for some time. Most people on Earth think only a god can do that, and they are right."

"I don't consider myself a god."

"No, but you are close."

"That seems a bit conceited."

"The ability to manipulate and communicate with energy is a godly trait. The power is granted by the Holy Spirit."

"I know Spirit granted the nine spiritual gifts, but I didn't realize it was the Holy Spirit."

"Think about it. He is an equal part of the trinity. He comforts us, helps us, guides us, reminds us, teaches us, comes alongside us, counsels us, intercedes and advocates for us."

"Is the Holy Spirit Archangel Gabriel?"

"No. Gabriel is one of Bath Kol's best messenger angels."

"Do the three of them work together?"

"Yes, but the only difference is that Bath Kol's voice is so silent it makes no noise. It is like pouring oil compared to water. You can hear water when it drips, but you can never hear oil."

"I think what you are trying to say is that Bath Kol is an inner knowing, not a thought, but a divine essence of energy. She does not speak in words such as Gabriel or the Holy Ghost, as both have taken human form before. She is similar to how God speaks, in a form that makes no sound."

"Well put."

"Freyja, are you considered a God."

"Depends, do you spell it with a big or little 'g'?"

"Big 'G'."

"Then no. I am considered a god with a small 'g'. There is a difference. Only God the Almighty is spelt with a big 'G'. All other gods are spelt with a small 'g'."

"I don't understand the difference. What do you mean?"

"Tamara, Bath Kol is telling me that you are familiar with a book called the Bible."

"Yes."

"She says that there are over one hundred references in the Bible about other gods, not to mention the belief of all the Greek, Roman, and any other cultures gods."

"No, I didn't know that."

"She says that God the Almighty said, 'That he was the one true God,' and to prove it, he silenced everything, and everyone, even the other gods."

"Interesting. Why are you telling me this?"

"Power to manipulate their followers, as in sheep, has been practiced before time itself. Rulers of any kind, of any world, do not appreciate their subjects to have a mind of their own, let alone have mystical powers that can overturn the throne."

"Your point being?"

"You understand how spiritual energy works, and that scares many people in your realm."

"I can't just forget what I know."

"True. That brings me to your request. Are you one hundred percent sure you want to go through with this?"

"Yes."

"Fine, it is done."

Chapter 54

"What do you mean she is gone?" Where did she go?" Lexi asked, trying to keep her voice from screaming.

Not answering her question, Freyja's servant said instead, "You are free to leave."

Turning her head to Kesia, Lexi said, "Leave, how can we leave without knowing where Tamara is?"

As the servant started to walk away from them, Kesia asked, "Excuse me. How do we get back to our friend Erland's?"

Turning slightly back towards them, she said, "The same way you got here."

"Lexi, I don't remember how we got here. What way did we come?"

Still thinking about Tamara, Lexi said, "We didn't. Remember Erland just had us think about Freyja, and we teleported to her quarters."

"Oh right. Maybe we could do that to find Tamara?"

"I've been trying, but I am still here with you."

"Maybe if we both try."

"Ya, that might work. Think about Tamara."

Nothing, they were both still in the queen's temple's hallway.

Making a huffing sound and shaking her head, Lexi said, "It is no use. Let's think about Erland and Edward."

Poof, instantly they were back at the patio table outside Erland's home.

Sensing their arrival, Erland and Edward came outside to greet them.

"Well, I see it went well," Erland remarked.

"How can you say that? Tamara is gone, and we do not know where to find her."

Edward came over to Lexi and asked, "Are you two, okay?"

Lexi started to cry. "Edward, I don't know what to do. She is gone. Where do we search for her?"

Erland stepped closer and said, "It is time for the three of you to go home."

As the blood ran out of Lexi's face, she said, "What are you talking about? We can't leave without Tamara."

Bluntly, Erland declared, "You can, and you will. Her fate has been decided. There is nothing more that you can do here. Now leave before you are rudely escorted out of Alfheim."

Kesia tugged on Lexi's sleeve and said, "Lexi, we have to leave. Look."

Lexi followed to where Kesia was pointing, and in the far distance, she could make out a swarm of enraged fairies flying towards them.

"What do we do? How do we get back to Earth?" Lexi said as she grabbed onto Edward.

"The horses, Lexi, we came on the horses."

Scared half to death from the angry faces coming closer and closer, Lexi gasped, "Oh ya,"

In an instant, Edward was on his night mare, Lexi was on Phantachus, and Kesia was on Lettfeti.

"Phantachus, take us back home to Edward's place, please." She clicked her heels into his side three times, and they were off like lightning.

A moment later, the horses landed at the entrance of the fairy door. The one they had come through, twice.

"Come on, you guys, get off and let's go home." Petting Phantachus, Lexi had enough time to say, "Thank you, my dear friend," just before the fairy door opened and their souls were back in their bodies in the counselor's room.

A knock at the door was heard, and then, "Edward, I need the room in five minutes."

Chapter 55

"Oh my God. Look!" Lexi was pointing at the couch.

"Holy Hannah! Where is she?" Kesia squealed as she opened her eyes and looked around. "Her purse is still on the floor beside where she was sitting. What's going on?"

Freaking out, Lexi said, "Edward, where is Tamara?"

Speechless, Edward got up to unlock the door, so his staff wouldn't get worried. "Grab all your stuff, including hers, and follow me."

Edward smiled at his staff and the client as he walked past them to his office. Lexi just looked down, trying not to make eye contact, and Kesia nodded to them as she hurried out the door behind Lexi.

Rushing into Edward's office Kesia was confused. "I thought that was impossible. I know that she didn't come back with us, but I would have thought that she would be like sleeping beauty and just not wake up."

"You guys, we have to go back. We can't leave her in Alfheim, Lexi said frantically as she remembered the fairy door was still in the counseling room, which now was being used.

"We're not going back. You saw the angry faces on the fairies. They were out for blood," Edward answered as he picked up the phone.

"Lexi, did Tamara tell you anything about where she was going or wanted to go?" Kesia asked just as Edward started to talk to the person on the phone.

"Detective Redington, we need your assistance. Tamara is missing."

"Who is this?"

"Oh, sorry, it is Reverend Hawthorne."

"Who?"

"Edward, Lexi's fiancé."

"Oh right. You said that Tamara is gone? Gone where?"

"That is the problem. We don't know."

"Then how do you know she is gone?"

"It's a long story. Can you come over?"

"Let me get back to you."

"Red, she is really gone, like disappeared."

"Sure, I have heard that before, and nine times out of ten, they just didn't want to be found."

"I hope in this case you are right. See you soon." Edward hung up the phone.

"So, when is he coming?" Lexi asked.

"I'm not sure. He said he will get back to me."

"You should have told him the whole truth over the phone," Kesia remarked.

Looking at the young girl, Edward had to remember that she didn't understand how crazy it would have sounded over the phone. *How do I keep finding myself in these situations?*

As she passed Tamara's purse to Lexi, Kesia said, "Lexi, look in her purse and find something that you can read her energy from. Maybe it will tell you where she is."

Taking the purse, Lexi said, "Oh, that might actually be a good idea."

Dumping the purse onto Edward's desk, Lexi spread out the contents. *What did Tamara say about psychometry? Oh ya, it had to be something personal, something that they touch often.* Lexi moved her wallet out of the way to reveal Tamara's car keys. "Oh, these will work."

Kesia asked, "Why did you pick her keys? Why not something bigger?"

Looking up, Lexi answered, "Tamara taught us that anything metal, and especially gemstones, hold the vibration of the person's memories the best."

"Fascinating."

"She told us a story about a guy who took his wedding ring off and put it into his shoe when he was on the court playing volleyball. He is not sure what happened because he lost it, or it was stolen. The point is, months later he bought a gold band at a pawn shop and wore it. One day someone asked to read his ring, and all the info was incorrect. Later, he remembered that it had been someone else's ring and had their info stored in it, not his."

"Couldn't he just clear the old energy out of the ring?"

"I think if it didn't have a diamond in it, he could have."

"Why not if it had a diamond?"

"Tamara said that a diamond is the only thing that cannot be cleared of the energy stored in it."

"I wonder why. How did she say that you can clear energy out?"

"If it is a room, you can smudge like the Indians do, using a feather and the smoke of a smudge stick."

"Right, I have heard of that before, but what if it is metal or a stone?"

"She said there are a few ways. You could intent the energy to be cleared while washing it under running water, Reiki it, or leave it overnight in the light of a full moon."

"Hey, what about if it is a person?"

"Then, if I remember correctly, she said that you could use Reiki, salt bath, prayer, or a chakra clearing meditation."

"Ooh, they all sound interesting. We'll have to try them sometime."

"Lexi, you might want to try reading her energy before Redington calls back," Edward said, worried that she would run out of time.

"Good idea, we'll talk more about this later, Kesia."

"Sure. I want to see what you do to read psychometry anyways."

"Kesia, can you please write down what I say?"

"Sure."

Edward passed Kesia a notepad and pen.

Holding Tamara's keys, Lexi sat back in the high-back chair she was sitting on, closed her eyes, and took a few deep breaths.

Rubbing the keys lightly, Lexi said the first thing that came to her mind. "I feel warmth and love."

Kesia wrote down what she said word for word.

Lexi took another breath. *Tamara, please tell me where you are.* Lightly rubbing the keys, she waited for anything, a feeling, a sound, a vision, or any thought.

Nothing.

She took another breath. *What sacrifice did you have to make?*

Nothing.

Fidgeting in her chair, she readjusted how she was sitting in case that made a difference.

It didn't. Nothing.

Desperate for answers, Lexi silently prayed, *God, please help me find Tamara.*

Hey, sis. You are not going to find her. She has to honor her sacrifice for the demand she made with Freyja to change her future.

Susannah, thanks for answering me.

No problem.

Is she coming back, Tamara, that is?

I don't think so.

Is she okay?

Yes.

Does she need my help?

Not right now. She might, though, but not the way you think she will.

Lexi tried to think of a better question to ask her belated sister. *What do I tell Detective Redington?*

The truth. He'll know what to do.

Is there anything else I should be asking you?

Not right now.

Okay, thanks. Hey, wait. Why couldn't I read Tamara's keys?

Because she is not Tamara anymore.

Chapter 56

Redington drove under the magnificent gateway that greeted you as you entered the cemetery. He had never been to Edward's and was astounded at the grandeur and care of the grounds. To his surprise, the funeral home was just as impressive. *And here I thought he was just an average Joe.*

As he walked up to the front entrance Kesia was just about to get into a cab.

"Hey, wait here a moment missy, where do you think you are going?"

Kesia looked towards the man coming towards her. "Why, am I under arrest?"

"Hey, watch that tone, young lady, or you just might be."

Kesia laughed.

Remington smiled at her as he got closer to the cab driver. "You're not going anywhere just yet." Red pulled out his wallet and paid the taxi driver, even though he had not completed his fare. "Come on, you can tell me what's been happening." Redington gestured for Kesia to lead the way.

Once into the entrance, Kesia said, "They are this way."

Redington followed her into Edward's office.

Surprised, Edward and Lexi looked their way as they entered.

"Ahhhh, thanks for getting back to me," Edward said, sarcastically to Redington.

"You're welcome."

Looking at Kesia, Edward said, "I thought you were going home."

"I was, but big guy here had other plans for me."

Looking at Redington, Edward asked, "And that is?"

"To keep her safe."

Lexi stood up from the chair she was sitting on and turned in Redington's direction. "You think that Kesia is still in danger?"

"I am not taking any chances at this moment. Greg is still at large and now you say Tamara is missing."

"Good point," Lexi said as she sat back down.

Redington pulled a third chair over for Kesia to sit in and then sat in the chair beside Lexi's. "Now tell me what you know so far."

The other three started to speak at the same time.

"Hold on. One at a time. Lexi, you go first." Redington pulled out his recorder. "On the record. Go ahead Lexi, tell me what happened."

"Well, as you know, Tamara was devastated from the ordeal with Greg. She said she needed to change her future."

Redington interjected, "You said, change her future?"

"Yes. That is what she said."

Edward and Kesia both nodded their heads to agree.

"And then what happened?"

"She said she needed to speak with Freyja."

"Do you know who that is?"

"Yes, Kesia and I met her."

Redington's eyebrow went up. "Okay, and then what."

"We all came here. Well, actually into the counseling room."

Redington looked in the direction where Lexi was pointing. He got up. "Can I see that room?"

Patting the air with his hand for Redington to sit back down, Edward answered, "No. It is in use with a client right now."

"Edward, it is considered tampering with evidence if someone else is in there. I am going to need to see the room."

"Yes, I know, but this is no ordinary case. We can go in soon. Lexi, tell him everything."

Looking over to Lexi, Redington said, "I'm listening."

Here we go again. Clearing her throat, Lexi said, "Red, we went to the fairy world."

Redington rolled his eyes in disbelief. "You went where?" He shut off his recorder. "What the? Is anything ever normal with you guys?"

Lexi looked at Edward for support.

Kesia piped up, "Hey, no judging. You're a cop. Act like one. Someone is missing, a friend."

Redington looked over to Kesia, "An acquaintance. And remember, I told you to watch your tone with me."

"Whatever, your job is to find her."

"Red," Lexi said. "I know it sounds crazy, but she really is gone. Her body that is."

"Her body?"

"Yes. When we came out of the meditation, she was nowhere to be found. She left her purse, cell phone, and keys."

At that moment, one of Edward's staff came into the office. "The room is available again."

"Thanks, Casandra."

Redington stood up demanding, "Show me the room."

Edward led the way back to the counseling room.

"This is where you guys were meditating?" Redington asked.

Lexi walked over to the circular couch and said, "Yes. Tamara was sitting right here."

"Lexi!" Kesia yelled. "It's gone."

"What's gone?" Redington asked with real concern.

Kesia looked at Lexi and pointed. "The fairy door. We left it right there."

Lexi looked around the room. "Edward, would your staff have moved it?"

"They might have. Let me go ask."

"What is a fairy door?" Redington asked, not sure if he really wanted to know the answer.

"It is a little whimsical wooden door about this high," Lexi held her hands, one above the other with about six inches of space between.

Redington wrote something on his notepad.

Kesia went over to where the door used to be. "How are we going to get her if the door is missing?"

"Lexi, what aren't you telling me?" Redington asked.

Lexi sat on the couch and put her hands over her eyes, then moved her fingers to her temples, and rubbed. Shaking her head, she said, "I don't even know if I believe it, and I witnessed it."

Redington sat down beside her. "You mentioned that she went to talk with a woman named Freyja. Who is that?"

Lexi looked into Redington's eyes. "She rules the fairies and elves. Well, technically her husband does, he is also her brother."

"Oh, my dear lord. Lexi, you are going to be the death of me. I swear. If I hadn't had other weird experiences with you, I would have had you locked up in the psych ward already."

Tears started to form in Lexi's eyes. "Red, we have to get her back."

Just as Redington was about to say something, Edward walked back into the room. "What did you say? Redington, if you made her cry, I am gonna. . ."

"What? What are you going to do, Edward?"

Lexi wiped at her tears. "Stop it you too. We have more important things to do than be petty."

"So, did they have the fairy door?" Kesia asked Edward, anxiously.

Coming to his senses. "No."

"Where could it be? We need that fairy door!" Kesia declared.

Redington got up. "I will need to take Tamara's belonging."

Lexi stood up, worried for Tamara's sake, and said, "But I need to make sure her stuff is looked after while she is away."

"I will figure something out. I'll call you guys tomorrow. Kesia, you'll have to stay with these guys for a few days. Just until I know you are going to be safe."

Looking at Lexi, she asked, "Is that okay with you?"

Looking at Edward, Lexi asked, "Can we stay here. I am not sure if my place is safe anymore."

"Ah." Stammering while thinking. *Dang it, I wanted it to be a surprise and it isn't finished yet.* "Sure. I'll figure something out."

Chapter 57

Kesia was looking at the books on Edward's shelves in his office while he was figuring out the sleeping arrangements.

Lexi was sitting on one of the high-back chairs staring out the window.

Touching a book, Kesia said, "Lexi, what do you know about Nostradamus?"

"Who?"

"You know, the old guy who could predict the future."

"Ah, I don't recall hearing about him."

"What? Are you kidding me? He is famous."

Kesia took the book down that she was caressing and sat down in the chair beside Lexi's. Opening the book, she said, "It says here that he was a French astrologist and physician. He was married twice, but unfortunately, his first wife and two children died. They think it was because of the plague. He remarried and had six more children."

Lexi turned from the window and looked at Kesia, interested now in what she had to say.

Kesia continued. "In 1547, he began making prophecies and wrote about them in rhymed four-lined stanzas called quatrains, which he grouped in hundreds. Eight years later he published his book, entitled Centuries, and named it that because each set of one hundred is called a century."

"He was a prophet?" Lexi asked.

Kesia nodded. "Not quite like the ones in the Bible, but yes."

"What is the difference?"

Kesia put the book down on her lap. "Well, my mom says that the prophets in the Bible are chosen and called by God. There are many references to prophets in both the Old Testament and New."

"What makes a prophet a prophet?" Lexi asked, questioning her last meditative conversation with Archangel Gabriel, *Lexi, you will become a prophet.*

Kesia took out her phone and typed in Lexi's question. "As my mom calls the internet the almighty oracle, let's ask." A moment later, Kesia said, "Wiki says, in religion, a prophet is an individual who is regarded as being in contact with a divine being and is said to speak on behalf of that being, serving as an intermediary with humanity by delivering messages or teachings from the supernatural source to other people. The message that the prophet conveys is called a prophecy."

"Hmm."

"In Christianity, a prophet (or seer) is one inspired by God through the Holy Spirit to deliver a message," Kesia added.

"Do people still believe that there are prophets amongst us?" Lexi asked, not really expecting an answer.

Kesia quickly searched the web. "It says here that some Christians believe that the Holy Spirit gives spiritual gifts to Christians. Some of these prophecies are tongues, miracles, and discernment (distinguishing spirits).

Lexi sat forward, closer to Kesia. "Tamara talked a lot about the nine spiritual gifts. In fact, many of her classes are based on these gifts."

"I wish I could have taken her classes," Kesia responded. "It continues talking about the gifts and gives proof in Matthew 12:32, it says, 'Whosoever speaketh a word against the Son of Man, it shall be forgiven him: but whosoever speaketh against the Holy Ghost, it shall not be forgiven him, neither in this world, neither in the world to come.' But Cessationists, whoever they are, believe that these gifts were given only in the New Testament times and that they ceased after the last apostle died."

Edward walked into the office just as Kesia was finishing what she was saying.

"Cessationists doctrine arose in the Protestant Reformation, initially in response to Roman Catholic miracles' claims. It was a major movement within Western Christianity in 16th-century."

"Kesia was just telling me about Nostradamus," Lexi informed Edward as he sat down at his desk.

"Ah, I studied him in seminary school. Here are a few facts you may not know. Christopher Columbus wrote an unpublished collection of prophecies because he was inspired by Nostradamus' work. Another, Nostradamus went to medical school but was expelled, and was not allowed to graduate because he had previously worked as an apothecary—now known as a chemist. This profession was banned from the University. And lastly, even though he moved towards the occult as a seer, Nostradamus remained a devout Roman Catholic, and there is evidence that he was opposed to the Protestant Reformation."

"But what made him become a seer?" Lexi asked.

Edward answered her with the only answer he knew of, "Some believe that Nostradamus was neither an astrologer nor a seer. Many believe he used a technique called bibliomancy."

"What is that?" Kesia asked.

"Taking past recorded information from older sources and then using astrological calculations to project its recurrence in the future, simply stating facts about history that will repeat itself. Today, many farmers use a similar method to predict the weather. You may know it as an almanac."

"Ya, they sell those little books in the grocery stores," Lexi said, knowing because she had glanced through one while waiting in line.

Kesia read from the book she was holding, "His last words were "Tomorrow I shall no longer be here." But this author makes a comment, 'but with us today are all the predictions that he made, most of which eerily came true.' Kind of creepy, don't you think?"

Edward responded with, "If you look at a thesaurus, "prophet" is connected to words like "seer," "astrologer," "fortune teller," "soothsayer," and even "witch.""

"That is not helping me, Edward. I want to know how one becomes a prophet," Lexi snapped.

Edward looked at Lexi with apologetic eyes. "Being chosen as a prophet is considered an honor, but not an easy task for imperfect humans to consistently maintain."

Lexi started to tear up, frustrated with the notion that Archangel Gabriel said she was to become a prophet. "Can there still be prophets today?"

Edward reached across his desk and touched her hand. "According to the Bible, prophets can still be called by God anywhere and anytime.

Edward pulled out his Bible and turned to Acts 2: 17-18. "In the last days, God said, 'I will pour out my Spirit on all people. Your sons and daughters will prophesy, your young men will see visions, and your old men will dream dreams. Even on my servants, both men and women, I will pour out my Spirit in those days, and they will prophesy."

Lexi looked deep into Edward's eyes, "So, you are saying that a person living today could become a prophet."

"Yes."

Chapter 58

"All right, you two. Enough of this prophecy talk for today. Lexi, come and see your surprise. You too, Kesia." Edward stood up and blocked the door. "Close your eyes, Lexi."

"But how will I walk if I can't see?"

Edward went over to her and put her arm through his, and said, "Close your eyes. I want it to be a surprise."

Guiding her, he walked towards the plastic that created a barrier from the funeral home to his living quarters.

Kesia opened the plastic like a tent flap for Edward to guide Lexi through.

She heard the plastic as it was being pulled back. Tempted to open her eyes, she closed them even tighter. "Oh, my God. I am so excited!"

"Drum roll, please," Edward called out.

Kesia played along and started to beatbox. (the art of using your lips, tongue, and throat to imitate the sounds made by a full percussion drum kit -cymbals, hi-hat, kick, and snare drums). She was really good at it.

"Okay, you can open your eyes," Edward said as he let her arm go.

Lexi slowly opened her eyes. Bringing her hands with intertwined fingers up to her heart, she said, "Oh Edward, this is amazing. I never could have imagined this."

"It isn't totally finished, the electricians and carpenters still have a few things they need to complete, but it is safe to sleep here tonight."

Lexi looked at the new door's intricate wood design that separated the funeral home and the stairs to Edward's living quarters. As she opened the door, it led to a widened stairway with beautiful wood and metal handrails attached to both walls. The stairs were white marble with black veins. Each step matched the one before. It was breathtaking. Lexi started to ascend. "I feel like a princess." Looking at the art on the walls, Lexi commented, "I haven't seen these before. They're beautiful. Are they new?"

"They're not new, I just pulled them out of storage."

Kesia read the signature on one. "You have another Rembrandt?"

"My grandfather loved his art."

As Lexi came to the upper landing, she squealed, "Oh, my. This is beautiful."

Edward had many of the upper floor walls taken down, creating an open great room theme. The kitchen, dining, and living room were now open to each other.

"How did you raise the ceiling?"

"The attic was above, and so the carpenters removed the floor in this area and created a high ceiling."

"With a skylight! Incredible!"

"Wait, there is more."

Edward guided Lexi and Kesia up a few more stairs.

"The furniture hasn't arrived for the great room, but the bedrooms are finished. I'll bring down some chairs, and we can relax by the fireplace. At least that is completed."

Lexi was tickled pink. The master bedroom had stayed the same, but the other rooms had changed.

"I hope I am not jumping the gun too much." He opened one of the doors, and inside was a nursery.

Lexi turned abruptly and hugged Edward, "Thank you! It is more than words can say. It is so cozy. I love the rocking chair."

Opening another door, Edward said, "Kesia, you will be sleeping here in one of the four guest rooms, or may I say children's bedrooms."

"Wow, baby. Five children. Edward, we will have to talk about that, two maybe, but five?" Lexi said, laughing.

Kesia excitedly said, "This room is Gucci and definitely extra! Wasn't expecting this glamour from you, Reverend."

"Thanks, I think," Edward said, hoping she meant something like totally rad.

Turning from the room to head back down to check out the kitchen, as her tummy started growling, Kesia asked "Hey, Rev? Do you have anything to eat? I'm hungry."

"I'll order pizza. I haven't had time to go grocery shopping yet."

"Awesome. I'll have a vegetarian, please."

Lexi added, "I'll have a Hawaiian."

"Three pizzas it is. I'm having an all meat one."

"It's your stomach," Kesia added jokingly as he walked away from the two girls.

Edward smiled and rubbed his tummy saying, "Nummy."

Since Edward got sidetracked talking about babies and pizza, Kesia brought down two chairs from a bedroom. "Here, we can wait for him in some comfort."

"Thanks." Lexi took a chair and joined her by the fire.

Just as Kesia was about to ask Lexi how she liked the new digs, Lexi's phone rang.

Chapter 59

September 24, in Switzerland.

"What? What is the matter? Is he okay?"

Movie star or not, the look on the nurse's face would have scared any new mother.

No one answered.

Anxiety quickly turned into fear. "What are you looking at? Does he have ten toes and fingers?"

The nurse looked over to her and nodded her head, yes.

"Let me see my baby!"

The doctor nodded to the nurse to let her see the baby.

Wrapped and bundled tightly in a typical hospital blue blanket, Isabella looked down at her newborn son for the first time. He was beautiful, jet black hair just like hers. He had his father's nose and lips. As she moved to get a better look, she saw a shimmer. She thought her eyes played a trick on her, so she moved him slightly again. It was as if his skin glimmered like moonlight. Pulling the blanket away from his face she noticed the nurse flinch. Looking at the nurse she was now very concerned, *What? What is wrong with him?* A bit frantic now she unwrapped her son and counted his toes and fingers. Ten, five on each. *What?* Turning him over to look in case he had a tail. *Nope.* Wrapping him back up, her anxiety faded. *She is crazy, that's all.*

The doctor called the nurse out of the room.

Isabella caressed her son's temple. *What should I call you?*

Just at that moment, the doctor came back in with the nurse. In a Swiss accent, he said, "Miss Jackson, we can do the operation tomorrow morning, I just need you to sign here please," and passed the clipboard and pen to her.

Isabella looked up. "What operation? What are you talking about?"

"Please, Miss Jackson. Think of your child. He cannot live like that. He will be the object of ridicule and laughed at. How do you Americans say? He will be the laughing-stock."

"What are you talking about? He is beautiful."

"Miss Jackson, I know every mother believes their child is beautiful, but come on. Do you really want him to go through life like this?"

Isabella was confused, he had ten toes and fingers, no tail, beautiful jet-black hair, maybe a little long for a newborn baby, but an operation, for what? "I don't understand. What do you need to operate on?"

The doctor looked surprised. "Why his ears of course."

Isabella moved the hair away from her baby's ears. "Oh, my!" Touching the tiny ears, she traced the outside edge. Pointed, like an elf.

"See, there is no way any mother would leave her child deformed when a quick little nip and tuck will cure it. It is called a Stahl's ear deformity."

Isabella looked at the doctor. "Please leave. I need a few moments alone."

"But Miss Jackson, I need your signature. The next opening is not for another month."

"Leave."

"You don't understand, the longer we wait the more scar tissue there will be."

"Leave."

Shaking his head, he said something in a mix of Swiss and German to the nurse and they both left the room.

Pulling out her phone she dialed Tamara. *She'll know what to do.*

No answer.

She left a message, "Tamara, this is Isabella. I had a beautiful baby boy. Please call me."

About half an hour later, the nurse came back in to check on her and the baby. "How are mamma and bebis?"

Isabella looked up from her son and said, "Good, thank you."

"You know you should consider the doctor's offer to operate. It is quick and easy. He won't feel a thing."

"I need to think about it."

"I will check back in an hour. You have until then to decide."

Isabella nodded.

Tamara, where are you, answer me. Isabella left another message.

The nurse came back precisely an hour later. "Well, what did you decide?"

"I didn't. I can't decide this fast."

"Miss, please think about your baby's life, and what he will have to go through or worse yet, always having to hide his grotesque ears."

Isabella covered her son's ears. "Shh, how rude. He can sense your tone. Leave me at once!"

Turning her face down to her sons, "Don't you listen to them, they are just jealous of your beauty. What should I name you? What would Hans have wanted?"

Isabella looked at her son and jumped when she heard Hans's voice in her head.

A son, he is so strong. Thank you, Isabella, for loving me so much that you would bring my son into the world. You need to call him Aias

Jackson Olof Magnusson. He will be considered royalty one day.

"Hans, is that you?" Isabella was looking around the room but could not see anyone.

It is Erland now, but yes. I don't have much time Isabella. You have to listen carefully. Call Lexi, she will tell you what is going on.

"Lexi?"

Yes. You will need her more than anyone. Go to her. Pack your bags now and go to her tonight.

"Hans, I mean Erland, you are scaring me."

Go, now!

Isabella could hear the fear in his voice and knew she wasn't imagining the conversation. Something in her gut told her to listen to him.

Getting slowly out of bed she got dressed and phoned her lawyer. "I need you to get me out of this hospital, tonight. I also need you to get my private jet ready to take myself and my son to America."

"Yes, Miss Jackson. Is everything alright?"

"It will be."

"What airport will you be landing in?"

"JFK in New York City."

Chapter 60

"Hello."

"Lexi, it's Isabella. I had a baby boy."

Leaning forward on her chair, she said excitedly, "Oh, my God. Congratulations! What did you name him? How much did he weigh? What does he look like?"

"Wow, slow down there girl. One question at a time. I called him Aias."

"Oh, I like that. His father would have liked that."

"Oh, he did."

"Ah, what? He did. . . Isabella did you speak with Erland?"

"Not exactly, but he telepathically spoke to me."

"When?"

"That is a weird question."

"Isabella, when?"

"A few hours ago. Why?"

"Did he say anything about Tamara?"

"No. Why? What is wrong? She won't answer my messages or texts."

"Oh, my God, Isabella, where do I start."

"From the beginning."

"Oh goodness no, that would take way too long. She vanished without a trace."

"What? When?"

"A few hours ago."

"Lexi, where are you?"

"At Edwards."

"His funeral home?"

"Yes."

"Okay, I am just touching down now. I'll see you shortly."

"You are here in New York?" But it was too late, Isabella had hung up.

"Who was that?" Kesia asked.

"A friend," Lexi answered, but was deep in thought about Isabella being kidnapped and having to go get her in Sweden.

Kesia jumped up when she smelled the fragrance of fresh bread. "Pizzas here!"

Edward came in a moment later with the three boxes. "I bought some root beer, I thought you might like that, Kesia."

"Thanks, sweetened iced tea is my favorite, but I will drink root beer from time to time."

"Edward, you're not going to guess who just called me?"

"Tamara."

"I wish. No. Guess again."

"I give up. Who called?"

Lexi was about to answer, but a bright light shone through the skylight and then disappeared. At the same time, her phone beeped, making her almost jump out of her skin.

"What was that?" Edward said looking up.

"Woo-woo, woo-woo, twilight zone. Creepy," Kesia said.

Lexi's phone beeped again. Looking down at it she read, 'What does a girl with a baby have to do to get inside this place?' "Oh, my God, it's Isabella, she is here." Not waiting for anyone, Lexi ran down the stairs.

Edward looked at Kesia, "That's who called?"

"I did hear her say Isabella earlier, so my guess is yes."

A moment later, Lexi was walking into the great room holding a bundle of joy in her arms. With his mama not too far behind. "Edward, would you be so kind to bring Isabella's things into one of the guest bedrooms? She'll be staying with us."

"Sure." Edward looked at Lexi and then at Isabella, "Congratulations."

"Thank you, Edward. It is nice to see you again."

"You too," he said, as he walked by her.

"And who might this be?" Isabella smiled at the girl who looked star-struck.

Looking over to where Isabella was looking, Lexi said, "Oh my, how rude of me. Isabella, please meet Kesia. Kesia, you can close your mouth now."

Blinking, Kesia pinched herself. "I can't believe I am standing in the same room with a famous movie star."

Lexi snapped her fingers, "Kesia, snap out of it. You're embarrassing me."

"It's okay, Lex. I am used to it."

Coming closer to Kesia, Lexi directed, as she passed Aias to her "Here, sit down and hold the baby. His name is Aias."

Clicking out of her star-struck trance, Kesia put her arms out and instantly forgot about Isabella when she looked at the beautiful little boy.

"Here, sit. You must be tired," Lexi pulled a chair over closer to Kesia for Isabella to sit next to them.

Edward came back into the room. "Nice chopper, of course you would ride in style."

"It seemed urgent that I get here as fast as possible."

"Uh-huh, I suppose it was." Seeing Lexi kneeling on the other side of Kesia so she could look at the baby, Edward said, "I'll get furniture in here tomorrow, I promise." He quickly went and retrieved a couple more chairs from another bedroom.

A few moments later, as he placed a couple slices of pizza on a plate for himself, Edward asked, "Isabella do you want some pizza, it's still warm?"

"Oh, that would be nice, thank you. Just one slice please."

"What kind, veggie, Hawaiian, or all meat?"

"Normally I would say all meat, but since I have had Aias, I can't stand meat."

"Yes!" Kesia said almost waking the baby. Moving the blanket, she saw his ears. Stunned she looked at Lexi.

Lexi looked over just as Edward passed a plate to Isabella.

"I see he has his daddy's ears," Edward said as if it was normal.

Kesia looked at Isabella, "You're Erland's Isabella. I should have put it together sooner. Man, does that guy have it bad for you."

Just as she was about to take a bite, staring at Kesia, Isabella said, "You know about Erland?"

"Know about him, I met him."

"You met him? Lexi, what is she talking about?"

"That is part of the long story."

"Start talking."

"Well, where do I begin?"

"Alexandra, just tell her the important parts. Oh, forget it. Isabella, the three of us went to Alfheim with Tamara. That is where we lost her and where we met up with Erland. He says hi by the way."

Isabella dropped her plate. It shattered on the floor making the baby cry. Taking the baby from

Kesia, Isabella said, "Shh, now, now. Mama is sorry, she was just surprised, that's all." Looking at Edward, she said, "Go on."

Lexi got up to clean the floor. "Edward, where can I find a broom?"

"Here, I'll go get it. I think you should answer Isabella's questions."

"Lex? What the heck is going on?"

Tears started to well up in Lexi's eyes. "Isabella, it is all a mess. Tamara was so upset over Greg that she insisted on going to speak with Freyja about changing her future."

"What happened to Greg?"

"Oh, my goodness, that is a really long story. Let's just say that he is not a good guy."

Kesia added, "And my uncle."

"Holy cow, a girl goes away to have a baby and all hell breaks loose. So, what did Redington do about Tamara? I assume he is looking for her."

"He is. He is also looking for Greg, he is at large."

"What did he do, kill someone?"

Kesia answered, "Yes, a friend of mine."

"I was joking." Looking at Lexi she said, "No way."

"Unfortunately, yes."

"Why?"

"For some tarot cards."

"Tarot cards?"

Lexi nodded.

Kesia said, "They were my mother's, and she gave them to me. He kept saying that the cards had special powers and that he had been searching for them for decades."

Shaking her head in disbelief. "Wow."

As Edward came back into the room with the broom he said, "Hey, I was just thinking about what Erland told me while the girls were with the queen. Have you noticed if he has any special powers yet?"

Isabella looked up. "What?

Chapter 61

It had been a week since Lexi told him about Tamara being missing, and still no sign of her.

Picking up his phone Redington called her.

"Well, it is about time," Lexi said, answering his call.

"Nice to talk to you too, Miss Constantine. Always a pleasure."

"You haven't returned my texts. I need to go and water Tamara's plants."

"Ya, I am working on it."

"Not fast enough. They will be dead before I get there at this rate."

"Hey, did Isabella call you?"

"Actually, she is here in New York. She had a boy. Why?"

"She called Tamara a million times."

"And you didn't call me, what if it was an emergency?"

"Hey, don't get mad at me, I don't make the rules. A boy, huh. Good for her."

"So, why did you call? It wasn't to tell me about Isabella, that we know."

"I was checking in on Kesia, how is she doing?"

"She is doing great. She is a natural babysitter. She adores him, ears and all."

"What ears and all? Do his ears stick out, you know they can operate on that now?" He thought back to when he was a kid. His own ears stuck out so far that the other kids called him 'bat ears.'

"Ah, not out."

"Not out? Then in?"

"No. Up."

"Up?"

"Yep, like a Vulcan. To be precise, like an elf."

"You're kidding, right?"

"Nope, he has his daddy's ears."

"Alexandra, we're talking about Isabella's baby, right?"

"Yes. He is adorable. Growing so fast. I swear he grew a couple of inches since she got here."

"I thought Hans was the father?"

"He is."

"You mean, he was?"

"No, I mean he is."

"Alexandra, he's dead."

"I know."

"Then why are you saying it?"

"His soul moved on into Erland's body."

"Alexandra, you say that as if it is normal. Who is Erland again?"

"The elf I told you about in Alfheim."

"No, you told me you went to the land of the fairies. What the heck am I saying. Man, now you have me talking like that is normal."

"Come see for yourself if you don't believe me. Actually, that is a brilliant idea. Then you have to believe our story."

Redington took a breath. *Here we go again.* "Alexandra, I don't believe in elves."

"You didn't believe in demons or ghosts either, but they were real."

"Honestly, Alexandra, elves. You want me to believe in elves?"

"You'll see."

"I am on my way."

Hanging up his phone he carefully got into his car because of his sore knee and started the engine. *What crazy stuff can she get me into this time?*

Traffic was a bit slow, so it took him longer than he hoped to get to Edward's place.

It was still business hours at the funeral home, so he just walked right in, nodding at the receptionist who poked her head out to say hi. He moved his coat aside so she could see his badge. "Is Edward in his office?"

"No, Detective, he is upstairs with the others. He said he was expecting you. Go right on up."

Opening the carved wood door, he was fascinated with the marble stairway. It looked like a cascading river of black gold running down from the top. Each step matched the next. *Fancy, pancy.* Moving faster, he took two steps at a time.

Isabella was at the top of the stairway waiting for him. "Hey, big guy, how have you been?" She gave him a hug once he was at the top.

"Iss, nice to see you. Wow, you look great! No one would ever know that you just gave birth a week ago."

"Thanks, Red, that is very kind of you."

Slipping her arm through his, she guided him over to the others. Kesia was holding Aias.

"So, this is the bundle of joy Alexandra was talking about." He stopped in his tracks. The sunlight was coming through the skylight and was shining on the baby's face. It wasn't sparkly like a diamond or the sun, but shimmered an opalescence radiance like moonlight.

"Beautiful, isn't he?" Lexi said as she saw the look on his face. "And here, look." Lexi moved the hair away from Aias's ears.

"Redington's eyebrows went up. He looked at Lexi then at Isabella, "She wasn't kidding, they are pointed at the top. They do look like elf ears. You can always get them operated on. I had mine done when I was a kid."

"You had pointed ears?" Isabella asked.

"No. More like elephant ears. Mine were enormous. So big I could have flown with them."

Lexi went over and looked at Redington's ears. "He isn't lying, there are stitch marks."

Swiping a hand at Lexi, Redington said, "Hey, back off, boundaries. Edward is in the room, he'll get jealous."

Edward commented with a "Ha, ha."

"So, you want me to believe he is an elf?"

"You can believe whatever you like," Lexi said. "But the truth is the truth."

"No. In the eyes of the law, the facts are the truth."

"Okay, two can play at that game. Tell me this then detective. Why does his skin glow like the sun?"

Redington had to think about that one. "I am sure there is a scientific explanation about that."

"And, what about how fast he is growing. He was eight pounds ten ounces a week ago, and now he is fourteen pounds."

"Ah, I would have to check with a doctor. I am sure it happens."

"He should be about the same weight as when he was born. Most babies lose weight at birth then start to gain it back shortly after. In a week he looks like he is five months old," Lexi exclaimed. "His dad became an elf and somehow that transferred to him."

"Alexandra, I am sure there is a perfectly good explanation that any doctor could tell you. I am sure he is human."

"Half-human," Kesia piped up. "Or half-elf, depending on who you are talking to."

"Hey, missy, don't take that tone with me," Redington smiled at her. "How have you been, kiddo?"

"Good. I miss my mom though. Can I go see her soon?"

"Ah, I'll get back to you on that one. Are they treating you good here?"

"Better than good. It is like I am one of them."

"Good."

"Red, we have to talk seriously about Tamara," Lexi said, motioning for him to come and sit on the couch that Edward had bought last week.

"About that. I haven't heard anything yet. I am looking, but nothing has come up about her vanishing."

"The cops aren't worried about her being abducted by Greg?" Lexi said in a voice a bit higher than normal.

"We don't know that. For all the cops know, you guys could be at fault."

"What? That is ludicrous! Why would we do something to our friend?" Lexi was panicking now. She never thought that she could be a suspect. "Oh, my God. Redington, you have to find her."

"I'm working on it. Have you found that fairy door yet?"

"You believe in the fairy door now?"

"Nope. Just checking."

"No, we haven't."

"Why can't you use a different one?"

Lexi looked at the others, "We hadn't thought of that."

"Just saying, as crazy as it sounds, maybe you could get some answers."

"Good idea. Edward, do you think you could have your carpenters make us a door. I am sure it doesn't have to be fancy."

"Draw me what you are thinking, and I'll get it done first thing tomorrow."

"Well, now that I know you guys are all okay, I'll be on my way."

"So fast Detective, you can't join us for dinner?" Isabella said as she laid on one of her award-winning smiles.

Smiling, Redington stroked the baby's head and said, "Maybe some other time." As he moved his hand away, he thought he felt a surge of electricity zap from the baby through to his fingers. Shaking it off, he said, "See y'all later."

Getting into his car, it took him a moment to notice but the pain he was having in his knee from twisting it the other day while on an investigation, was gone. Shaking his leg, nothing, no pain in his knee. *That's weird.*

Chapter 62

The next day Edward had one of the carpenters make a fairy door, saying that it was a gift for the baby.

Passing the tiny door to Lexi, Edward admitted, "I had to tell a white lie."

"Why?"

"I was embarrassed to tell the carpenter the truth."

"What would you tell a parishioner to do if they confessed a sin?"

"A priest would tell the penitent to repeat a prayer so many times.

"Why would someone go tell their sins to a priest?" Kesia asked.

"For spiritual healing and for the purpose of receiving absolution," Edward said, answering her.

"Does a person only confess their sin if it is for lying?" Kesia asked innocently, not having a religious upbringing.

"No. First, note that a priest is Catholic, and the person could confess if they lie, cheat, steal, or even murder."

"Isn't that kind of crazy?" Kesia said, shaking her head. "How does a person who commits murder get absolution?"

"This topic was another one I had to study in seminary school. Catholics believe that sinning not only breaks God's laws, like in the Ten Commandments but wounds the sinner spiritually. It's like the person's soul is infected with millions of deadly germs."

"Okay, that is weird," Kesia said as her eyes widened in disbelief.

"Kesia, if a person believes something, especially if it is ingrained from childhood, that belief is real to them until proven otherwise. If a person grows up all their life practicing confession, then after the priest forgives their sins, their soul will shed the weight of their suffering."

"So, all Greg has to do is go to a priest and confess that he killed Trina and he is forgiven?"

Edward raised an eyebrow in recognition of her question. "Only God can forgive a person for their sins. A priest will give him or her a penance to perform. A penance can be something like being nice to your enemy or to volunteer every day for a week. It may be to visit a nursing home or hospital one day a week for a month, or it may involve any one of the corporal or spiritual works of mercy. Usually, it is a set of prayers, such as saying the 'Our Father' or the 'Hail Mary'."

"That's it? Can't a priest go to the cops and report the 'sin'?"

"Many religions practice confession and follow the same rules of confidentiality as a counselor or doctor. Though, a priest is even more bound to secrecy. They cannot even tell the authorities if someone admits they are going to hurt themselves, another, or a child is involved. To be precise, a priest cannot break the seal to save his own life, to protect his good name, to refute a false accusation, to save the life of another, to aid the course of justice (like reporting a crime), or to avert a public calamity. He cannot be compelled by law to disclose a person's confession or be bound by any lawful oath he is asked to take, as in being a witness in a court trial."

"I get it that confessing your burdens can free a person from the pain they are having due to holding it in, but it's not fair that a man like Greg can get away with murder if they don't find him."

Lexi interrupted before Kesia got even more upset. "Edward, I think for your penance you should help Detective Redington for a full day on any case he chooses."

Edward looked over to Lexi, "My sin wasn't that bad." Changing the subject, he said, "What are you going to do with the fairy door?"

To get her mind off of her conversation with Edward, Kesia looked up fairy doors on her phone. "Hey, you guys, did you know that fairy doors first appeared in 1993 in Ann Arbour Michigan as installation art. People from all over the world came and visited so that they could sign quest books in restaurants or leave behind little trinkets in the hope of a dream to come true."

"Cute," Lexi said helping to lighten the heavy aura in the room left behind from the deep conversation they just had.

"This is interesting. They say in the United Kingdom and Ireland it is bad luck to call them by name, so instead they were called Little People or the Hidden People. It says that most nations around the world have their own version of this magical creature. For example, the Cherokee Indians in North Carolina refer to fairies as Yunw Tsunsdi. These little people are effectively elf-like natives. Fairies are also known in Cuba, Asia, Philippines, Greece, New Zealand, Indonesia, Romania, Argentina, Canada, and the Mayans in Mexico have a legend about the Alux (aloosh)."

Lexi was enjoying what Kesia was telling her about the fairies.

"It also says that not only elves but pixies, brownies, gnomes, sprites, leprechauns, goblins, trolls, dwarves, and ogres live in the fairy realm."

Edward, shaking his head, said, "Are you sure we have to go back there?"

"Yes, Edward, we do," Lexi confirmed.

"Hey, Edward. Maybe you weren't lying after all. It says that fairy doors inspire a magical season of the holidays all year round, and ignites the imagination, and behavior control of young children. After we are done with it you can give it to Aias."

Isabella was just walking into the room when she heard her son's name. "What are we giving to my son?"

Kesia answered, "A fairy door. That way not only Edward wasn't lying, but Aisa and you could visit Erland."

"How sweet of you to think of that, Kesia," Isabella said, taking the fairy door from Lexi. "So, how exactly does this work?"

Chapter 63

"Are you sure you want to look after Aias for me Kesia?" Isabella said feeling a bit anxious as she was about to let someone else look after her son for the first time.

"Of course," Kesia said as she wiggled her finger under his chin. "Who wouldn't want to look after this cutie pie." Speaking to the baby she said, "Right Aias, you are the cutest baby ever."

Isabella looked at Kesia holding her baby.

"Go! He'll be alright. I promise." Kesia ordered.

Lexi touched Isabella's shoulder. "She'll look after him, Iss. It will be alright."

Isabella nodded her head yes, even though her heart said no.

"Kesia, I want you to take this fairy door with you wherever you go. Don't let it out of your sight," Lexi said sternly.

"Is there a reason I have to protect the door?"

"I am not sure, exactly, but my gut just tells me that it is important."

"Whatever you want Lexi. I'll protect it as if it was a second baby."

"Great. Okay gang we are ready to go. I'll say a little relaxation meditation to get us started and then we will focus on the fairy door and go through it. Once there I will call our flying friends to take us to Erland."

Edward placed the fairy door against a wall and sat on the couch in the living room between Lexi and Isabella.

"Okay, take a deep breath and relax your body. Get yourself comfortable on the couch." Lexi paused a moment before continuing. "I am going to count to three. One, in your mind we will hold hands. Edward you will be in the middle holding Isabella's and my hand. Two, we are tiny and able to fit through the fairy door. Three, I open the fairy door, and we safely walk through it."

On the other side of the fairy door. Lexi looked at Edward and Isabella, only to be surprised because Kesia and Aias were with them. "What are you doing here?"

"I don't know. I think Aias has powers. He came through and since I was holding him, so did I."

Isabella took Aias from Kesia. "Hey, you. You want to meet your daddy, don't you."

The baby smiled.

"Did he just smile at you?" Edward asked.

Isabella nodded.

Looking at Lexi, Edward said, "Isn't that a little early for him to be doing that consciously?"

Lexi just shrugged her shoulders. "Don't ask me."

"Well, we're here now, so I might as well come with you guys," Kesia said.

Lexi just stared at Isabella.

"Well Lex, they are here now so we might as well just get started and go find my man."

Lexi nodded. *Phantachus, please come with three of your companions that the others can ride.*

A moment later, Phantachus, Lettfeti, night mare, and a new ride named Gulltaoppr for Isabella and the baby appeared.

The group mounted their rides by thinking to be on their backs.

"This way, follow me," Lexi said to the others as she lightly clicked her heels three times into Phantachus's sides.

They were flying high above the meadow when Freyr riding Skírnismál and Freyja riding Hofvarpnir appeared in front of them, blocking their way.

"You must go back," Freyja said to the group. "It is not safe for you here."

"We are here to see Erland," Lexi said. "We need to find out where Tamara went. Hey, you are who I should be asking. Where is Tamara?"

"She is where she asked to be."

"Where is that?" Lexi asked, not backing down from finding out where she went.

Freyja turned her head behind her, saw what was coming, and said loudly, "You must go back now. That is an order."

Isabella not accustomed to taking orders said, "I demand to see Erland!"

The queen turned her head slowly and looked at Isabella. "Is that Erland's baby?"

Isabella held on tighter to him. "I do not have to answer you, you are not my queen. I will only speak with Erland."

"You will not find him at his home."

"Why not?" Isabella asked.

"He is at war."

"With whom? Erland wouldn't hurt a fly. I don't believe you."

"You have made things much worse now that you are here. It was bad enough, but to bring the baby, that was foolish."

"What does the baby have to do with anything?" Isabella asked holding Aias even closer.

"He is the reason for the war."

"Enough!" Freyr said cutting them both off from speaking. "We do not have time for this, they will be here soon."

Not understanding the seriousness of the situation, Lexi asked, "Who will be here soon?"

"The dark elves."

Trying to understand what was going on Lexi confirmed what she thought she heard, "The dark elves started a war because of Aias?"

"Yes. Erland broke the rules, and the dark elves are after the baby. If they find him here, you will lose him forever," Freyr replied getting frustrated that these mortals weren't leaving.

"I don't understand," Lexi said. "What does a tiny human baby have to do with starting a war?"

"Half-elf," Freyr said. "The baby is a half-elf and lives in the mortal world. That is forbidden."

"Isabella, I think we better leave. We can't take a chance that Aias could be hurt," Lexi said as she motioned for Phantachus to turn around.

Isabella nodded her head and motioned for Gulltaoppr to turn around when Erland appeared riding a fire dragon.

"Isabella, what are you doing here. It is not safe."

"Hans." As she thought him, she and the baby were in his arms. Hugging him as to never let him go. "Looking down she said, "This is your son, Aias."

Erland knowing that Isabella would always think of his soul as Hans, looked down at his son. Tears welled up as he brushed a finger over his son's. Aias grabbed on to Erland's finger and held tight.

Frantically, Freyja said, "Erland you must take them back now before it is too late."

Looking at his queen, he nodded. He whistled and the fire dragon disappeared into thin air.

Lexi screamed, "Oh, my God, where did they go?"

But it was too late for her, Edward, and Kesia to escape.

Coming fast towards them was a flock of phoenixes carrying Dökkálfar warriors—dark elves with ghostly pale skin, glowing red eyes, and clad in blue-grey armor.

Mesmerized by the vision in front of her, Kesia said out loud, "The German word for nightmare is Albtaum. It means 'elf dream.' It is believed that nightmares were a result of an elf sitting on the dreamer's chest."

"Kesia, snap out of it," Edward said concerned for her sanity.

"Edward," Lexi said, "They look like vampires, their skin is so pale."

Freyr's army of fairies and light elves appeared between them and the dark elves, guarding their King.

Freyja said quietly, "They are very brutal and cruel by nature, having little mercy when it comes to cheating, battling, or anything dealing with the life of another being. They have little respect for even their own kind. We must be on guard. Our lives are at stake."

"Edward leaned over and said to Lexi, "Honestly Lexi, if this wasn't a dream, I would be really upset with you right now."

Freyja turned to Edward, "Are you mad? If you get hurt here, you will feel it when you get back to your realm. If you die here, you will be dead in both realms."

Edward was now scared for their lives.

The leader of the dark elves sent a telepathic message that all could understand, *I am Aelfric, I hereby order you to stand down.*

Freyr answered, "You are trespassing on our land. I demand that you surrender, and we will allow you to return to your world unharmed."

Aelfric laughed. *You are outnumbered, ten to one. We would slaughter you. Give us the half-elf and we will spare your lives.*

Knowing that Erland had taken Isabella and the baby away, Freyr said, "I am the King of Alfheim, a God from Vanaheim, you do not want me to bring the wrath of the gods down upon you."

Aelfric considered his options and knew that the old laws were stronger than a King, god or not. *If you protect this child, then you are considered a traitor to our ways and will be held accountable for this child's welfare, actions, and secrecy. Are you prepared to pay the price for this half-elf?*

Freyr knew the laws, the first and most foundational law, the Law of Divine Oneness—the interconnectedness of all things. Law of Vibration—everything is in constant motion. Law of Correspondence—as above, so below. As within, so without. Law of Attraction—like attracts like. Law of Inspired Action—real, actionable steps to invite what we want into our lives. Law of Perpetual Transmutation of Energy—everything in the universe is constantly evolving or fluctuating. Law of Cause and Effect—the direct relation between actions and events. Law of Compensation—you reap what you sow. Law of Relativity—in reality, everything is neutral. Law of Polarity—everything in life has an opposite; good and evil, love and fear, warmth and cold. Law of Rhythm—cycles are a natural part of the universe. Law of Gender—everything has its masculine (yang) and feminine (yin) principles. He knew that the law Aelfric was referring to was the law of Cause and Effect. Aias was going to cause a ripple effect in the human world. "I am," he replied.

So be it. As of today, let it be known, that King Freyr has declared the birthrights of a half-elf in the realm of Earth. He has stated that he will be solely responsible for the cause and effect this will have in that world.

With that said, the dark elves retreated and disappeared from where they had come.

Edward looked at Lexi, and then at the King. "So, does that mean we can go home?"

Freyr looked over at Lexi, Kesia, and Edward. "I am granting you three to be the guardians of Aias. Keep his powers from the mortals a secret at all costs." And then the King, Queen, and all his army vanished into thin air.

Edward sat on night mare and looked around him. "Alexandra, I think we had better get back to our world."

Lexi clicked her heels three times and the three of them were back at the fairy door. Thank you Phantachus," Lexi thought as she petted his nose. Lightly kissing his head, she said to the others, "hold hands we are going home."

Chapter 64

Once back at Edward's, Lexi was relieved to see that Isabella and Aias were sitting there on the couch waiting for them to wake up from the meditation.

"Oh my God!" moving over to hug Isabella, Lexi squealed, "I thought you might have disappeared like Tamara. Thank God you are okay. I don't know what I would have told Redington."

After hugging Lexi, Isabella cleared her throat, "I have to tell you all something."

"Great. Just great." Edward's happiness to see Isabella and the baby turned instantly defensive. "What is it this time? I am not sure what else I can handle. God is pushing me to my limit."

Isabella looked at Edward and said, "And they call me a drama queen."

Lexi lightly hit Edward's shoulder. "Go on Isabella, Edward can handle it."

"Hans is here. I mean Erland."

Edward's mouth dropped open. Kesia clapped her hands and Lexi started to look around.

"Where?" Lexi asked startled.

"How?" Edward said at the same time.

"I do not know all the details of how it works. All I know is that he brought Aias and me through the fairy door, and stayed with us."

Kesia looked at Edward and Lexi with eyes that meant, get it together you guys. "That is wonderful for you, Isabella."

"Great another ghost," Edward remarked. A second later he felt a hand grip his right shoulder. "What the? Fine. You are welcome to stay here too Erland. Just don't scare my clients."

Kesia started to laugh uncontrollably.

Edward looked over at her. "What is so funny about that?"

Kesia between breaths said, "Your clients are dead, what could a ghost do to them?"

Edward's face went red. "You know what I mean."

Edward felt a couple of hard taps on his bicep.

Isabella laughed, "Erland is chuckling. He thinks you are funny."

Humiliated, Edward got up and walked over to the kitchen. "Anyone want a coffee?"

Lexi quickly got up, "I'll come and help you."

Once in the kitchen, Lexi asked, "Hey, what do you think the king meant about the Law of Cause and Effect?"

Edward finished pouring the water into the coffeemaker and pushed the button. "In seminary school, they taught us that in the Bible it refers to the Law of Sowing and Reaping. Galatians 6:7-8 says, 'God is not to be fooled, whatever someone sows, that is what he will reap. If his sowing is in the field of self-indulgence, then his harvest from it will be corruption. If his sowing is in the Spirit, then his harvest from the Spirit will be eternal life.'"

"I forgot for a moment that I was going to marry a minister. Of course, you would refer to a Bible verse," Lexi hugged him as she said it.

Kesia had heard their conversation as she walked into the kitchen. "So, what you are saying is that if a person smokes, he may develop a cough or cancer. If he overspends, he may go hungry or bankrupt. But, if he eats right and budgets wisely, he will have money for his groceries and live a long life."

"Are you sure you are only sixteen?" Lexi asked.

"Almost seventeen," Kesia beamed.

Edward smiled and agreed with Lexi's remark by nodding. "At school, one of the classes we had to take was a counseling course. We learned that the Law of Sowing and Reaping can be interrupted. People can interfere by stepping in and rescuing irresponsible people. A person who continually rescues another person is considered codependent and healthy boundaries are repeatedly broken."

Isabella yelled from the other room, "Erland says to tell you that your thoughts, behaviors, words, and actions create specific effects that manifest and create your life as you know it. Each and every decision you make and action you have taken has set events into motion creating predictable and specific effects that you are now experiencing in your lives."

Kesia added to the conversation, "My mom used to talk about this, but she called it a Sanskrit word, Karma. Which means action, work, or deed and refers to the sum of all deeds done through the person's mind, speech or body. . . either in this life or in a previous life."

Isabella yelled again while holding Aias up as he pretended to walk. "Erland says, every human thought, word, and deed is a Cause that sets off a wave of energy or vibration throughout the universe, which in turn creates the Effect whether desirable or undesirable. This vibration not only affects our thinking, but it also travels outwards and creates responses from those it's directed towards, which then manifest their reactions right back at us. In other words, even though you might not voice a specific emotion, your thoughts create a vibrational emotional energy towards something or someone, and you

can't stop this vibration once you've released it.
. . such as the phenomena of Cause and Effect."

Edward shook his head and looked at Lexi, "It must be my destiny to experience all this craziness."

Isabella yelled over again, "Erland says that people tend to think of destiny as something unavoidable and unchangeable, but destiny is affected by Cause and Effect, which means that you influenced your destiny, Edward. He says to think of your thoughts as lined up dominos. Whichever domino you knocked over first, or thought first, will trigger the downfall of the next, and so forth."

"So, what you are saying is that if Susannah, Alexandra's sister, didn't get buried at my cemetery, our path would not have turned out like this?"

Isabella spoke the words as Erland was telling her, "If you don't throw the pebble in the pond in the first place, there'll be no ripple."

"I think she means that if you didn't think the thought, or take the action, it couldn't have manifested," Kesia said trying to decipher the meaning of Erland's words.

Edward looked at Kesia, "Ya, I got it. Thanks."

"Just trying to help," Kesia said forgetting that some people don't like being reminded of simple facts. "I am sure Erland meant all of our thoughts and actions, not just yours."

Isabella yelled again, "Erland says that if we are not happy with the Effects we have created, then we must change the Causes that created them in the first place. You can do that by transforming your thoughts, which will change your actions, therefore you will start creating a new life."

A light bulb went off in Kesia's head, "I get it! Freyr rescued us by accepting the consequences of a half-elf living amongst the mortals, Cause and Effect, every action has an outcome."

"Really? Sixteen," Edward said as he lovingly took hold of her shoulder.

Lexi put her hand to her mouth. "Oh my God, Edward. Freyr stopped a war to save not only us but his people. He is counting on us to accept and honor the responsibility to be Aias's guardians."

The three of them looked over to the baby, who looked like he was about to take a step on his own.

"He can't do that, he isn't even three months old," Lexi whispered. What have we gotten ourselves into this time?"

Chapter 65

Lexi's phone rang as Aias took a step. Freaked out because he was so young to be able to do that, she fumbled with her phone, "Hello."

"Alexandra, where are you right now?"

Lexi heard the fear in Redington's voice. "I am at Edward's watching the baby take a step by himself. Why? What's up?"

"I'll be right over."

"O. . .kay," but he had already hung up.

Anticipating where she was, within minutes Redington was walking into the funeral home and up the stairs. As he entered the living quarters he said, "I need you all to have a seat."

"Well, hi to you too," Lexi said sarcastically. "It is always a pleasure."

Redington waved at her to have a seat. "I don't have time for pleasantries. Kesia, it is your mom. She is in the hospital."

Kesia stood up. "What?"

"We just got word at the precinct that there was a break-in at her house, and she is beaten up pretty bad."

"I have to get to her."

"I would take you, but I am still on duty."

"Lexi, can you take me?"

Edward cut in. "I'll drive."

"You're not leaving without me," Isabella said dialing a number on her phone. "I need a limo that can fit six at this address." She gave the person on the other end Edward's address.

"Six?" Who else is coming?" Lexi asked.

"Erland."

"Whose Erland?" Redington asked confused.

Lexi looked over. "Remember, I told you about the elf in Alfheim. Erland is Hans, Isabella's Hans."

"He is here?"

"It is a long story."

Isabella's phone beeped. "Our ride is here."

"That's impossible?" Redington stated.

"Hey, when you have money, anything is possible, and who said we were driving. The chopper is waiting for us outside. Everyone, go get what you will need for a day or two, and meet me outside in five."

"I can't pack in five minutes," Lexi mumbled as she took off for her room.

"Then you will be left behind," Isabella called out as she picked up Aias and his baby bag.

Lexi was out of breath as she ran to the chopper. "Oh my God. I made it."

As the helicopter took off, Lexi put her head on Edward's shoulder and closed her eyes.

The hum of the propellers was hypnotic, and she went into a deep trance state.

Lexi, you must pay attention. Lexi was dreaming that Susannah was talking to her. They were playing in the yard. She was about five and remembered this moment. Susannah was pushing her on the swings. She was pumping her feet so she would go higher when Susannah stopped pushing.

Hey, why did you stop Susannah? I want to go higher.

She remembered her sister's response.

You can do it on your own now Lexi, you don't need me. Ask and you will receive. Cause and Effect.

Susannah disappeared from the dream.

Tears welled up in Lexi's eyes as she wept for her sister.

Bath Kol, you are the voice of God, are you not?

Yes.

I am sad.

Why?

Because of all that happens around me. Things that I cannot change even though I want to.

How do you mean?

Like Aias. He is an innocent child, born to circumstance. He does not deserve the coming torment of others.

Lexi, remember that he has chosen his life path. It is his right to live it.

But what if I know it will be a hard path and there is another, a much easier one. It breaks my heart that I cannot take his hand and lead him down it.

Why do you think you cannot help him?

I am not his mother. I have no rights to him. Even if I were his grandmother, I have no rights to help.

How do you know this?

It is a human law that only the guardian has control of the welfare of the child. Unless it is sexual or physical abuse, I cannot help him or his mother unless asked, even if she were to end up in a psych ward. Unless she gives the authorities written consent for me to know something or help her, I wouldn't be allowed to.

And this is what makes you sad?

Lexi thought about it. *Does God know that this is a messed-up system?*

Cause and Effect is a universal law. God knows better than anyone. Don't you think that he can see a clear path and the answers for each and every soul? That if he had a human heart, it would break seeing his children go through their trials. Even he cannot act unless someone asks.

I never thought of it like that. But? A child has a voice and may ask, but the parent, no matter if they are sane or have undiscovered genetic mental issues is still in control of that child's welfare until the child is of age. There has to be a better way.

Lexi, each soul's path is unique. Only that soul's subconscious knows why it chose that life's path.

But what happens when it hurts so bad because you have no control to help?

Ask God to learn your lesson early and have the ability to shift your thoughts, words, behaviors, and outcomes to pleasant ones that serve your higher purpose.

Is it that easy?

Lexi, your past predicts your future, and your present creates your past. Change your present actions and your past will change, creating a brighter more successful future.

Lexi's body bumped and woke her out of her trance state as the helicopter landed. *I wonder why those thoughts were in my head?*

Susannah's voice came into her mind, *Prophecy comes in many forms, Lexi.*

Chapter 66

The helicopter landed on the roof of the hospital.

"Who knew there was a hospital in Jersey Shore?" Edward stated. "I thought it was a resort town."

Kesia informed him by saying, "It opened as a private hospital in the early 1900s, but was recently taken over by a family, and now serves the residents of western Lycoming and eastern Clinton counties." Barely finishing her sentence and almost flying out of her seat, Kesia jumped out as soon as the pilot opened the door.

Lexi and the others had to run to keep up.

"You guys go ahead, I'll meet you shortly," Isabella said not being able to run after her.

Lexi turned and nodded.

Lexi and Edward saw the direction Kesia had gone and tried to keep up. They entered Kesia's mom's room just as Florence opened a swollen eye.

"Mom. What happened?" Kesia gently grabbed her mom's hand, holding it tenderly.

Florence couldn't talk. There were tubes coming out of her mouth.

A nurse came in hearing the beep from Florence's monitor. "Hey, what are you all doing here, this is a restricted area?"

"I am her daughter," Kesia said with tears streaming from her eyes.

Florence tried to say something but only winced as she moved.

"Okay, everyone out. Your mom needs her sleep. You can come back in when she is out of her critical condition. There is a waiting room just over there." The nurse pointed. "You can see her room, and I will come regularly to tell you how she is doing."

Edward helped Kesia out of her mom's room. "Kesia, we are here now, your mom will be okay. Let the nurse do her job. We only want the best for your mom, come on I'll help you."

Kesia nodded and allowed Edward to guide her to the waiting area.

Isabella walked in as a nurse came and gave something to Kesia.

"What is it?" Isabella asked. "What did I miss?"

Kesia opened the brown paper bag, stuck her hand in, and pulled out something she knew all to well. Her deck of tarot cards. "Do you think they were after these again? Do you think Greg has something to do with this?"

"Lexi, I think you should call Redington. I think he should know what we have," Isabella said as she looked at the cards.

"That might be a good idea."

"Hey, and ask him to send a guard to stand outside Florence's room."

Lexi looked at her friend. "Do you think she is still in danger?"

"Let's not take a chance."

Lexi walked over to a more private area to call.

Kesia shuffled the cards while thinking about her mother's welfare. She turned over the seven of pleasures. In the Rider deck, it would be the seven of cups. Kesia knew when this card appeared it meant a temptation was being offered, but it was a temporary pleasure that could lead to permanent damage.

Isabella asked, "What does that mean?"

Kesia looked over and said, "My mom needs to stay strong in her beliefs, no matter what is being offered to her."

"That sounds serious."

Kesia looked at the card. "It is."

"Do you know what she will be offered?"

Kesia picked another card. Her face went white as a ghost.

"What? What did you pick?"

Kesia turned over the god Mercury.

"What does that mean?"

"It is equivalent to the death card."

"Oh, Kesia, I am sorry. I am sure it means something else," Isabella said as she gave Aias his bottle. "Turn over another one. This time ask what we can do."

It was the seven of riches.

"What does that mean?"

"We wait."

Lexi put a hand on Kesia's knee. "Hey, you, don't go there. We can win this war."

Kesia made a weak smile.

"Pick a card. It will be how we do this."

She turned over the King of Riches just as the doctor came over.

"Kesia, your mom needs an operation to stop the internal bleeding, it is very risky and very expensive."

Isabella and Lexi spoke at the same time. "I'll pay for it."

The doctor looked over and smiled. "You have great friends Kesia, your mom is in good hands."

A moment later, Kesia watched as her mom was wheeled to the operating room.

Lexi tapped her knee again. "She'll be alright. You'll see." Lexi didn't know why she was saying something that most would say was foolish, but somehow she knew that Florence was going to be alright.

Just as the gurney was being wheeled past the group, Aias flung himself onto Florence, grabbing at her hand.

Barely able to move, Florence felt his tiny fingers around hers. There was heat like no other she had ever felt.

Isabella scrambled to gain control and pull her son back.

"That was weird," Lexi said.

Isabella looked at her in shock. "You will never believe what Erland just said."

Chapter 67

Lexi was waiting for Isabella to divulge what Erland said when her phone rang. "Wait, don't tell anyone without me. I have to take this, it's Redington."

"Alexandra, It's about Tamara."

"Redington, you do know that hello is usually said before talking."

"If I had time to wait for all the hellos, I would get nothing done in a day. Do you want to hear what I have to say or not?"

"Of course."

"We arrested one of Genovese's men yesterday. I can't tell you all the details but during the interrogation, he mentioned that his part was to help a Julian D'Angelo leave the country."

"Did he say where he had taken him?"

"Bangalore, India."

"Wow, that is an interesting place to decide to escape to."

"With over a billion people in the country and over eight million in that city alone, he could disappear, and no one would find him."

"I see."

"How is Kesia doing?"

"She is holding up, but her mom is in the operating room as we speak. She might not make it."

"Let's hope it doesn't come to that."

"Do you think Greg, I mean Julian, had anything to do with Florence's break-in?"

"Maybe. Genovese's man said something else that I found intriguing. No one else listening to his confession caught what he was actually saying."

"Don't keep me in suspense, what did he say?"

"He mentioned that his boss needed cards."

"Wow, what did you guys offer or have to do to him for him to reveal so much?"

"That, my dear Scarlet, is a trade secret."

"Cards, huh. Interesting. Red, Kesia has the cards."

"She does?"

"Yes, they were with her mom here at the hospital."

"That means you guys are in danger. Has the officer arrived yet to guard Florence's room?"

Lexi looked. "No, I don't see anyone yet."

"Okay, Alexandra, he will be there shortly."

"Great. You know what is best. If you think she needs protecting, then I trust your instincts."

"Take care will ya, and don't get killed today."

"Thanks for the words of encouragement. I will keep that in mind."

"Lex, I mean it. I don't know what I would do if you died."

"Lex? Well, this is serious, you never call me by my nickname. It almost feels like you have a heart."

"I mean it. Take care of yourself and don't do anything stupid."

Lexi took a breath. *What if I had met him first?* "Don't worry, Edward will look after me."

That burned a bit. He hated being reminded of him. "Ya, his cross will ward off all kinds of evil."

"Funny. But you might be on to something. I will remember to use a cross if I need protection."

"Alexandra, I have to go, but call me when you find anything out about Florence's wellbeing."

"I will, and detective."

"Ya."

"Thanks for caring."

Redington's heart melted. *If she only knew.* "Just doing my job."

"Uh-huh."

The line went dead.

"So, what did Redington have to say?" Isabella asked.

Kesia and Edward looked over and listened.

"He said that Greg is in India."

"India?" repeated Edward.

"Bangalore, to be precise."

"What could possibly be in India that would make Greg want to go there?" Edward asked out loud.

"Beats me," Isabella answered.

Just as Kesia was going to say something the doctor walked up to them.

"It's a miracle. Your mom made it through the operation with flying colors. She is going to make it."

Kesia hugged the doctor. "Thank you so very much!"

"My pleasure. You can see her in a few minutes. The nurse will come and get you when it's time."

"Awesome. Thanks again."

Edward shook the doctor's hand before he left. "Thank you."

"That is good news Kesia, I told you she would be alright," Lexi said giving Kesia a hug.

"Okay, okay. I am dying to tell you," Isabella said excitedly.

"Lexi let go of Kesia and turned to Isabella. "Oh ya, Erland told you something. What was it?"

"That it was Aias's touch that healed Florence."

Edward made the sign of the cross.

Lexi stood there confused. "What do you mean?"

"His touch. It has magical healing powers."

"Are you sure?" Lexi said still not believing what she was hearing.

"Yes, Erland told me. It is the main ability of an elf."

"Fascinating. Can he heal anyone?"

"No. He is far too young for that, but maybe when he is older."

Lexi stood there staring at the baby who in only a few weeks looked like he was almost two. *God works in mysterious ways.*

Chapter 68

"She is sitting up, you guys can come in now," Kesia said to the others.

Edward, Lexi, Isabella, and Aias walked into Florence's room.

"Mom, these are the people I have been talking about." Kesia introduced them all to her mom.

"Nice to meet you all. Thank you for taking such good care of my daughter."

"It's our pleasure," Edward said. "You've raised quite a remarkable girl."

"Thank you. I think so too." Florence smiled at Kesia.

The nurse came in and checked on Florence. "You are the buzz around here Florence."

"What do you mean?"

"You are a miracle. The doctor said you are going to be released today. He can't believe how fast you healed. It is like God himself touched you. Even your bruises are almost gone."

Florence forced a smile as the nurse checked her over.

When the nurse left, Florence confessed, "I really don't understand it myself. I was on death's door yesterday and today I am walking out of here."

Isabella smiled, knowing her son helped save a person's life.

"Mom, there is something I need to tell you."

"Yes dear, what is it?"

"I am going to India."

The whole group turned from Florence to stare at Kesia.

"What?" They all said at once.

"Greg is there, and I need this to be over with. They are not going to stop coming after the cards. We have to do something. I can't let him hurt you again." Tears started to run down her face.

"No, you are not going to India," Florence commanded.

"Mom, I am not a child anymore. Plus, we have family there. I can stay with them."

"You have family in India?" Edward asked.

"Yes. Mom did our ancestry online and we both did a DNA test a few years ago. I have been conversing through email and zoom with many family members."

"You don't look Indian," Edward stated.

"Well, you know that I come from a gypsy background. I told you about my ancestral grandmother Clementina."

"Yes, I remember. She is Tatiana's mother," Lexi said. "How could I forget your family. I have your ancestral aunt's 'Archangel Gabriel' painting in my living room."

"Right. Well, gypsies originated from India, and our DNA proves that."

"Fascinating!" Isabella exclaimed. "I can have a jet ready in an hour."

"Wait! There is no way my daughter is going anywhere without me. I almost died. If you are going then so am I."

Lexi could feel the excitement in the room. "Oh my God, we are going to India. How exciting!"

Edward looked over at her. "What are you talking about? I don't want you to go."

"Come on Edward, we only live this life once. Let's go."

Edward looked at his fiancée. *Why do I feel like I am going to have to go with her just to keep her safe?* "Alexandra, I have a business to run and renovations to complete. I don't think we should go." *Our adventures seem to always have a dangerous side to them. Life needs to get back to normal.*

Lexi looked at Edward, then to Kesia, "I'm in."

"Lexi, what about your drawings for work? You still need to work, don't you?" Edward said, trying to keep her here safely in New York with him.

"I can draw from anywhere in the world. My company's employees are all still working from home. As long as I have the internet. I am good to go."

Edward was desperate. "Alexandra, I can't go on like this. You are going to have to choose. Me or these crazy adventures."

Lexi stood still, staring at Edward.

Isabella nudged Edward, "Come on Edward, lighten up. Come with us."

"Isabella, with all due respect. Stay out of this. Alexandra, what are you going to choose?"

Lexi took a breath. *Hey, Sis. He's not bluffing. Think this over carefully.* Lexi took another deep breath and looked at Kesia, Florence, and Isabella, then back at Edward. "Edward, I love you very much and can't wait until we are married, but until then I have to follow my heart. Right now, it is telling me that I need to go with them to India. I pray that you will not hold me to make a decision between you and going because I will choose to go."

Edward's face went white. *She chose to go. I can't believe she chose to go.* Not saying anything, Edward walked out of the hospital room.

Lexi went to go after him, but Isabella grabbed her arm. "Lex, he'll take you back. Just give him time. He loves you and just wants you safe."

"I know. I just wish he didn't react like that. I live in New York City. Anything could happen to me at any time. If it is my time to go it won't matter where I am."

Kesia came over to Lexi. "I understand if you don't want to come. It is okay to stay here Lexi, I really will understand."

Lexi looked at this amazing girl and couldn't imagine not going to help her. It was as if something deep inside of her was telling her to go to India with Kesia. That something important was there waiting for her. As if it was part of her destiny to have this experience. "Thanks, Kesia. That means a lot to me, but I know I am going with you to India. He'll get over it. He loves me." *He'll get over it, right Susannah?* But there was no answer.

Chapter 69

November 06, in India.

The flight over to India was more luxurious than Lexi could have ever imagined. Flying with a multi-millionaire actress was incredible. The plane Isabella chartered was a G6.

Kesia was using a computer on the airplane while it was in flight. "I can't believe you have the internet up here, Isabella."

Isabella answered, "From what I understand, it is being tested. The company has permission from the officials governing the federal communications to test its satellite internet."

"I have been looking up The Gulfstream G650 or better known as the G6. This baby is remarkable. Did you guys know that this long-range jet travels at more than ninety-two percent the speed of sound, delivers an incredible range of seven thousand nautical miles, and since we are on the G650ER, it gets additional five-hundred nautical miles?"

"No," Lexi said smiling at Kesia's inquisitive mind.

"Its cruising speed is five-hundred and sixty-six knots. I wonder how fast we are going?"

"Push that button and ask," Isabella said while feeding Aias, who was spitting out the mashed peas.

Kesia pushed the button.

"Yes, this is the captain, how may I assist you, Miss Jackson?"

"Hi, this is Kesia. Will you kindly tell me what speed we are flying at?"

"Yes, Miss Kesia. We are currently flying at four-hundred and seventy-eight knots. The wind is slowing us down a bit."

"Thank you."

Lexi asked, "Is that good or bad?"

"I am sure the captain knows what he is doing. It is slower than what this plane can do, but I am sure the three of them know what they are doing," Kesia said matter-of-factly.

"The three of them?" Lexi questioned.

"Yes, it says that when crossing the Atlantic, there are always a captain, co-pilot, and an additional pilot."

"Good to know we are well looked after."

Kesia nodded. "Hey, this is interesting. It was published from Bowditch in 1984."

Lexi looked up from the magazine she was about to read to listen.

"The term knot dates back from the 17th century when sailors measured the speed of their ship by using a device called a 'common log.' This device was made from a long piece of rope with equally spaced knots, and attached to one end was a piece of wood shaped like a slice of pie. The end of the rope with the wood attached to it was lowered into the water from the back of the ship and allowed to play out freely from the coil as the piece of wood fell behind the ship for a specific amount of time while it sailed. When the specified time had passed, the rope was pulled back in and the number of knots on the rope between the ship and the wood were counted. The speed of the ship was said to be the number of knots counted. One knot is one nautical mile per hour."

"I did not know that," Lexi said being polite to Kesia. "How far is that compared to a mile?"

"A knot is speed, Lexi. What you are asking is called a nautical mile, which is 1.852 kilometers or 1.1508 miles."

"Oh, well, you can teach an old dog something new. Thanks. I will try to remember that."

Florence cut in. "Kesia, let her rest. I am sure she isn't interested in that kind of stuff."

Kesia looked at Lexi, who mouthed, *It's okay. I like that stuff.*

Kesia smiled but stopped talking so her mom could rest.

Lexi took a moment to look around at the craft they were flying in. Not only was it fast, as she learned from Kesia, but this particular plane's interior was magnificent. Upon entry to the craft and facing down the aisle there are two rows of three swivel chairs, one on the right and two on the left of each row. Lexi found it convenient to be able to turn her chair backward and face Kesia, it made it so easy to talk to As you enter the craft you walk down an aisle that has two rows of three swivel chairs, one on the right and two on the left of each row. Lexi found it convenient to be able to turn her chair backward and face Kesia, it made it so easy to talk to her. She also noticed that a flip-down table could go between the six chairs and make a dining room table.

On her way to the washroom, Lexi walked towards the back of the plane where she noticed there was a console on one side with a TV on it and a comfy couch that could fit three people on the other side of the aisle.

She passed through a state-of-the-art kitchen, where a flight attendant was preparing some food for them. As she entered the bathroom, she was blown away, not only did it look like it was made of gold, it also had a full shower in it. Peeking through an adjoining door, she found a bedroom at the back of the plane.

Coming back to her seat she asked Isabella, "What did this cost you to charter?"

"Almost seventy-two thousand dollars, give or take a few pennies."

"Oh my God, that pays for our trip home, right?"

"No, that is just to Frankfurt. From there we need to gas up and continue on to Bangalore."

"Isabella. What the hey. We could have flown commercial."

"Are you kidding me? I am not taking over forty hours to get there. This flight will only take nineteen."

Lexi sat back and smiled. *To live the life of the rich and famous.* "Thanks, Iss," Lexi smiled at her generous friend.

"What is money for if you can't enjoy it?"

After eating a five-star meal, Lexi closed her eyes.

Hey, Lex, you are going to love India. Susannah said to her.

Why is that? Lexi thought back.

You'll see. Susannah giggled. *And you thought Tamara was intuitive.*

Lexi's heart skipped a beat.

Chapter 70

"*I* texted my cousin, and she will be picking us up from the airport and taking us back to her place," Kesia told the others when they landed.

After passing a thermal screen and pulse oximeter test, the group was allowed entrance into the country.

Bangalore was a metropolis.

As she was reading the information she Googled, Kesia excitedly said, "Hey Lexi? Did you know that Bangalore is in the Karnataka state?" Before Lexi could answer, she added, "It is the capital city, has more people than New York City but in less space, and it is widely regarded as the "Silicon Valley of India."

Smiling, Lexi answered, "I do now."

Zeenat, Kesia's twenty-five-year-old female cousin, had picked them up in a very modern van that could fit all of them and their luggage.

After driving through hectic traffic—even for a New Yorker—Lexi asked her, "How do you like living in Bangalore."

In her thick Indian accent, she replied in well-spoken English, "As a travel agent, here is what I tell my clients. Bangalore is known as the 'garden city,' with its year-round favorable summer weather, stunning parks, and magnificent buildings. It has a perfect mix of modern and authentic traditions, with its advanced technology, backstreet markets, and fascinating culture. Lexi, I love living here."

To Lexi's surprise, Zeenat's home was a contemporary cozy three-bedroom townhouse that her parents owned. They were away on business, so their room was given to Kesia and her mom. Isabella and the baby stayed in the spare room, which was also used as an office, and Lexi was given the hide-a-bed in the living room.

Once everyone was settled in, Lexi said, "I don't know what I was expecting but, I thought India was more of a third-world country."

Zeenat joked, "Were you expecting us to live in tin shacks with cardboard doors?"

"Ah, sort of. I wasn't expecting everything to be so. . . American. . . this looks better than the way many people live in the United States."

"I will take that as a compliment."

"I'm sorry, I didn't mean it as an insult, I was just, ah," Lexi changed her wording, "Media back home makes it out like people in India are very poor."

"Lexi, the average income is around twenty-four thousand a year. To an American that is poverty, but our expenses here are not as high as yours."

"Well, I have had my eyes opened. From now on I will only believe what I see in person. Thank you."

Zeenat smiled at Lexi but said to the whole group. "Before you get too busy with your own purpose for coming here, with Isabella's help I have planned a little sight-seeing adventure starting tomorrow."

Kesia clapped her hands. "So, exciting! I can't wait."

The others were also excited to see India, but Lexi was thrilled to be seeing it through Zeenat's eyes.

The next morning their first stop was back to the airport for a short flight to Delhi. They used a private taxi for the rest of the day. The first place they visited was Sikandra, to see the tomb of Akbar.

Zeenat explained, "Akbar was the third 'Mughal Empire' emperor, who reigned from 1556 to 1605. What might interest you is that he was considered the most famous and enlightened of the Mughal Emperors."

Keisa added from her search on Google, "Lit! Akbar was only thirteen years old when he became emperor. Hey, get this, he was a descendent of Genghis Khan, who was the ruler of the Mongol tribe and Timur ruler of Iran and Iraq. Hey, this is dope too. As tradition, Akbar managed the construction of his own tomb right up until his death, whereas his son had to finish the construction."

"Cool," Lexi commented.

Next, the group explored Fort Agra which belonged to the Mughal Dynasty.

"Built as a military structure in 1565 by Emperor Akbar, with later additions by Shah Jahan, the stunning Agra Fort, also known as Agra's Red Fort, is an interesting mix of both Hindu and Muslim influences," Zeenat informed the group.

Zeenat was an amazing tour guide, her knowledge was incredible on the history of each place visited.

"Here is Khas Mahal's Private Palace. Look at its splendid copper roof. And here is the Anguri Bagh, also known as the 'Grape Garden.' It is a jigsaw-patterned garden with numerous fountains, water channels, as well as screens that once offered a private area for the emperor and his entourage."

Kesia happily added, "Hey y'all, notice the octagonal Musamman Burj tower. It says here that it later served as Shah Jahan's prison, right up until his death."

Lexi couldn't believe how beautiful it was and how much history was here. *Oh my god, Edward would have loved India. It is amazing!*

The next morning, two miles away, the group visited the Taj Mahal.

Zeenat explained to the group, "This is also known as the world's most famous testimony to the power of love. It is named after Mumtaz Mahal, the favorite wife of Emperor Shah Jahan, this most beautiful mausoleum took twenty-thousand workmen and seventeen years to complete."

"It is magical," Lexi commented. "You can almost feel the love."

Near the end of the day, they walked the 'Old City,' which was behind the 17th century Jama Masjid mosque. There they encountered a tangle of narrow lanes filled with a variety of wares, including spices, clothes, saris, jewelry, shoes, crafts, and snack stalls. Lexi and Isabella were in their glory.

Continuing along their journey, they encountered the 'Mankameshwar Temple' dedicated to Lord Shiva.

Zeenat shared with the group, "It is said that in the temple is a Shiva Lingam, a Sanskrit symbol, covered in silver. It was founded by Shiva himself in the Dvapara Yuga when Krishna was born in Mathura."

"You're talking about the Hindu Deity, the Hare Krishna, the god of protection, compassion, tenderness, and love?" Kesia asked for confirmation.

"Yes, we have many religions in India. The main dharmic religions are namely Hinduism, Jainism, Buddhism, and Sikhism."

Kesia was now curious, "What is the difference between these religions?"

"Jain Dharma or Jainism traces its spiritual ideas and history through a succession of twenty-four leaders or Tirthankaras. A Tirthankara is an individual who has conquered the saṃsāra, the cycle of death and rebirth on their own and made a path for others to follow."

"I have never heard of that one," Kesia said.

"The basis of Sikhism lies in the teachings of Guru Nanak and his successors. This religion originated in the Punjab region of India. You will know the people who follow this faith by the dastār (turban) they wear. The five Ks (panj kakaar) are five articles of faith that all baptized Amritdhari Sikhs are obliged to follow. Number one, called Kesh: Uncut hair, usually tied and wrapped in a dastar. Number two, called Kanga: A wooden comb, usually worn under a dastar to always also keep one's hair clean and well-groomed. Number three, called Kachera: Cotton undergarments, worn by both sexes, the kachera is a symbol of chastity, also historically appropriate in battle due to increased mobility when compared to a dhoti (loose trousers). Number four, called Kara: An iron bracelet, a symbol of eternity, strength, and a constant reminder of the strength of will to keep hands away from any kind of unethical practices, and number five, called Kirpan: An iron sword or dagger. In the UK, Sikhs can wear a small dagger, but in Punjab, they might wear a traditional curved sword from one to three feet in length. Kirpan is only a weapon of defense, used to serve humanity and to be used against oppression."

"Interesting," Kesia said.

"You are probably more familiar with Asian Buddhism and Buddha. But I bet you didn't know that it originated here in ancient India, it is a Sramana tradition."

"No way," Kesia said, fascinated.

"True. It is based on the original teachings and philosophies of Siddhārtha Gautama."

"And what about Hinduism," Kesia asked Zeenat.

"Hinduism is based on Sanātana Dharma. In Sanskrit it means 'the Eternal way,' which refers to the idea that its origins lie beyond human history."

"Now that religion is more up my alley," Isabella said.

"Hinduism is also based on Vaidika dharma, the dharma related to the Vedas."

Isabella eagerly told the group, "I have arranged a surprise for everyone, with Zeenat's help of course."

Kesia jumped up and down, "I love your surprises! What is it?"

Zeenat answered for Isabella, "She has graciously granted us all a Jyotisha reading."

Kesia looked confused, "What is that?"

"I think you call it back home a Vedic astrology reading," Zeenat answered.

"Is that like Western astrology?" Kesia asked.

"Similar, but you may be surprised that your birth sign will not be what you are expecting."

"I was born April 10th, 2004. My zodiac sign is an Aries" Kesia told her quickly.

"We'll see," Zeenat smiled.

The group ended their day traveling to Jaipur.

Chapter 71

At breakfast the next morning, Zeenat informed the group, "Jaipur is known as the pink city of India and is the capital of Rajasthan. It is famous for its forts and palaces."

"Very pretty," Lexi said, looking out the window of their hotel, for all she could see were terracotta-colored buildings. "I can see why it is called the pink city."

They started their day's adventure at the Jantar Mantar.

Zeenat shared her knowledge, "Jantar Mantar literally means, instruments for measuring the harmony of the heavens." With a smile, she said, "Kesia, what did you find out about it?"

"It was built in the 18th century and is an equinoctial sundial."

"Oh, that's fascinating, because it looks alien to me, with its moon shape structure and stairs going everywhere," Lexi added.

Kesia informed everyone, "It consists of a gigantic triangular gnomon (blade), which is the part of the instrument that casts a shadow. Guess what?"

"What," Lexi said, playing along.

"The hypotenuse is parallel to the Earth's axis."

"What on earth is a hypotenuse?"

Kesia chuckled, knowing Lexi was playing with her. "It is the longest side of a right-angled triangle."

"Oh. I am so glad you told me that." *I really didn't know that and felt stupid for asking, but I needed to know what she was talking about.* "So, what I am to understand is that what we are looking at is a ginormous sundial, right?"

"Yes, and it says here that this Mantar is intended to measure the time of day, correct to half a second," Kesia informed her.

Zeenat added, "As you may know, astrology is based on the celestial placement of the stars and planets at the moment of your birth."

"What does this Mantar have to do with Vedic astrology?" Lexi asked Zeenat.

"Only that it represents time. It is extremely important to know the exact time within seconds of your birth for a true Vedic astrology reading."

"What if I don't know my exact time of birth?" Lexi asked. "I think I have an approximate time."

"A difference of ten minutes can be detrimental if you are relying on the accuracy of your reading, Lexi."

"Really?" Lexi questioned.

"Yes. Many Hindu people live their lives according to Vedic astrology. They follow the chart and decide all their future advents like, who they marry or what job or career to be in. Their chart is so precise that it can even tell a person when their life's path may take a turn for the worse or when it is at its optimal."

"People really follow it that strictly?" Lexi challenged.

"So much so, that the family would have prearranged their children's marriage based upon their children's charts."

"You're kidding, right?"

"No. A male can even tell the sex of his firstborn child."

"What? That's unbelievable." Lexi caught herself saying, "Great, now I sound like Edward."

Kesia asked, "What happens if you don't have a good chart?"

"In that case, there will be ways to balance your energy."

"Lit!" Kesia exclaimed. "When do we get our reading?"

Zeenat smiled. "I am happy that you are excited. It is next on our adventure."

The group showed up at Mukesh Vashisth place, a master astrologer, known as a jyotishacharaya.

After everyone was seated, Zeenat explained, "He will use a variety of charts to further refine your individual horoscope. Please fill out this form." She passed a clipboard to the adults, as Aias was taken by a young girl to play in the other room.

Lexi filled out the form to the best of her knowledge.

Name: Alexandra Elizabeth Constantine
Born: May 28th, 1986
Location: Brooklyn, New York. USA
Time: 12:30pm

After the group gave back the clipboards, Mukesh's assistant entered the information into the computer and said something in the Hindi language.

Zeenat translated, "She says that it will take a few moments for each of your charts to be created."

Zeenat also translated for Mukesh as he spoke to the group. "Welcome. In Sanskrit, the word Jyotish translates to 'science of light,' and refers to the profound and mathematically sophisticated form of astrology, originating in the ancient Vedic traditions of India."

Everyone sat attentively as she translated.

"I am sure you have heard the word Yoga. It is a sister science of Jyotish, along with Ayurveda."

"Lexi nodded and said, "Yes, those are quite popular modalities in the USA."

"In the Veda custom, these yoga-related practices are used to lessen or strengthen the influence of specific planets in a yogi's life. Kesia you were asking what happens if someone has a negative chart."

"Yes."

"Such practices include mantras, meditation on yantras, yogic breathing exercises, and asanas to balance the person."

Kesia nodded and kept listening.

"On a deeper level, Vedic astrology provides insight and perspective on the yogi's strengths and weaknesses, thereby providing a framework and guidance for yoga practice. This lifetime's chart will be affected by the Karma you accumulated from your previous life."

The assistant passed out the computer analyzed charts to the group.

"Karma," Lexi repeated.

"Yes. Cause and Effect, good intent and good deeds contribute to good karma and happier rebirths, while bad intent and bad deeds contribute to bad karma and bad rebirths," Zeenat explained.

Lexi said, "Isn't that coincidental, we were just having this 'karma' conversation back home." Looking down at her chart, she read, Taurus. "I think you made a mistake. I am a Gemini."

Zeenat answered, "In Western astrology you are Gemini, but you are Taurus in Eastern."

"What? How is that possible?"

"Eastern astrology emphasizes the rising sign at the precise moment of birth, rather than the Western 30-day sun sign. To be more precise, the difference between the sun signs in the two systems of astrology is said to be 24 degrees, meaning that one might identify with a different constellation."

"I don't understand. Are you telling me that I am not a Gemini, that I am actually a Taurus?"

"Yes."

"Wow, that makes a difference in reading my horoscope."

Zeenat nodded.

Kesia said, "Mine says I am a Pisces, not an Aries."

Isabella asked, "It sounds like the date and the exact time of your birth is what makes your sign different?"

"Yes, Mukesh is telling me that in Vedic astrology the dates are all from the 15th of the month to the 14th of the following month. Where Western is approximately somewhere around the 20th of the month."

Isabella nodded, knowing that it had to be that simple.

Zeenat continued, "Eastern astrology considers the wobble of the Earth over the past two thousand years, and the wobble has changed the planet's position by approximately twenty-two to twenty-four degrees."

"The wobble of the Earth? "Lexi asked.

Zeenat nodded yes, "Another difference is that we enter the Eastern chart through what is called the "ascendant," the constellation that is rising on the Eastern horizon at the time of a person's birth."

Kesia and Lexi both nodded that they understood, which really, they didn't.

Each person in the group had their Vedic astrology chart explained by Mukesh. He started by telling their personality traits first.

As Lexi was the last one to be read, she heard her personality traits and said, "I don't think so. That doesn't sound like me."

Zeenat translated. "Lexi, your time of birth must be wrong. Can you check with your mom to see your accurate time?"

"I'll call her." Luckily, it was later in the day and with the time change it was early morning the day before back in New York City. "Hi, mom."

"Are you having a good time in India?"

"Yes. It is beautiful here."

"Wonderful."

"Mom I need you to check my baby book, please." Lexi knew it was kept in the kitchen with Susannah's. It was a funny place for them to be kept, but Olivia loved reading them.

"Oh, let me get it. What are you needing to know?"

"My exact time of birth."

"12:43 pm."

"Thanks, mom. That is all I need. I am in a meeting right now, but I will call you tomorrow."

"Alright, dear. Say hi to everyone for me."

"I will. Love you, mom."

"You, too."

Lexi wrote down the time and gave it to the assistant.

Moments later her new chart was given to Mukesh.

Zeenat translated.

This time, everything he said was so precise and accurate, it sent chills down Lexi's spine. "Wow, that is freaky."

Mukesh showed Lexi her chart, it was rectangle, not circular like she had seen in her Western reading. He continued by reading Lexi's Rasi (main chart), Navamsa (marriage, partnership, and direction of life as years progress chart), Dasamsa (profession, achievement, status, and skill chart), and Trimsamsa (misfortune, injuries, enemies, and disease chart).

"Did I hear you correctly? There will be a misfortune concerning my marriage?" Lexi asked, worried now that Edward may not be so forgiving when she gets back home.

Chapter 72

"You're doing what?" Lexi asked Kesia the next morning.

"Mom and I are going to trace our gypsy ancestry. Our ancestral lineage follows the line all the way back to our grandmother, Clementina. We. . . mom and I, want to know more about her." Kesia added, "You are invited to join us."

"Will you still be looking for Greg during your travels?"

Isabella spoke up, "Lexi, I paid to have a private investigator look for Greg, or Julian as he is now going by. The guy found him a few days ago near here. We believe he is researching his heritage since it is believed that the gypsies originated in this area of Rajasthan."

"Oh, this should be interesting, and so exciting for you guys, Kesia and Florence."

Kesia answered for both of them, "Yes, not only will we find Julian, but we will discover more about our heritage."

"What have you found out so far, Isabella?" Lexi asked, knowing that she would already be ahead of the game.

"Ah, I am glad you asked. So far, I have been informed that there are two main types of Rajasthan gypsy tribes. The Kalbeliya tribe are famous for their serpent-like folk dance moves and the Bopas tribe are famous for their story-telling songs. My source says that if you analyze the dance of the Romani people living in Europe, they have similar hand and dance movements as the Kalbeliya gypsies here in Rajasthan."

"Kesia, didn't you tell me that your ancestral grandmother danced?" Lexi asked for confirmation.

"Yes, she did."

"A clue, so where are we going first?" Lexi asked.

"Road trip through the Aravalli Mountains to Ajmer," Kesia said excitedly.

Isabella patted Lexi's shoulder and said, "I knew you couldn't resist the adventure."

Smiling, Lexi answered back, "You've got me hooked now. I am this far, why not see where this road leads to. I would hate to miss out on all the fun."

Isabella had hired a private driver with a van to take them to Ajmer.

As everyone was getting into the van, Lexi said, "Aren't you coming with us, Zeenat?"

"No. Some of us have to work. Enjoy!"

Lexi watched as Kesia hugged her goodbye, saying, "Thank you for all that you have shown me, Zeenat. I will keep in touch, and if you ever get a chance to come to America, I will be your tour guide,"

"Thank you, I will keep that in mind."

The trip took about two and a half hours. As they entered Ajmer, Lexi was intrigued with the old building and ruins on top of the Hill. "What is that?" Lexi asked the driver as she pointed to the enormous historic structure.

The driver in his broken English said, "The majestic Taragarh Fort."

"Hey, Kesia, can you look it up for me," Lexi asked.

Kesia was already on it. "Also known as the 'Star Fort,' this fortress was built in 1354. It says here that the intricacy with which the artisans of that time worked on the carvings is beyond imagination."

"I have to go and see that while we are here," Lexi said while having a Déjà vu sensation come over her. "It feels like I have lived through this present situation before. I am having a deep connection to this place."

The driver stopped the van.

"What are we doing?" Lexi asked, surprised by the sudden stop.

"I can take you no further."

"What? Why?"

"You are filled with the devil. Out! Out! All of you."

"What about my money?" Isabella said. "I paid you handsomely to take us to our hotel."

"No. Out!!! You did not pay me for this."

"What about my baby? You are going to make my child walk in this heat?"

"Out!" He yelled, throwing their baggage on the side of the road.

"Wait!" Pulling on his arm. "Why do you say I am filled with the devil?" Lexi begged.

"I know this word Déjà vu. You have the power of 'already seen.' The power of precognition or prophecy." With that, he sped off, leaving them there in his dust.

"Lexi, honestly, you couldn't have kept that information to yourself," Isabella joked as she gave Aias a treat from her bag.

Lexi stared after the driver.

"Well, I guess you get your wish, Lexi," Kesia said, staring up the hill at the Taragarh Fort.

Lexi turned to see what she was referring to. "Ah, I guess I do."

"I'll wait here," Florence said. "It is too hot, and I don't like the thought of trekking up there. Plus, someone needs to look after the luggage."

The group started up the hillside, stopping at a ticket counter. A man came out of a souvenir shop and held up bottles of water. "Americans, yes?"

Kesia said, "Yes," as she paid him for a bottle. "Good idea."

Nodding to the others, "You'll be glad you have these," he said as he pointed to more water bottles.

"Thank you," Lexi said.

"Here, you will want this too."

Lexi took the stick from the man. "Ah. What would I need this for?"

"You'll see."

Within the walls of the fort, Lexi was mesmerized by a beautifully designed tall gateway. Welcoming you on a platform midway up, were two huge carved elephants, one per side. As she walked underneath them, they looked like they were kissing.

As luck would have it, just up ahead, there was an English-speaking tour guide sharing the marvels of the palace.

Lexi could hear her telling her group, "The Garh Palace is a fine example of Rajput architecture, notice the frescoes."

Lexi looked to where she was pointing.

Quickly, she and the others followed quietly behind through the labyrinthine layout of regal rooms and hallways. To her amazement, she saw incredible murals painted on the walls. But the most remarkable and memorable room was what the tour guide called 'Badal Mahal.' It was a room on the second floor of the palace. It reminded her of a kaleidoscope, every inch of its walls was covered with paintings. As she looked up, she saw on the ceiling, a band of red, and just below it—where the ceiling meets the walls, were the miniature ragamala, featuring scenes of hunters and wild animals. The ceiling portrayed courtly life and Hindu mythology, and portraits of Hindu gods. Lexi heard the guide tell her group that at the very center of the ceiling was a scene from the Raas Leela, showing Lord Krishna surrounded by gopis.

It was breathtaking.

The images reminded Lexi of the extraordinary art in the Sistine Chapel in the Vatican City. Though here, the art had an Orientalist style, hinting at foreign influences, while other paintings suggested a Deccani influence.

Lexi was happy for her years at university studying art, it came in handy at times like this.

The guide informed the group that there were actually three palaces within one, Badal Mahal, Phool Mahal, and Chhattar Mahal.

Lexi's Déjà vu sensation came over her again when she was looking at the art in the Chhattar Mahal. There were also courtly scenes, but it was the Hindu mythology paintings that gave Lexi shivers as she looked at them. There were paintings of Lord Vishnu (A prominent Hindu god), Lord Shiva (another important god in Hinduism), Lord Surya (the Sun god), and many more paintings rich in colors comprised of red, gold, and indigo, which gave Lexi a feeling of a peaceful paradise.

"Lexi, Lexi," Kesia said shaking her.

"What? What happened?"

"I don't know. One moment you were following us through the palace and the next thing I knew, you weren't."

"Where am I?" Lexi asked.

"I am not quite sure."

Lexi looked up at the painted story on the ceiling as she followed Kesia out. It was mostly painted in red, with royal figures, horses, and carriages. *Hmm, maybe I was an Indian Princess in a past life.*

Chapter 73

"We have to go. Mom is waiting for us,"
Kesia said, as she hurried back down the hill.

"Hurry y'all, I found us a ride," Florence said
as she watched them run towards her. "But there
is a catch."

A bit out of breath, Lexi asked, "What's the
catch?"

"He will only take us to Pushkar."

As their luggage was already in the bus, Lexi
entered the festively colored metallic blue
Ashok Leyland and was greeted by a group of
foreign travelers. She was extremely happy that
it only took about ten minutes to get to Pushkar,
as one of the men were hitting on her, telling her
how beautiful she was.

As she got off the bus, she was surprised by
another beautiful city in India. *Why haven't I
ever heard of these places?*

As it was near evening, the vision she encountered was an old-world charm. A pink sunset was the backdrop. Built on the hill, the tiered blue homes and temple's colored lights shimmered and danced upon the water of the lake. Chanting, drums, and gongs could be heard creating a mysterious feeling.

Kesia came up to her, "In Sanskrit, it says that Pushkar means blue lotus flower."

"Fascinating," Lexi smiled, loving the intel Kesia could find on Google.

"It is believed that the demon Vajra Nabha killed Brahma's children, Brahma, in turn, struck him with his weapon, a lotus flower. Vajra Nabha died with the impact, and the petals of the lotus fell at three places. One of them is here, where the petal gave birth to this lake."

The man who had been hitting on Lexi came up to them and added, "This is a sacred lake of the Hindus. It is also among the five pilgrim sites or dhams for people following Hinduism. The most famous temple here is the Brahma temple."

"Thank you for sharing that with us," Lexi said without a smile, trying not to encourage him.

"My pleasure."

Lexi looked at the small city and noticed the many different series of steps leading to the lake. "Isn't that a nice way to go down to the lake."

"Kesia looked to where Lexi was looking and asked, "Do you mean the stairs?"

"Yes. Look, they are everywhere."

The man said, "There are fifty-two ghats leading down to the sacred water. It is believed that a dip in the sacred lake will cleanse a person's sins and cure skin diseases. That is why I am here." He moved his sleeve up to reveal psoriasis. "I am praying for a miracle."

"Fascinating," Lexi said.

Kesia's laughter conveniently interrupted Lexi and the man, "It says here that man-eating crocodiles used to be a menace in this lake, resulting in the deaths of many people, and even though pilgrims were aware of this fact, they considered it as lucky to be eaten by crocodiles."

The man not taking the hint that Lexi wasn't interested, added, "A story tells of a ninth-century Rajput king chasing a white boar to the lakeshore on a hunting expedition. In order to quench his thirst, he dipped his hand into the lake and was astonished to see that the Leukoderma marks on his hand had disappeared."

"Hey, this is interesting," Kesia said, "According to Vedas, Brahma originated directly from the Supreme Being. Seated on a lotus, Brahma has a reddish-golden complexion, four bearded heads, and four hands. His four faces represent the four Vedas, and his hands are pointed in the four cardinal directions, each one holding sway (causing change) over a quarter of the Universe. He is, therefore, known as the god of wisdom."

"Isn't that incredible," Lexi said, staring at the lake.

"What?" Kesia asked looking up from her phone.

"I should have said, coincidental."

"Why?"

"Well, we just had our Vedic astrology done, and now we are here learning about Brahma and the Vedas."

As she carried her son down the ghat, Isabella called out, "Lexi, Kesia, come down here with Aias and me."

Lexi was enjoying watching Florence cautiously dip a finger into the lake, Kesia swishing the murky water around, making a tiny whirlpool, and Isabella struggling to take Aias's shoes off so she could dip his feet in, unfortunately the enjoyment was short-lived.

Lexi's mouth dropped open when the water around Aias's feet instantly turned crystal clear and sparkled as he touched it.

Giggling, Aias laughed louder as he splashed the water with his feet, this time turning it a beautiful hue of pink.

"Holy Hannah!" Kesia stated.

Looking directly into Isabella's eyes, Lexi quietly said, so she didn't attract attention from the many people bathing around them, "What in God's name is going on?"

Chapter 74

The man hitting on Lexi saw the water change colors and came over to them. "I have seen magic like this before, but not on Kartika Purnima."

Lexi looked at him and denied everything, "I do not know what you are talking about."

Looking at Isabella he said, "Pilgrims come to this festival to bathe in the holy water of Pushkar's lake and be absolved of their sins. Those who bathe on the day of the full moon are said to receive special blessings." Looking at Ais, he said, "Your son, what else can he do?"

Not sure if she could trust this man, she answered, "I do not understand, he is a baby, he can only do things that a baby can do."

"I see. And how old is your baby?"

Isabella tensed up. *If I tell the truth, he will know.* "Ah, three."

"Um-hmm, in size yes, in age no, and in his divine abilities not even close."

Lexi stepped in front of Isabella and Aias. "Sir, I think you should mind your own business."

Before anyone could speak, he touched Aias. The man's psoriasis instantly disappeared. "My name is Abbas. There hasn't been a person, or should I say baby of this caliber in a few years. The last man was Sathya Sai Baba, and he died in 2011."

Protecting Isabella and the baby, Lexi said, "What are you talking about?"

"I am talking about someone who can heal," Abbas said as he pointed to Aias. "In time he will be able to do more than just miraculous healings and changing the color of water, he will be clairvoyant, and have the ability of bilocation, materialization, and even resurrection."

Not knowing what he meant, Lexi asked, "What is bilocation?"

"The ability to appear in two distinct places at the same time."

Lexi looked at the others. "Are you trying to tell us that he is omnipotent and omniscience?"

"Yes. I believe he might be a reincarnation of Sri Dattaguru. At the very least he is a yogi."

"Who is Sri Dattaguru?" Lexi asked, not being able to help herself. Her curiosity was getting the best of her.

"He was a Hindu god," the man answered.

Kesia piped up, "You said he might be a yogi. Why would you think that? I thought a yogi meditates and practices stretching?"

Abbas laughed, "That is funny. You Americans are funny."

"I was serious," Kesia said, not amused with his laughter.

"Have you ever heard of the book Autobiography of a Yogi?"

"No," they all answered at the same time.

"It is a book that introduces the methods of attaining God-realization and spiritual wisdom of the East. There are many different abilities that a Yogi can develop. You should read it. It is very enlightening."

Lexi nodded, being polite.

"I would like to invite you all to come and join us at the temple. It is similar to what you would call a monastery."

"Where is this temple?" Lexi asked.

"Not too far from here. It is called Jagatpita Brahma Mandir."

Getting shivers, Lexi looked at the others. They nodded yes at her.

"Sure. We will come."

"Great, but first you must bathe in the Pushkar Lake. It is Kartika Purnima after all."

Lexi looked at Kesia and Florence, "I guess we need to join Isabella and Aias in the water."

After they bathed, the group followed Abbas back onto the bus and took their seats.

Noticing the Ferris wheels as they drove around. Lexi asked, "Is this part of the Kartika Purnima festival?"

"No, the Pushkar fair is celebrated after. Here you will see over twenty-five thousand camels all dressed up, paraded, shaved, entered into beauty contests, raced, made to dance, and traded. It is a huge carnival, with an array of musicians, magicians, dancers, acrobats, snake charmers, and carousel rides to entertain the crowd."

Lexi looked at the grounds as they passed by.

Abbas told Lexi and her friends, "In Hindu mythology, a legend associated with this day is Lord Shiva killing three demons, Tripurasura–Vidyunmali, Tarakaksha, and Viryavana, after which the peace was restored on Earth. It is believed that gods celebrate the day in heaven by lighting diyas, a lamp, and hence the day is known as Dev Diwali."

Kesia googled the three demons, "It says here that for a hundred years the three brothers meditated standing only on one leg. For a thousand more years they lived on air and meditated. They stood on their heads and meditated for another thousand years. Pleased at this difficult tapasya, Brahma granted them a wish. They asked for immortality, but he would not grant that, so he granted their next wish. 'Grant us the following: Let three forts be made. The first will be of gold, the second of silver, and the third of iron. We will live in these forts for a thousand years. These three forts, built in different worlds, shall align once every thousand years.' The golden fort was built in heaven, the silver fort was built in the sky, and the iron fort was built on earth. The other gods became jealous, and figured out a way to be rid of these three brothers. They created a man and taught him a religion that was completely against the Vedas, by giving him the impression that there was no separate place—*Svarga* (heaven) or *Naraka* (hell), that both were on earth. They taught the man that rewards and punishments for deeds committed on earth were not inflicted after death. They then had the man go to Tripura and teach the demons this new religion. As the three cities aligned, and to the other gods rejoice, the demons ended up being dislodged from the righteous path and destroyed by the Pashupatastra weapon, and the three brothers."

"Fascinating," Lexi said.

Moments later, after ascending several marble steps that lead to a gated archway, Lexi and the group arrived at their destination, Lord Brahma's temple. It was built from large stone slabs and blocks, that were joined together with molten lead.

As they entered, Lexi stared down at the black and white checkered marble floor. As an offering to Brahma, the floor had been inlaid with hundreds of silver coins, with devotee's names inscribed on them.

Lexi noticed that many of the worshipers and devotees were leaving food.

Noticing, Abbas said, "During this special celebration, it is custom to leave an offering to the gods."

Lexi said, "Oh," just as something caught her attention from her peripheral vision. Turning, she thought she saw. . . *It can't be, could it?* Thinking she knew one of the monks, her adrenaline kicked in, and she set off to run after the monk, but was abruptly held back by Abbas.

"You cannot follow them."

"But that was my friend," Lexi said, fighting to get away from his grip.

"I am sorry, it is not permitted."

Isabella seeing Abbas grab Lexi's arm, and confused by Lexi's strange behavior, asked, "What's going on?" As Isabella turned in the direction Lexi was about to run, all that Isabella could see was the back of a monk's red robe entering a sacred room. Then it all made sense when she heard Lexi scream, "Tamara!"

Chapter 75

"Lexi," Isabella said grabbing her friend's arm. "Calm down. It can't be."

"Iss, I am sure it was. We have to go see."

"I am sorry, but as I said that is impossible," Abbas said again, still standing in her way. "You would go to jail."

"Lexi, really, what is the chance that she would be here of all places?"

Looking at Isabella, she said, "Really good."

Isabella was going to say something as her phone rang. Pointing a finger at Lexi to stay put as she said, "Hello."

"Miss Jackson, it is Detective Redington. Where are you guys? I have been trying to reach Alexandra on her phone, but she is not picking up."

"Oh. Hi, Red. That is odd. I am standing right here beside her, and I didn't hear it ring. We are in Pushkar."

"Well, I am glad to hear that. Hey, wait. Isn't that in India?"

"You are clever, Red. Yes, it is. Hey, stop her. Lexi, no!"

"Isabella, what's going on?"

"Red, I have to go. Lexi is about to go to jail if she goes through that doo..r."

"Isabella, what is going on?"

"Lexi thinks she found Tamara. Oh, thank God."

"What? What happened?"

"He stopped her before she went in."

"Who stopped her?"

"Abbas."

"Who is Abbas?"

"The man who saved Lexi from going to jail."

"What the heck is going on? Put Alexandra on the phone."

"Lexi, it's for you."

"Who is it?"

"Red."

Answering the phone Lexi said, "How do you do that?"

"Do what?"

"Have spidey senses. You always seem to know when I am about to do something crazy."

Red shook his head, "I don't know. I guess it is a coincidence."

Still staring at the door, she said, "Red, it was Tamara. She's here."

"Are you sure?"

"I'm positive."

"I'll have the authorities check it out."

"Thanks, and Red."

"Ya,"

"It's nice to hear your voice."

"Yours too. Put Isabella back on, will ya?"

"Sure."

Isabella took the phone back and said, "Yes, Detective."

"The reason I called."

"Oh, ya. Why did you call?"

"We have a lead on Julian. The guy you hired called me today."

"He was supposed to call me. I am the one paying him."

"What were you guys thinking? Julian's dangerous, Isabella."

Ignoring his last sentence, "I am helping Kesia and Florence. So, where is he?"

"They are there too. Are you all mad?" Redington hesitated, but said, "He is going to be at the Kalbeliya dance celebration tomorrow."

"Do you think that he is following Tamara?"

"What are the chances that all of you, Julian, and Tamara are all in the same place?"

"As Lexi would say, really good."

"I am going to make sure a couple of undercover cops are at that event. And Isabella, don't let Alexandra do anything stupid."

"Red, when have you ever known Lexi to listen to me?"

"Right. Good point. Well, be careful. I'll see you guys tomorrow."

"Red, did I hear you right, you'll see us tomorrow?"

No answer, he had already hung up.

Chapter 76

Detective Redington had called Isabella from New Delhi and was on a train the next morning to Ajmer, then transferring to Pushkar. *What are the chances that all of them, Julian, and Tamara are all in the same place? Not even if you don't add me into the equation. Are coincidences real? Here I am following a lead to catch Julian and find Lexi in the middle again.*

Wasting time, Redington looked up the word 'coincidences.' The meaning of the word coincidence depends on the beliefs of the person involved. Many people believe that Fate, Mystery, the Universe, or God causes coincidences. The dictionary definition is 'the occurrence of events that happen at the same time by accident but seem to have some connection.' Another site, a 2015 study published in New Ideas in Psychology, reported that coincidences are "an inevitable consequence of the mind searching for causal structure in reality."

That's it, there is no such thing as coincidence, we all just have the same common goal, finding Julian.

Redington was in Pushkar mid-afternoon. He hired a taxi to take him to meet with his contact at the Pushkar Police Station.

"Detective, over here." An Indian man wearing a khaki-colored uniform and a navy peaked cap was waving at him to come over.

"Was it my blond hair that gave me away?" Redington asked.

"And your height."

Redington looked around him, most of the Indian men came up to his chin.

"I am Officer Raju Narula."

"Detective Ferguson Redington, but my friends call me Red."

"These two undercover officers will be with you tonight at the event, Seshadri and Venkatesh."

"Nice to meet you guys. Officer Raju, there may be a twist to the investigation."

"What would that be?"

"Julian might be in Pushkar for another reason."

"Which is?"

"His ex-fiancée, Tamara Reeve might be here, and if she is, he's looking for her."

"You said she 'might be here.' Do you know for a fact that she is?"

Redington looked down for a second before answering, "No. I was hoping you could have one of your guys see if she is here in Pushkar."

"Where was she last seen or where do you expect us to look?"

"My sources say that she is now a monk in the Jagatpita Brahma Mandir."

"Officer Redington, I do not know the laws in your country, but here monk's identities are protected. We cannot confirm your request."

"I see. Well, it was worth a try."

"My men will pick you up before the event and take you there. But know that they will drop you off a block from the entrance and once you are inside, you are not to make contact with them unless you see Julian." Passing Redington a tiny mic, "Here, wear this and you can tell them anything necessary, but this is a one-way transmitter, you will not be able to hear them."

Redington took the piece and was escorted out of the Police Station by the two undercover cops and taken to a local hotel.

Later, Redington arrived about twenty minutes prior to this evening's event starting. He was expecting an indoor event, but to his surprise, it was out in the desert.

As dusk neared, there were hundreds of people gathered to watch the event. *How am I going to find him in this crowd?*

Scanning the audience, Redington couldn't see Julian. *Ah, right. Scan for a white guy. This will narrow the field.* Which it didn't, most of the people watching were European tourists.

Redington could hear the beat of a drum as three women came out in bare feet. They were wearing a traditional patterned black and red skirt that swirled wide as the ladies swayed and danced to the music. As the sound of a snake charmer's instrument started to play, the ladies moved their arms as if they were snakes. The gold and diamond bracelets on their arms sparkled in the moonlight as they moved around the sand. Their long red veil flowed like fiery hair as they moved seductively. It was bewitching to watch.

Shaking his head to come out of the semi-state trance that the dancers created, Redington started to walk the perimeter to see if he could see Julian.

"Detective!"

As Red turned he spotted Lexi running over to him. He put a finger up to his lips to shush her.

Coming up to him, she whispered, "Sorry. I was just excited to see a familiar face." Looking around she said, "We haven't seen him."

"Julian?"

"Yes, who else would it be?"

"Ah, now there is the attitude that I have come to love."

Lexi blushed, not that Redington could see that in the moonlight.

Kesia came rushing up, giving Redington a big hug.

"Fancy meeting you here, little one. How have you been?"

"Good."

Florence, Isabella, and Aias came up and said hi.

Redington looked at the child in Isabella's arms. "What are you feeding that kid, steroids? Isn't he supposed to be about this big?" Redington moved his hands about two feet apart.

"He takes after his father's side," Isabella laughed.

"I can't talk now, I have to find Julian, but I'll call after the show and catch up."

Just as he was about to walk away there was applause and the host of the event came on the microphone and introduced the ladies. The one name stopped all of them in their tracks, Clementina Masones.

Turning to look at the lady in the middle, Kesia whispered, "She looks just like the painting."

"What painting?" Redington asked.

"The one my mom has that Tatiana did of her mother."

"It can't be," Florence said staring in disbelief.

They all watched as a man from the audience came up on stage and gave the lady a bouquet of flowers.

"Oh my God, that's Julian," Lexi said before the others could say the same thing.

Redington talked into his earpiece, "That's him. The man on stage. That's him. Get him!" Not knowing if the undercover officers heard him, Redington made his way through the crowd to the center stage just as Julian left the lady with a hug.

"He's getting away," he yelled, hoping the cops were listening.

Running now in the direction Julian was heading, Redington lost sight of him. The two officers had caught up to Redington from another direction.

"Sorry, we almost had him, but it was like he disappeared into thin air," Officer Seshadri said in broken English.

Redington searched the area but could not find any trace of Julian. Heading back towards the dancers he saw Kesia and her mom talking to the girl named Clementina.

Spotting Redington, Kesia waved him over. "You'll never guess."

"She's related to you."

"How'd you know?"

"Lucky guess."

"But do you know how?" Kesia said smiling.

"Ah. . . nope."

"She gave me her website and it has her history and lineage on it. She is a descendant of Dominic, Clementina's firstborn son. The website says that Dominic and his mother Clementina, who she is named after, escaped and fled to Europe. Not knowing where to go they headed East and ended up here in India."

"Wow, now what are the chances of that happening?"

"Still don't believe in coincidences, Detective?" Lexi asked. "Not only did you find us here, but you also found Julian and more of his family."

"Here Detective, read this. It was given to Clementina from Julian." Kesia handed him a folded piece of paper.

Redington opened it.

> Meet me in my hotel's lobby.
> I have more to add to your lineage.

Looking at the logo on the paper, Redington knew what Hotel Julian was staying in. Speaking into his earpiece, he told the undercover cops.

Chapter 77

Later that evening, Redington caught up with the girls. "Pushkar police have Julian in their jail. We finally got him."

"I knew you'd catch him," Kesia said.

Turning to her, he asked, "How did you know? Did your tarot cards tell you?"

"No, Lexi did."

Blushing, Lexi said, "Kesia, that was supposed to be between you and me."

Redington looked at her, "How did you know?"

"You wouldn't believe me if I told you."

"Try me."

"I dreamt it."

"You dreamt it?"

"Yes. Back in New York, a few weeks ago."

"You dreamt about me?"

Now Lexi was really blushing, "Red, it is not what you think. I don't dream about you. You were just in my dream."

"Ah huh, sure. Whatever you say, Alexandra."

Kesia laughed at the two of them. "When are you two going to admit that you like each other?"

Lexi looked over and said, "Kesia, don't you start. It's bad enough that he teases me. I'm engaged to get married, remember?"

"Ah, about that," Redington asked. "Where is Edward anyways? I thought he never lets you out of his sight."

"He is back home." *Mad at me.*

"He let you come all this way without putting up a fight?"

Lexi lied, "Yes. He trusts me." Crossing her fingers, she thought, *It's only a white lie.*

"Good for him. Man, if I was marrying you there is no way I would let you come all this way without me."

Lexi quickly changed the topic, "So, did you find anything out about Tamara?"

"No. Locals here honor their monks. I hit a dead end."

"Hmm. Well, I can't let it go. We are here in the same city that she is. There is no way I am leaving without seeing her."

Knowing that look on Lexi's face, he said, "Ah, what shenanigans are you cooking up now?"

"I don't know, but I have to go back to the temple where I saw her. There must be a way that I can speak with her."

"I don't have to head back just yet. I'll go with you. I'll pick you up at ten tomorrow morning at your hotel."

"That would be great."

Isabella heard what they were saying and said, "I am going to meet with Abbas tomorrow. He wants to tell me more about Yogis. He is insisting that I make sure to teach Aias all that he needs to know."

Kesia added, "Mom and I are going to meet up with Clementina. I am so excited to learn more about that side of my family."

"So, I guess that leaves just you and me, Alexandra. If she is here, we'll find her," Redington said.

Lexi nodded confidently but felt a bit nervous to be alone with him again. *Lexi, don't be crazy, Kesia doesn't know what she is talking about, you love Edward. Nothing will happen.*

Redington picked up Lexi precisely at ten.

"One thing about it, your next wife will never worry about you being late," Lexi laughed as she got into the taxi that he came in.

"You said, I am remarrying. One wife was enough."

"Ah, don't worry, Red, you'll find someone who can put up with you."

"I know I could, but why put myself through that again. Always needing to watch what I say, do, wear, or have a honey-do-list. No, I am happy being single."

Lexi smiled, knowing full well that what she dreamed would come true. *Redington relaxing on the beach chair with a margarita in one hand and a slim hand holding onto his other from another chair. She couldn't see the woman's face because it was covered by a big straw hat, but she saw the diamond on the lady's wedding ring finger, and it was big.* "If you say so, Red."

Lexi almost ran up the stairs to the temple.

"Slow down, you aren't going to gain access with that speed. From what I've seen, monks don't do anything in a hurry."

At the entrance, Redington showed his badge and asked to speak with someone who could talk to the monks for him.

A few moments later a young lady came up to them and said, "Hello. I am told you need to speak with one of the monks. Do you know the monk's name?"

Lexi answered, "Tamara Reeve."

"I am sorry madam, but that doesn't sound like a name our monks here would be called by. Do you know her Dharma name?"

"What is a Dharma name?" Lexi asked.

"It is a new name the person chooses or has chosen for them when they are ordained into the monastery."

"Oh, my goodness. I never thought of that." Turning to Redington, Lexi said, "Now what do we do?"

"May we speak with the monks?"

"I am sorry, but even if they were here, you wouldn't be able to talk with them, since they worship most of the day."

"If they were here?" Redington repeated.

"Yes, the group of monks that were here this week have gone back to their monastery this morning. We have a new group that comes and worships every week."

"Where did they come from, this specific group I mean?" Lexi said, worried that her chance to find Tamara was slipping away.

"Ah, I think I heard someone say they were from Nepal."

"Where in Nepal?" Lexi cried out desperately.

The young lady shook her head, "We are never told that."

Lexi started to cry.

"Ah, madam, I did hear someone call an American monk Sophea. It is a Buddhist name and means - She who is a clever and wise one."

Lexi thanked the girl.

Redington held onto Lexi as she cried.

"We were so close. I know it was her."

"Well, we did find out some important information to track her down."

Lexi looked up. "We did?"

"Yes. We know she is going to Nepal, has joined a Buddhist monastery, and that her name is now Sophea. That is more than you had a few moments ago."

Lexi wiped away her tears. "Yes, I guess it is."

Redington hailed another taxi.

"Red, are you coming with me to Nepal?"

Chapter 78

"Lexi, you must come home. Your wedding is just around the corner, and we have much to do," Olivia was saying over the phone.

"Mom, I have to find Tamara."

"Have you spoken with Edward yet?"

"No. He won't take my calls."

"Lexi, honey, you have to come home. You have to fix this or you may not be getting married at all."

"Mom, don't worry. Edward will forgive me."

"Did I tell you that I stopped by the funeral home the other day?"

"No, you forgot to mention that part."

"Well, I did. A mother needs to make sure her baby is taken care of."

"So, how is he doing?"

"That is what I am trying to tell you. Lexi, he wouldn't see me either."

"What?"

"Lexi, you have to come home asap. You have to fix this."

"Oh my. This is worse than I thought. He really wouldn't see you?"

"I wouldn't lie to you, Lexi."

"Not even a white lie to get me to come home."

"No, not even a white lie. A lie is a lie in God's eyes. White or not."

Great, I am going to hell then. "Mom, I will take the next flight back to New York."

"Good. You be careful."

"Don't worry, I'll have a bodyguard with me."

"You're joking."

"Sort of. Redington is going back to New York, I'll catch the same flight."

"Detective Redington?"

"Yes."

"Oh, Lexi, don't tell Edward. He is already mad at you."

"Oh mother, you worry too much."

"I have seen how that man looks at you with lust in his eyes."

"More like distaste, mom. He likes me as much as you like your neighbor next door. . . oh wait. Aren't you dating him now?' Crap. Mom, don't make my life any more complicated than it is. Redington is just an acquaintance."

"Lexi, I think he is more than that. Be careful! You are a beautiful woman."

"Love you mom, see you soon." Lexi hung up before her mother could put any crazier thoughts into her head.

Turning back to the group, she heard Isabella say, "Well, we are off to the airport tomorrow to Sweden and then to Switzerland. It's time for Aias to meet the rest of Han's family."

Kesia came up to her and took Aias, "I am going to miss this little rascal."

"What are you and your mom doing, Kesia?" Redington asked.

"We are going to stick around here a bit longer and meet more of our family. Clementina says our family here is quite big."

"Are you really going to Nepal, Lexi?" Isabella asked.

"Ah, it will have to wait. I am needed back home."

"Is your mom, okay?" Worried now that she knew Lexi had just gotten off the phone with her.

"Oh. Ya, ya. She needs me to take care of some business." *Close, but that wasn't even a white lie.*

"Oh good, you can fly back with Redington," Isabella said, happy to know that Lexi wasn't going to Nepal alone.

Red looked at Lexi, and jokingly said, "Can't live without me, huh."

Kesia stated without laughing, "Come on you too, I told you already, you like each other. We all know it."

Within moments of liftoff, Redington was snoring beside Lexi.

Taking a fashion magazine that she had bought out of her purse she started to read it as Redington's head tilted towards hers and found a resting spot on her. Not sure what to do, she slowly turned the pages.

The flight attendant came over and passed her a pillow, "For your husband."

"Ah, he's not my. . ." but never finished her sentence and took the pillow.

As soon as Redington moved his head, she stuck the pillow between them.

Hours later she woke to the smell of a meal being served. Her head was resting on his chest. Embarrassed she moved off of him, wiping her mouth from a bit of drool that had seeped out over her lip.

Passing her a napkin, Redington said, "Did you know you snore?"

"Yes, I remember you telling me that months ago when we were hiding in your friend's cabin."

"You know Alexandra, people are going to start to talk if you keep sleeping with me."

Lexi sat up straighter. Fuming she said, "Red, your ego is bigger than a house and it is going to get you killed one day, and not from a bullet."

Redington laughed.
"It will be by my bare hands."
Redington laughed so loud, the couple beside him said something in another language, and it didn't sound friendly.

"Alexandra, you keep getting me involved in these cases that I end up having to solve. If I didn't know better, I would say you are hitting on me."

"Hitting on you? I'll be hitting on you with my fists you mean."

"Hey, I have witnesses, you were resting your pretty little head on my chest. Drooling away. Here look, I still have proof, a wet spot." Redington flexed his chest and pointed to a little spot on it.

Lexi blushed and took a bite of her meal. *Men!*

Chapter 79

After clearing terminal four's customs at the JFK airport, Lexi texted her mom that she had arrived and was on her way to level 1 to pick up her luggage and would text as soon as she was at the cell phone parking lot for her to pick her up.

"Mom can give you a ride home if you want," Lexi offered to Redington.

"That's okay, I wouldn't want to inconvenience her. I can catch a taxi."

"No, I insist. Mom would love to hear how you caught Julian."

"If you are sure that it will be no trouble then, I would love to tell your mom stories about you."

"Me? I didn't catch him."

"She doesn't know that."

"Funny. She wouldn't believe you anyway."

"You would be surprised how convincing I can be."

Lexi smiled at him as they walked to the Blue Lot pickup area.

Dropping his phone on the ground just as Lexi texted her mom that she was there, Redington was a moment behind her.

To her surprise Edward drove up. She watched as Edward took one look at her and then saw Redington walking up to her. His face changed from happy to see her to instant anger. She watched as he drove away fuming.

"I thought you said he was cool about you being in India?"

"Ah, I guess I was mistaken."

"From the look on his face, he wasn't expecting to see me. Didn't you tell him I caught Julian?"

Lexi whispered, "Ah, I didn't talk to him."

"What? I didn't hear that."

Lexi punched Redington in the arm, "Ow, that hurt my hand," she said, as she flinched from the pain.

Redington laughed, not feeling a thing.

Olivia drove up smiling, not knowing what had just happened.

Getting into the car, Lexi said, "Mom, I thought you said you weren't speaking to Edward."

"Well, I decided to try again. I left a message this morning with his assistant saying that you were coming in today. Why? What happened."

"He just drove by. By the way, we are giving Detective Redington a ride home."

Olivia turned to look for Edward's car, but he was nowhere in sight. "Detective, so nice to see you. I hope your flight was comfortable."

Smiling as he got into the back seat, he said, "Actually, it was horrendous."

"Really, what happened?" Olivia asked as she drove away.

"I had to listen to this passenger snore and to make things worse she drooled on me."

Olivia started to laugh. "Oh, my. She used to do that as a child. I thought she would outgrow it."

"Nope. She didn't."

Lexi turned to Redington and stuck her tongue out at him.

"Lexi put the Detective's address into the car's GPS, would you?"

"Sure. Red, what is your address?"

After telling her, Redington said, "Most people don't know that the borough of Queens is named after English Queen Catherine of Braganza."

"I knew that," Lexi said.

Not having been to Redington's place, Lexi was surprised that he lived in the community of Rockaway Beach, a neighborhood on the Rockaway Peninsula of Queens on Long Island.

"I didn't know that you were Irish," Lexi said knowing the largest ethnic group there was Irish.

"I'm not. I'm English."

"Then why do you live there? It's a far jaunt to work?"

"It is the largest urban beach in the United States that offer surfing and scuba diving."

"You surf?"

"On my days off, I do."

"Rockaway always reminds me of a charming New England port town," Olivia commented.

Redington looked around, "It does."

Olivia pulled up to a condo building with a blue awning protecting the entrance.

Lexi got out of the car as Olivia popped the trunk for Redington to retrieve his luggage.

"Nice place. Do you rent or own?"

"That's a personal question."

Lexi looked around. "Breathtaking views, 24-hr doorman, private off-street parking, and a business center. Pretty nice, Red."

"You didn't mention that it has a fitness center, locker rooms, and best of all, Lexi, I can walk out of my door and I'm on the beach! You'll have to come and visit sometime."

"You didn't answer my question."

"I own."

"What do you do on the side, I'm sure the police force doesn't pay you a salary to afford this place."

"Espionage. I am a secret agent."

Lexi laughed. "Right."

Redington shrugged his shoulders and grabbed his bag.

"Thanks for the lift, Mrs. Constantine," Redington said as he passed by her car window.

Undoing it a bit more she said, "No problem. It was my pleasure."

Not wanting the travel to tire her mom out, Lexi came over to the driver's side, opening the door saying, "Mom, I'll drive us to your place."

Redington turned and waved as he entered the building.

"Well, that was unexpected," Lexi said.

"What was, dear?"

"I never would have put him living here. Not with the car he drives."

"What does he drive?"

"An old rusted-out car."

As they were about to pull away from his condo, Redington drove out from the parkade.

"That one," Lexi said pointing.

"Dear, that is a classic. Your dad loved those cars. It's a 1967 Chevrolet Impala SS."

"Well, what do I know. It just looks old to me and needs a paint job. Beige, who would want a blaa color like that?"

"I think you call it Sierra Fawn, Dear."

Looking at her mom, "How would you know that?"

"As I said, your dad loved that car. I should have let him buy it, for it would be worth a small fortune by now."

Chapter 80

"Sophea! Worship is not the time for astral traveling," a fellow Buddhist monk said to Tamara.

Coming back to the present moment, Tamara, now called by her Dharma name, Sophea nodded her head and started to pray.

For the request she made to Freyja to change her future, Freyja had teleported Tamara's body and soul to Nepal, Kathmandu to be more precise.

Shortly after materializing onto the front entrance of a Buddhist Monastery, Tamara was accepted into the sanctuary. She humbly agreed to be trained in their Vajrayāna school and eventually be granted full monastic vows in Newar Buddhism. According to Vajrayāna scriptures, the term Vajrayāna refers to one of three routes to enlightenment, the other two being Śrāvakayāna and Mahāyāna.

Sophea was given a red robe to wear and was shaved bald. *The custom of shaving your head is known as tonsure. Tonsure is performed as a ceremony of initiation into a new religion and symbolizes the surrender of one's worldly ego and fashion. It has been practiced since the medieval Roman Catholic era, but many years later was abandoned.*

She had to learn a new language, Newar, or as it is officially called, Nepal Bhasa. She enjoyed this lesson. Another class was dedicated to Siddhārtha Gautama who lived in ancient India around the 5th century BC. He was a mortal man but after his death was known by the name of Buddha, which means 'Awakened One' or 'Enlightened One.' To Sophae's surprise, the rubbing of the Buddha's belly, to bring good luck, wealth, and prosperity is folklore and the legend derived from the Chinese proverb of the laughing Buddha. It is not an Indian belief or custom.

She also learned that in 1926, five monks, along with their Tibetan guru, were expelled from the country. The reason being that the government objected to one of the men being born a Hindu and converting to Buddhism, but the more likely reason was due to the monks making alms rounds (begging) in Kathmandu. To make an example of them, the police arrested the monks and ordered their banishment. They were marched to the Indian border under police escort, and all Buddhist practices had to stop.

It wasn't until 1946 that a Sri Lankan goodwill missionary visited Kathmandu and interceded on behalf of the monks. The delegation emphasized that Nepal was the birthplace of Buddha and that his followers should be free to practice their faith in India, where he was born. Shortly after, the ban was lifted, and the monks were allowed to return to spread the Buddhist faith.

The Buddhist's faith was to learn how to achieve Nirvāṇa. A concept in Indian religions that represents the ultimate state of salvation, the liberation from repeated reincarnations.

Sophea's new lifepath was now to learn the lifelong practice of Dhamma, also known as Dharma, which means *cosmic law and order but also includes the teachings of the Buddha.*

Each day started at 4.00 am. Upon awakening, she would meditate for one hour, followed by one hour of chanting. Then at 6.00 am, she would walk barefoot around the neighborhood while the local people earned merit by offering her and the other monks food. *Bhikṣu (a male monk), the Sanskrit term translated as "monk," literally means "beggar."*

Then at 8.00 am, Sophea and the monks would return to the temple and sit together to eat their breakfast. Before noon, all monks would eat a light lunch. *This is the last solid food they are allowed to consume until sunrise the following morning.* At 1.00 pm, classes in Buddhist teaching would begin. At 6.00 pm, they would begin a two-hour session of meditation and prayer. Finalizing the day at 8.00 pm, where she and the other monks retired to their bed-chambers to do homework.

A couple of times a year, the monks were invited to worship at other monasteries and temples. This year they were invited to Jagatpita Brahma Mandir in Pushkar, India. That is when she was reminded of the cost of her wish to change her future, and who she had to leave behind. How could she forget the coincidence of seeing her friends from her past and hearing Lexi's words, *but that was my friend.*

Lying down to go to sleep for the night, Sophea couldn't help but think about her friends back home.

Closing her eyes, she imagined Kesia. Instantly she was there, in New York, at Kesia's school. She forgot that Kesia was still in school since she seemed so mature for her age. Grade twelve, senior year. It seemed like yesterday that she, herself, had graduated. Sophea smiled as a cute boy came up to Kesia and asked her to be his date at prom.

The thought of young people brought her to think about Aias and Isabella, and instantly she was in Switzerland. She knew that elves matured quickly, but she didn't know that half-elves did. *Wow! Isabella is in for a treat with that one. I can't wait to see what you do in this lifetime, little one,* she thought to him as she blew him and Isabella a kiss.

The kiss brought her to check in on Edward and Lexi's love for each other, and instantly she was . . . *where is this? Nice digs, Edward! Good job on the renovations.* Well, he seemed to have forgiven Lexi for her little excursion to India, but he is still mad at Redington for going there and spending time with his soon-to-be wife.

Ah, Redington. You mysterious man you. Who would have thought that you actually have a heart and could fall in love again? Too bad she is taken.

Shifting her position in bed, Sophea started to contemplate. *As they say, be careful what you pray for.*

They all seem to be in good hands. Lexi is learning how to accept her ability to see the future. She has come so far from the day I met her. If she only knew how much further there was to go, I wonder if she would continue on this path?

Life has so many twists and turns. One minute life seems normal, and then bam, it shifts, and you are headed in a new direction.

I am blessed that I was granted my wish and could start anew, and I wish Greg, or whatever his name is now, all the best, and that God will be kind to him on judgment day.

I pray that I learn how to stay in the present moment, as taught here at the Buddhist school. That what I see in my future is just that, future, and that to stay in the present moment—is a true gift. I pray that I have made the right choice and won't ever regret my decision.

A noise came from another room and interrupted her dream.

Sophea, Bath Kol said. *It is your destiny to become all that you can be. Your life's path started long before going to Peru and being blessed by a Shaman. It began as a soul in Heaven.*

Sophea closed her eyes again as the shivers ran through her body. She knew Bath Kol was right, that her soul's journey in this lifetime was far greater than just being a teacher and marrying a man. Lying there in her modest bed, she knew that her destiny, her life's path was far from over. This was just a new chapter in her book.

Excerpt from
Book 4
Healing of a Soul
Chapter 1

July 10th – Wedding Day
Lexi

"I hear wedding bells," Sherie said in her cute southern belle accent as she came into a small room that Lexi was using at the front of Edward's church.

As Oliva watched Isabella place the headpiece on her daughter, she wiped a tear from her eye, and said, "I am so glad that you and Edward made up. I was a little worried that you would become an old spinster."

"Mother, a spinster? Really? I'm not that old."

"Well, you are thirty-six."

"Mom, you know my career took priority, and besides that, most the men I work with are gay."

Wiping at another tear, Olivia said, "Well, I have no need to fret about it now, you're getting married. I just wish your sister and dad could have been here."

Looking in the mirror at Olivia, Lexi responded, "Mom, you're going to wreck your make-up. I think it is time for you to go and get seated."

Olivia kissed her daughter's head, thinking, *thank God Isabella could sub in for Tamara,* but whispered, "Your dad would have been so proud."

Lexi smiled awkwardly at her bridesmaids as her mom left the room. To shift the room's vibe, she said, "You all look so beautiful."

Lexi had designed the teal floor-length, V-neck silk dresses to match her wedding gown. She loved how the matching tulle showed off the intricate aquamarine gemstones that were hand-sewn throughout the netting. The ladies looked stunning in their very chic gowns.

Looking at herself in the mirror, Lexi looked like a Greek goddess in her one-of-a-kind backless wedding dress. The V-neck gave way to a cinched waist. The flow of the floor-length gown was spellbinding, as she moved, the light silver tulle fabric shimmered and glittered like stardust overtop of the white silk lining. It reminded her of beautiful ice crystals that shimmered brilliantly in the sun. And instead of a veil, Lexi wore a sparkling crystal tiara with matching earrings that dangled from her ear lobes.

She had also designed the men's attire. Edward's silver and gray tux matched her dress. Little Aias, who now looked five, was the ring-bearer, and looked adorable in his dark gray suspender shorts, matching vest, and teal bowtie. The best man and the groomsmen were wearing identical outfits but with pants, not shorts.

The minister performing the ceremony was a good friend of Edward's dad, Reverend O'Malley. The ladies were waiting patiently for one of the ushers to come and tell them when he was ready to start the ceremony.

Lexi looked at the clock on the wall. *Fifteen minutes late, really.* "I thought it was supposed to be the bride who is running late. What is taking them so long?" Lexi said, getting antsy.

"I am sure they are just waiting for stragglers to come in and get seated. Edward probably thinks that it is you who is late," Isabella chuckled.

Lexi looked again at the clock. Five more minutes had gone by. "Okay, something is wrong. Kesia, please go and find out what is taking so long."

Kesia quickly went out the door.

A few moments later, the door opened.

While looking at her make-up in the mirror, Lexi said, "So, what is taking so long?"

"Alexandra."

That wasn't Kesia's voice. Turning, she saw Detective Redington staring at her. Startled, she asked, "What are you doing here?"

"Lexi, I am so sorry. I just came from a crime scene. It's Edward. He was there. He's . . ." Not being able to finish his sentence before she fainted, he barely heard her say, "Oh my God, the prophecy is coming true!"

Not remembering, Isabella asked as she went to catch Lexi, "What prophecy?"

Trying to catch Lexi, but as she missed, Kesia answered, "The prophecy that Mukesh read in Lexi's Vedic Astrology Chart while we were in India, he predicted that there was going to be a misfortune concerning her marriage."

Acknowledgments

Thank you to Diane, my friend and mentor for being a beta reader and gifting me with your enlightened feedback.

A very special thank you to my mom, Linda. Thank you from the bottom of my heart for spending hours reading my manuscripts over and over again. You are amazing, and such a pleasure to have in my life.

I would also like to thank my Aunt Diane and my grandmother, Anne. You both mean so much to me, and I so appreciate you pre-reading the manuscripts and giving me feedback.
Love you two!

And I can't forget my husband, Nick. You are the most patient man I know. Helping me come up with ideas for the books and finding more mistakes even though it has been edited five times already. Thank you for believing in my dreams and letting me play and bring them to life. I am so happy to have you as my soul mate.
Love ya, Babe!

Companion Book
ISBN: 978-1-7770818-8-1

Canadian Author

Constance Santego, author of the *Nine Spiritual Gifts* Series.

As well as being a wife, mother of two adults, a grandmother, an author, and an artist, Connie has owned a few day spas, retail stores, a manufacturing company, a café, yes—a castle, and a college.

For fourteen years, Constance Santego owned an accredited college that taught natural health and healing, energy concepts, and spiritual metaphysics in the beautiful Hawaii of Canada, Kelowna, BC.

Having her bachelor's degree in Holistic Studies, Constance has published many non-fiction books (Secrets of a Healer Series, Your Persona, Fairy Tales Dreams and Reality, Angelic Lifestyles) and a fiction series based on the Nine Spiritual Gifts.

Constance continually strives to educate herself in the wonders of the Nine Spiritual Gifts taught in the Bible and its relevance in today's modern world, as well as working on her Ph.D. in Integrated Medicine.

Also Available

For additional information on
Constance Santego's wide range of
Motivational Products, Coaching Sessions,
Spiritual Retreats, Live Events, and
Educational Programs
Go to
www.ConstanceSantego.ca

Play the 'Ikona' game and test
your Virtues and Sins.

Keep in touch with Constance via the web:
Instagram - Constance_Santego
Facebook - ConstanceSantego
Twitter - ConieSantego
YouTube Channel - Constance Santego

Subscribe and receive free information &
Meditations

www.ingramcontent.com/pod-product-compliance
Lightning Source LLC
Chambersburg PA
CBHW051309190726
48290CB00001B/78